REVENGE
The Damien Palmer Investigations
Book 3

Stuart Holland

REVENGE
The Damien Palmer Investigations
Book 3

Chapter One

The early morning rays of sunlight bathed Damien Palmer's bedroom in a pale, golden light, bringing the promise of warmth into the room. It was not yet six o'clock in the morning but Palmer was already awake, his troubled mind keeping him from the luxury of more than the few hours of sleep that his body had demanded. Even as he had been sleeping, his mind continued to work out the permutations of the case he was involved with. It needed to be resolved in the next few days, though the probability of a successful conclusion seemed bleak enough. With those first few rays of light penetrating the cool darkness of the late-summer night that was even now fading into history Palmer wondered where the light would begin to shine in the case he was working on.

It had all seemed so different a few months previously when the woman had telephoned him to ask his advice. He really had thought he would be able to help her. After all, missing people were one of his specialities and it was not as if her husband had been gone that long either. Admittedly two months would have been long enough for him to leave the country but his passport was still at home and it had not seemed that he had prepared for a period of time away from home. Palmer's first impression had been that the man, Stephen Green, had made absolutely no preparations to leave his wife. More likely it had been a spur of the minute decision. A close examination had shown none of his clothes were missing and neither were his personal effects. That had been six weeks previously when Green's wife, Dawn, had contacted Palmer. At first Palmer had thought the nervous woman was slightly paranoid. As time had elapsed his first impressions had, for some unfathomable reason, taken root in his mind.

Now, nearly two months into the investigation, Palmer was on the brink of admitting defeat. Green had not been seen at work since the day he had disappeared and it appeared no one knew where he was. Moreover, it was becoming increasingly difficult to understand what he was living on, for the couple had a joint account and he had made no drawings on the meagre balance that had existed at the time of his disappearance.

Palmer had considered many angles in the case. He'd interviewed friends and family and there had been nothing to help him. His good friend, Eddie Marston, was a somewhat short man, slightly overweight, with a chubby face and a squat nose on which perched a pair of wire-framed spectacles. Marston had spent hours watching people but to no avail. Even an article in the local papers had failed to draw a single response. As he lay in bed this particular morning and as the rays of light filtered softly into his bedroom, Palmer contemplated the next move. It was not a move he intended to make immediately for he had an arrangement with his lady friend, Karen Shaw, for a day out. He had plans to take a stroll in Richmond Park and then enjoy a picnic together. He considered such a day would be the perfect tonic after the rigours and demands of the past few weeks. First there was the meeting to face with Dawn Green, a meeting Palmer was not relishing. She would be arriving in just under three hours. Palmer lay there on the black, silk sheets and as he did so, the woman beside him stirred.

Karen Shaw was an attractive woman. A few years younger than Palmer, she was a slender woman, standing some five feet and nine inches tall. What made her particularly attractive was her long, sandy hair. Her hair reached down to the middle of her back and flowed over her ample breasts. Now, as she stirred, the duvet fell away from her, revealing her lightly tanned flesh, naked on the black silk sheets. Palmer turned to the woman as she opened her eyes and stroked her leg tenderly.

'Did you sleep all right?' His question was spoken softly.

'Mmm, and you?'

'Hardly a wink, I just can't get the Green disappearing act out of my head.'

'What time is it?'

'About six thirty, you can go back to sleep if you want.'

As if by way of reply she turned away from the investigator and pulled the duvet back up over her body.

'I'm going to make some coffee. Fancy a cup?' Palmer leaned over and kissed the back of her head.

'No, just a couple more hours sleep.'

'Okay, sweetheart, I'll be downstairs when you want breakfast.' Palmer slid out of his side of the bed and pulled on the boxer shorts that had been discarded during a passionate moment the previous night. The air was warm and he allowed the cotton bath-robe to hang over his shoulders without tying it with the waist height belt. Silently he padded out of the bedroom and down the stairs to the kitchen. With care he almost closed the door and started to fill the coffee maker. A few minutes later the pleasing aroma of freshly brewed coffee filled the air. As carefully as he had closed the kitchen door, Palmer opened it and took the mug of steaming coffee into his study.

As he opened the door he looked with satisfaction at the shelves filled with leather-bound tomes, each one holding a memory for the sleuth. He turned to face the window and placed the mug on the coaster sat next to the blotter that occupied much of the top of his elegant, if somewhat ostentatious, oak desk. To the far side of the desk sat a black box, seemingly incongruous in the room, yet the laptop enabled Palmer to perform many of his investigative tasks from the comfort of the leather-upholstered swivel chair that waited for him in the space between the desk and the window.

Palmer walked behind the chair and looked out of the window onto the grassy area that mercifully broke up the urban sprawl in which he lived. As he looked out of the window, and not for the first time, he longed to return to the days when he had lived in the leafy suburbs of Dorking in Surrey. The memories of those days still remained - they always would. He'd been 21 years of age when he'd married Penny. She'd been a middle manager at the bank where he was a junior clerk, and the fact she was five years older than him had only become a problem after they had married. On reflection, the marriage had been impetuous, but they had been happy enough. It was only six months later he had discovered his wife, Penny, was having an affair with another colleague at the bank. Palmer was struggling with his job at the time and her expectations of the marriage far outweighed what he could provide, both financially and emotionally. She had little patience for a 'loser', as she often called him, and he had been numbed but not totally surprised when a few months later she had moved out.

The divorce had followed soon afterwards. She had no hesitation in admitting the adultery but as it was mostly her money that had gone into buying the house in the first place there was never any question she would end up receiving it back as part of the settlement. So Palmer had made a new life for himself. He'd quit his job as a bank clerk and taken to learning the skills of a Private Investigator. It had not been easy and his apprenticeship under the auspices of a somewhat arrogant and ageing experienced sleuth was far from happy. After some bungled cases, and one in particular that had nearly ended up with a teenager losing her life, Palmer decided to strike out on his own.

Moving from his home in Sutton to the more urban side of the Putney area he began '*DW Palmer Investigations*' from the office in which he was now sitting. Before he'd done so, he'd already met Eddie Marston and their friendship, something Palmer never treated lightly, had continued and grown. Then, in one of the lull moments in his career, as he liked to call the frequent early periods when there was no work to do, Palmer had decided to learn more about the world of computer technology. The Internet applications course had been interesting and he'd started dating the seminar leader. That relationship had developed over the past couple of years and now it seemed he and Karen Shaw were becoming, what to Palmer was so loathsomely termed, an item. Perhaps, he now reflected, his desire to move back to leafy Surrey would become a reality if this relationship worked out, but that was one of life's imponderable questions.

Palmer turned to his desk and sat down in the leather chair. He opened the top right drawer and pulled out the manila envelope that held the case notes relating to the disappearance of Stephen Green. Palmer instinctively knew there must have been something he had overlooked. With a flash of inspiration that sometimes occurs in the fresh morning light, he decided to re-check the copies of the bank statements Dawn Green had let him copy. He recalled from the previous times when he had examined them that most of the Green expenditure went on the usual household bills. As he scanned the half dozen sheets of the statements that covered the most recent three months, he began to make notes on the pad of paper in front of him. The regular outgoings were of little interest and were ignored. What Palmer focused on were the cash withdrawals and the cheques. In particular he noted the cheques that had been written. The cash amounts were small by comparison and he knew that twenty pounds dispensed from a wall-mounted machine was likely to be for immediate use anyway. The cheques, though, were more interesting. In the first month there were just four of them and Palmer calculated they came to about three hundred pounds in total. Again in the second month there were four cheques that came to a total of nearly four hundred pounds. Then, in the last month, there were eight cheques totalling well in excess of one thousand pounds.

Palmer scratched his head as he looked at the notes he'd made. The details of the cheques were anonymous but it seemed odd that there were so many more of them in the weeks leading up to Green's disappearance. Palmer looked again at the statements as if seeking further assistance from them. Then, and again for no apparent reason, he began writing down the cheque numbers against the dates and amounts he had already listed. When he had finished he let out a low whistle. The cheques had not been cashed in sequence.

Indeed in the weeks leading up to the disappearance, there had been three cheques drawn on the account, two that were over two months old, and the third from the previous month. Palmer sat quite still for a few moments as he absorbed the knowledge he had just gained. It was the breakthrough he had been waiting for. It was nearly eight o'clock and Palmer absently reached over to the telephone sat on a small table beside his desk and dialled the number on the top of the manila envelope.

'Good morning, Mrs Green, it's Damien Palmer.'

'Good morning, Mr Palmer, what can I do for you so early in the day?'

'Yes,' Palmer sounded momentarily surprised at the time, 'I'm sorry it's so early but I wanted to catch you before you came to see me. Do you have the cheque stubs for your current and previous cheque books to hand?'

'Yes, I think so. I know Stephen left them here.'

'Good, would you mind bringing them with you?'

'Of course, but how will they be of help to you?'

'I don't know, but there may be something in them.'

'Oh, I see, well I'll bring them. It was nine o'clock, wasn't it?'

'Yes, that's fine, I'll see you in an hour, and once again I'm sorry for having disturbed you so early.'

'That's all right, Mr Palmer, I was up anyway. The truth is I haven't slept much since it happened. I'll see you in an hour.'

'Goodbye then.' Palmer replaced the receiver and went upstairs to get dressed. In the bedroom, Karen Shaw was stirring.

'You look happy,' she said as she rolled over to look at him. 'Don't tell me you've cracked it.'

'No, but I think I'm onto something. I'd bet right now that Green's been planning this for some time and he's gone off with someone. It's beginning to add up but we won't know for sure for a few days at least.'

'Oh well, at least we can have our picnic without you worrying about the case the whole time.'

'Yeah. Once Mrs Green's been we can go out. What say we go to Richmond Park, have a stroll and take the picnic there?'

'Mmm, sounds fun to me. What's the weather like?'

'It's already warm, and the sky's blue and clear. It should be pretty hot later on.'

'Perfect. What time is she coming round?'

'Nine. That gives us an hour for breakfast. She shouldn't be here for long, so I reckon we'll be on our way by about half past.'

'Right, give me ten minutes to get up. I'll do the picnic while you're talking to your client. That way we'll save some time. I want to make the most of my day off.'

'Yeah, me too.' Palmer had been dressing as he spoke. 'Coffee, cereals and toast, or something cooked?'

'Coffee and toast for me.'

'Jam, marmalade, or pate?'

'Marmalade, and no fat.'

'Yeah, I know you're on a diet.'

'No, just watching the calories. There's no point in eating more fat than you have to.'

'Okay, breakfast in ten minutes.' Palmer reached over, kissed the woman affectionately and then left her to dress. She heard him almost run down the stairs and as she began to dress, she heard the familiar sounds of Palmer at work in the kitchen. He was, she thought, a somewhat messy person in that particular room, though she had to admit he always cleared up afterwards and his culinary skills were better than most.

Breakfast was an unhurried affair and the plates and cups had been cleared away some minutes before the doorbell sounded. Palmer walked down the hallway and opened the front door. The radio in the kitchen could just be heard from behind the closed door.

'Mrs Green, do come in.' The woman crossed the threshold and shook Palmer's hand in greeting. 'Shall we go into my office?'

Palmer's smile was effusive and friendly. He closed the front door and ushered the woman into his study. 'Now, would you like coffee, or tea perhaps?'

'No thank you, Mr Palmer, I've only just finished breakfast. Now, those chequebooks you wanted to see. I have the stubs here.'

She reached into her handbag and was handing Palmer the counterfoils before he had reached his own side of the desk.

'Please, take a seat. Ah, the cheque stubs. Now, if you don't mind, I'll just have a quick look at these.' Palmer sat down and took the stubs off the woman. He spent a couple of minutes examining them. Finally he looked up and smiled. It was supposed to be a disarming smile but Palmer instantly noticed it made the woman nervous.

'Mrs Green, these are most useful. I noticed a couple of days ago,' Palmer lied, 'that some of the cheques drawn on your joint account had been drawn out of sequence and it puzzled me.'

'But surely that is just down to when the recipient decides to pay them in?'

'Sometimes and if the amounts were small I would agree with you. But the three cheques in question come to nearly a thousand pounds and two of them have been drawn almost two months out of sequence. It may be nothing but again, from my experience I would have to say it is odd.'

'And those cheques, what do they tell you?'

'There is very little to go on from the stubs. Of course it may be your husband doesn't always write his cheques from the top of the book but not many people write cheques from a book in a random sequence. I notice most of the cheque stubs contain the date and amount and details of the payee, but for the three cheques in question the details are blank.'

'But that can't be. Stephen always wrote down the details. He checked them back every month to the statements. It was something he always insisted on and he was quite fastidious about it.'

'Did you ever look through the counterfoils?' Palmer was leaning forward in his chair.

'No, I always left the financial things to Stephen. He was so good at that kind of thing and I'm useless at it.' The woman seemed more nervous than ever. 'What are you saying, Mr Palmer?'

'Well, I can't be sure, but it is at least possible your husband has moved at least a thousand pounds out of the account shortly before he disappeared. If that is the case then it is good for us.'

'Why is that, Mr Palmer?'

'Because we can find out where he paid those cheques in and it will give us a clue.'

'I see, and how do you do that?' Palmer was flicking through the counterfoils of the second chequebook. When he had done that he looked up.

'Please be candid with me, Mrs Green. When I first met you, you said you were struggling financially. How long has this been the case?'

'About two years I would say. Stephen was always going on about high interest rates and things and how we couldn't afford to go away on holiday.'

'I see. Now then, this is what I would like you to do. Go to your bank manager and ask him to retrieve the details of these three cheques.'

'Can he do that?'

'Oh yes. I want you to say it is important he does it today if possible because you need to find out where they were cashed. I notice that you bank at the Midshires branch on the High Street. Ask for David Carstairs, he's a friend of mine. Tell him you need the information for me. I'm sure he'll help you, only you must really stress it is of the greatest urgency.'

'Very well, Mr Palmer and then what do I do?'

'Well, I am out today, but when you have the details if you telephone and leave a message on my machine I'll call you back when I have a chance. Of course it may take a few days for you to get the information we need, it just depends on how busy the bank is.'

'I see. Well, Mr Palmer, thank you for your time. I'll keep you informed.' The woman stood from her chair and took back the counterfoils Palmer waved in her direction.

'Not at all, Mrs Green, and believe me, we will find your husband and soon.'

'Let's hope so, Mr Palmer.'

'Please, allow me to show you to the door.' Palmer stood up and in a moment was ushering the diminutive Dawn Green out of his study. As he closed the front door behind his client, the kitchen door opened.

'Well?' It was all Karen needed to say.

'Well, I reckon he's been siphoning money off the account for the past couple of years at least. God knows where it's going, just small amounts each month mostly. You know, I think he's been planning this for some time. I reckon he's got another woman somewhere. The question is - where?'

'So do we get to go on this picnic? Incidentally it's a good job we didn't opt for Epsom Downs. The local radio news is warning of traffic chaos up there this morning. Apparently a woman's body was found near the gallops first thing and the police have cordoned off the entire area.'

As she spoke, the phone rang. Palmer was about to reply concerning the picnic when he heard the first ring. By the third intrusion he was standing behind the desk.

'Damien Palmer, good morning, how can I help you?' His voice sounded almost monotone, if not slightly impatient. As he spoke, Karen joined him in the office.

'Good morning, Mr Palmer, I'm David Hartley-Brown of Castle Point Systems.'

'Good morning, Mr Hartley-Brown, how are you?' Palmer wrote the name and the company name on the pad of paper. Karen was standing by the desk and looked with interest at what he'd written.

'I am well, Mr Palmer, and yourself?' Hartley-Brown sounded somewhat impatient.

'I'm very well, thank you. Now what can I do for you?'

'I have a problem, Mr Palmer, a problem of the utmost urgency.'

'Go on,' Palmer's interest was increasing if only because his girlfriend had written on the notepaper, the three words "I know them".

'Well, Mr Palmer, I am the Managing Director of Castle Point and I have an employee, quite an important employee, who has gone missing. Not only that but she appears to have taken a very valuable piece of equipment with her. I was wondering if finding her was the kind of work you involve yourself in?'

'That depends, Mr Hartley-Brown. Ordinarily it is the kind of work that comes my way, but I take each case on its own merits.'

'I see, so it's down to money is it?' Again the man on the other end of the phone sounded somewhat abrupt, as if he were under a good deal of stress.

'No, Mr Hartley-Brown, you misunderstood me. It is not just about money. It is more to do with what I consider to be the chances of locating the missing person. After all, it's your money and despite what you may read in the press about private investigators, I would not wish to mislead you into spending a lot of money if I thought the case was hopeless.'

'I see, well in this case, Mr Palmer, money is no object. What is of vital importance to me is that I find the woman and the piece of equipment in the next seventy-two hours. Now, can you help me or not?'

'Without talking to you further, Mr Hartley-Brown, I really don't know.'

'Look, I don't really like talking about this over the phone. You never know who might be listening in. Could you come to my offices?'

'One moment, Mr Hartley Brown, I'll just check my diary.' Palmer covered the mouthpiece with his hand and rapidly told the woman beside him the gist of the conversation. Her eyes opened wide as she listened.

'Damien, you've got to see him. Do you know what CPS do?'

'Not a clue, do you?'

'Yes. Look, this could be big money for you. If we could visit him this morning then we could still have a walk and a picnic in Nonsuch Park.' There was a quiet urgency in her voice.

'You sure?'

'Yes. I'll tell you why later.'

'Mr Hartley-Brown, I'm sorry to have kept you waiting. How are you fixed for today?'

'Now you're talking my kind of language, Mr Palmer. This has top priority on my schedule, so name your time.'

'Where are you?'

'Cheam Village, just behind the station. Do you know the area?' Karen was listening to the conversation, standing just a few inches away from the telephone. She nodded vigorously to Palmer.

'Yes, I know it. Let's see, it's nine thirty now, would eleven o'clock be okay?'

'That would be fine, Mr Palmer. Please use our car park. I'll have someone waiting for you. What do you drive?'

Palmer went on to describe his maroon coloured Escort and also gave Hartley-Brown the registration number.

'Eleven it is, Mr Palmer.'

'Until eleven o'clock, Mr Hartley-Brown. Goodbye.' Palmer replaced the receiver and looked at the woman beside him. 'Are you sure you don't mind?'

'No, just so long as I can come with you and we can have the picnic afterwards.'

'Why the interest in Castle Point then?'

'I looked at them a few years ago. They're innovative, heavily into the hi-tech end of computing and rumour has it they've been doing some special work recently. It's all very hush, hush, but if you have contacts in the right places you get to hear things. So do you think it's linked to the special stuff?'

'I doubt it. It's more likely to be a storm in a teacup. It's Tuesday today so this woman, whoever she is, might just be sick, or decided to have a day off, and she just happens to have the equipment with her. I doubt it's going to add up to much.'

'But why did Hartley-Brown insist it was urgent?' The woman sounded intrigued by the situation that had arisen.

'I have no idea, and I suppose that's what intrigues me. Right, if we're going to meet this chap at eleven, we'd better get moving.'

'I suppose so. I need a couple of minutes upstairs. I won't keep you waiting long.'

'Okay,' Palmer was already walking towards the door of the room. 'I'll put the picnic stuff in the car and come back to lock up.'

Chapter Two

Five minutes later and they sat in Palmer's maroon Escort and had begun the journey towards Wimbledon, Sutton, and then Cheam. It was a journey that was familiar to the investigator. He had made the same journey to Sutton on countless occasions as his relationship with the woman beside him had developed. Her flat, which was near to the centre of Sutton's main shopping centre, was small, modern, and quite luxurious in its appointment. On the back seat lay Palmer's top-opening brown attaché case, his constant companion when visiting clients. The road from Putney to the top of Wimbledon Common was slow, the last of the rush hour traffic mingling with the first of the shoppers. Once they had navigated the Tibbets roundabout and joined the road that skirted Wimbledon Common the traffic eased and Palmer made better progress. Almost without noticing the sumptuous dwellings that faced the common he drove as fast as the road conditions allowed. The trees that lined the side of the Common were in full leaf and the yellowing darkness of the grass indicated that it had been a long, hot, summer. The day was warm and Palmer had the sunroof open to increase the car's ventilation.

Passing through the still-quaint setting of Wimbledon Village he steered the car down the main hill that leads into the very modern shopping centre of Wimbledon itself. The grandly named Centre Court shopping mall, that stood where once the Town Hall had graced the very epicentre of the town's life, was soon behind him as he entered the part of town where the twenty miles per hour speed restriction had been imposed. It irritated the man behind the steering wheel that he should have to travel so slowly, but the rumour was that the security cameras in that part of town had been fitted with speed detectors. The restricted zone seemed to take forever to traverse before Palmer was able to improve his progress through the older, less opulent end of the town. From there he passed quickly through South Wimbledon and on to Sutton.

Instead of taking his familiar route into the heart of Sutton he opted for the bypass. The traffic was not heavy and Palmer made good progress along the bypass until he reached the turning for Cheam Village. The village reminded him of a much earlier period, and indeed some of the buildings still fronted their Tudor beams and construction, though the modern highway had destroyed much of the ancient character that had once surrounded the place. Picking his way to the heart of the village Palmer turned left, the road taking him back towards the railway station that had been built right on the edge of the village as it had started to sprawl. He passed under the bridge that carried the rail track from Sutton to Epsom and turned left to bring him back to the station itself. It was a few minutes to eleven and by now Karen was showing him the route to follow.

'Right,' she said, 'Castle Point is just round the corner on the right and the entrance to the car park is at the end of the block. It's pretty considerate of him to make sure you'll be able to park in there though. From what I can remember it's a tiny space, with room for not more than half a dozen cars.'

Palmer found the entrance and in a moment saw that the woman was right. As he drove towards the parking space that was empty a dark-haired girl of about twenty approached him.

'Mr Palmer?' Her query was polite, although she sounded as if she was demeaning her position in the company by becoming a car-park attendant.

'Yes. Mr Hartley-Brown is expecting me.'

'Yes, yes. We've reserved that space for you. I'll wait here and show you inside to his office.'

Palmer parked the car quite easily and in a moment both he and Shaw were being escorted by the not unattractive twenty-something into the office.

'It's a bit of a narrow corridor in here and we have to go through our kitchen to get to the offices. I'll take you straight to Mr Hartley-Brown's office if that's okay.'

'Fine by me,' said Palmer, as he wondered to himself where else she might have taken them.

'It's up on the third floor. Follow me.' Palmer did as he was bidden and after climbing two narrow flights of stairs with Shaw close behind him the dark-haired girl knocked on the second door that they came to.

'Mr Palmer's here, Mr Hartley-Brown.'

'Excellent, excellent, thank you Carol. Mr Palmer, good of you to come so promptly, do come in.' The balding managing director came from behind his desk to welcome the investigator into his office.

'Mr Hartley-Brown, Damien Palmer, and may I introduce my colleague, Karen Shaw?'

'Colleague hey? Yes, yes, of course, delighted to meet you. Do come in. Coffee, tea, a cold drink?'

'Coffee would be fine,' Palmer responded first.

'Coffee for me as well,' Karen was just entering the office.

'In that case,' continued Hartley-Brown as he fussed around his guests, 'that will be three coffees if you don't mind Carol.'

'Certainly.' The dark-haired woman left the office and Hartley-Brown shut the door. As he did so, the smile on his face turned to something altogether more serious.

'Now Mr Palmer, I won't beat about the bush. I'm a busy man, and doubtless you are too.' Palmer waved his hand in an unassuming manner as if being busy was a relative thing, which it was. 'We're a small company of fifty people. There are half a dozen people involved in Administration and secretarial work. Then there are three directors including myself. We have three divisions, development, support, and research. Ostensibly we sell a financial management package and that keeps the development and support teams busy. We have over fifty major installations including most of the major banks and other big financial institutions.'

'And your research team?'

'That is why I phoned you. There are just four people in that. There's the manager, Katherine Delaney. Then we have two full timers, James

Hawton and Brian Stavers, both been with us for about four or five years and good at what they can do. Finally, there's a contractor, name of Mark Hammond. He's been here about five years as well, and he is the genius of the group.'

'So I take it that it's Hammond who has disappeared?'

'Why do you say that?'

'Well, it's usually the contractors or geniuses who just get up and go.'

'No it's not actually, but I see your reasoning. Actually it's the Manager, Katherine who's gone missing. She was last seen on Thursday last week. According to Carol, my PA you understand, she was working late on some reports when Carol went home. The others in the research team had left by then, so there was only Katherine in the office at half six. Carol was working late finishing off a very important document for me to have the following morning. Anyway that was the last time Katherine was seen. She didn't turn up on Friday and didn't phone in sick, not that she's ever had a day off sick in seven years. And what's more there's no reply from her home number or her mobile. They both ring but there's no response.'

'And you mentioned something about some missing equipment?'

'Which is what I'm coming to. The research team have been working on something a bit different to our usual stuff and I was due to give a demonstration of it next Tuesday. Anyway, we were going to have a dry run of the demonstration last Friday, only she didn't turn up. It was mid-morning before Brian came and told me the laptop was missing.'

'So, why is that important?'

'Because it was the machine where the package had been loaded. It was all wired into the network ready for our dry run.'

'But you will have a backup of the software won't you?' It was Karen's turn to join in the conversation.

'Of the software yes, but without the card in the machine it's useless.'

'So let's get this straight,' said Palmer. 'Your research manager has gone missing and a laptop computer with a new bit of software has gone with her?'

'That's about the size of it, yes.'

'And you think she took it?'

'I should have to say that it's possible, though until last Friday I would never have said such a thing.' Hartley-Brown was looking at Palmer evenly as if trying to sum up the character of the investigator.

'Which means all I have to do is locate the missing person and everything should come out in the wash. You're sure she's not ill?'

'Positive. I even visited her house yesterday just to check. She wasn't there of course. I have her details here for you,' Hartley-Brown reached forward and handed Palmer a sheet of paper.

'No, I don't suppose she was.' Palmer looked briefly at the sheet of paper before turning to his client.

'Okay, Mr Hartley-Brown, level with me. Just what is on that computer that makes it so special?'

Hartley-Brown was about to respond when there was a soft, polite, knock at the door of the office. The dark-haired personal assistant entered the room carrying a tray of coffee, and an envelope.

'This was just delivered for you, Mr Hartley-Brown, bike courier said it was urgent.'

The woman placed the tray on her boss's desk and left the room, closing the door carefully behind her. Hartley-Brown handed the cups round before continuing. As he spoke he absent-mindedly began to open the envelope.

'Well, Mr Palmer, I take it you are not into computers as such?'

'No, but my colleague here is, which is why I brought her.'

'I see, and what I am about to tell you must not leave this office, Christ…' he had just removed the contents of the envelope. His hand started to shake as he handed the single sheet of paper to Palmer. 'You'd better see this.' Hartley-Brown sat down heavily in his well-worn chair. Palmer looked at the sheet of paper. The message was typewritten on three lines in a bold, large, font. It was as stark as it was simple:

I REQUIRE £2,000,000 FOR THE SAFE RETURN OF YOUR EQUIPMENT. I WILL CONTACT YOU AGAIN IN 48 HOURS. HAVE THE MONEY READY.

Palmer handed the note to Shaw and looked at Hartley-Brown.

'You were about to tell me what was on the computer.'

'A new package, and you must understand it is a combination of hardware and software. Without the hardware, which is actually a plug-in card, the software is useless.'

'And what does this all do? You have my word that what you say stays between these walls.'

'Well, if I said it allowed the owner to link up to any bank in the world, or virtually any other system, and for that person to read any information they wanted and indeed to make transactions if they wished, would you understand me.'

'I think so.' Palmer was sitting back in his chair, his index fingers locked under his chin as he looked with a degree of disbelief at his client.

'It's top secret stuff, financed by HMG, and of course its main intention is to locate the hidden assets of those who would try to harm this country, but in the wrong hands it could be disastrous.'

'So why here, and why no special security precautions?'

'We had the right connections, and we had the country's two specialists in this kind of work already with us. They've made huge inroads into the financial markets for us over the past few years. And there was no added security because there was no need. Absolutely no one outside the research team and myself knew what we were building.'

'I take it the experts you mentioned are your research team, Hawton and Stavers?'

'Not quite, but you were right with Hawton – a genuine whiz kid on programming. No, the other one is Hammond. He's a system's designer like you will never have seen before. He designed the card from top to bottom and did all the testing on it.'

'And Delaney?' Karen was intrigued by what she was hearing.

'Katherine Delaney is a manager. Actually she heads up the research and development teams. She's not technical in the strictest sense of the word, but she can operate any of our systems.'

'So, she knew what was on the laptop?' Shaw continued the questioning.

'I would imagine so. There's been monthly development reports passing her desk and coming to me. And yes, in answer to your next question, she would know what it was worth to this company.'

'So, where was the card made?'

'Don't know, the MOD saw to that, or some other office. They took Hammond's design and got the prototype produced. We only took delivery of it a week last Monday and they'd just loaded the software and done a few tests. The demonstration to myself was due last Friday.'

'So why did you get me involved now, why not then?' Palmer was concerned at the delay that had been incurred by Hartley-Brown's indecision.

'Because Miss Delaney is a friend and someone I trust. For her to do this is beyond belief,' and Hartley-Brown stabbed a finger at the sheet of paper Palmer had returned to the desk. 'And I couldn't be sure she wasn't ill until after the week-end.'

'Fair enough, and have you told the MOD?'

'Good God, no, to admit to what's happened would be the end of this business. It is absolutely vital we get that machine back before whoever has got it works out what to do with it.'

'And if it is Miss Delaney who has it, how long will that take?' Shaw was showing more concern than Palmer.

'That depends. A few days maybe, I don't know.'

'And this demand, can you pay it?' Palmer was still sitting back in his chair.

'Just about, if we had to, but it would virtually wipe us out.'

'I see. So what do you want me to do Mr Hartley-Brown?'

'Well, find the woman, obviously, and get the laptop back for me.'

'That sounds simple enough. Are you sure you have told us everything?'

'I think so, at least everything that is of use to you.'

'In that case, what I suggest is this. Miss Shaw is a software designer, and she has a flair for performing systems audits. I would like you to take her on to perform an audit of your systems, which I guess will take a few days at most. She will need full access to all your systems and so forth and it will give her an opportunity to talk discreetly to some of your staff. You never know something might come out of it. Meanwhile I will get onto finding Miss Delaney. I have a guy who works for me who is extremely competent at finding people. As for myself, I regret that I am already occupied on another matter which will take a few days to resolve, though I will have time to assist my two very capable colleagues if they need me. Is that acceptable to you?' Palmer sat forward and his final sentence carried a good deal of force.

'Well I guess so, though I had hoped for your personal service, on account of your reputation. And the ransom demand?'

'Well, you can't talk to the MOD, nor the police for that matter, so for now I would sit tight and wait to see what further contact there is.'

'I guess so, and when will Miss Shaw start?'

'Tomorrow morning at nine a.m. sharp.' Palmer looked at his girlfriend as if seeking support.'

'Sure,' she said, 'and not a word of this to anyone. Stick to Mr Palmer's idea. I should be in and out of here by the end of the week. In fact, a couple of days should be enough.'

'In which case,' said Palmer calmly, 'unless there is anything else we must be getting on. The sooner I attend to my other business the sooner I can help out here, if necessary, though frankly I suspect my colleague will locate Miss Delaney in a very short space of time. Incidentally, how old is she?'

'She's 36 years old, and no, there's nothing else I can think of. I take it that I can phone you if I think of anything. Hartley-Brown sounded like a tired man, defeated by the events of the past few days.

'Of course, my card has my home, mobile and fax numbers on it, and an email address if you need it.' Palmer handed his client the small white business card.

'In which case I will see Miss Shaw tomorrow morning.' Hartley-Brown showed them to the door of his office and called his personal assistant to escort them from the premises.

'See you tomorrow,' Karen commented as she said farewell to the dark-haired PA.

'You're coming back?' the voice sounded surprised.

'Oh yes, your boss wants us to perform a system audit. God knows what for but probably something to do with getting some sort of industry recognition or something.'

'Oh,' the PA sounded as if the whole matter was substantially beyond her level of comprehension.

'Well, until tomorrow, then.' Karen opened the passenger door of the Escort and shut it as Palmer started the engine.

'It sounds like this could be fun. How do I square a couple of days off work?' Her query was genuine, for she had only booked the single day off as holiday.

'I'll phone them in the morning. Right, show me how to get to this park. I'm starving and that picnic in the back smells too good to be true.

Chapter Three

The car park behind the memorial that guards the entrance to Nonsuch Park was almost empty when Palmer pulled into it. The journey from Castle Point Systems had taken less than ten minutes and despite the fine weather and warm sun it was still too early in the day for the sun-worshippers to take their lunch breaks from work and stroll through the well-kept gardens, soaking up the final rays of the summer sun. Palmer parked the car and then, with Karen helping him to carry the bags containing the picnic, they headed into the main area of the park in search of a bench on which to sit as they ate lunch.

They watched as a couple of magpies flirted with each other, dancing in and out of the longer grass several yards ahead of them. They ate the sandwiches and salad that Karen had prepared, and throughout the meal their conversation consisted of small talk. When they had finished, and by now the magpies had flown away to entertain another couple sitting on a bench well out of earshot, Palmer changed the topic of conversation.

'You are happy about going into Castle Point aren't you?'

'I guess so, but I haven't got a clue what I'm looking for, or how to do a system audit. Apart from that it will be a breeze.'

'Well, first off we need to know just what equipment they've got, what they're running on it, exactly what's gone missing, and anything else you can think of. Get serial numbers, product names, anything that looks interesting.'

'Sure. That shouldn't take long.'

'No, it probably won't. But the trickier bit might be talking to some of the employees. We're not going to be overly interested in the support guys, or the development team, but talking to some of them might through some light on this thing.'

'And Katherine Delaney?'

'I think we'll let Eddie deal with that one. Actually I could try ringing him.' With that Palmer extracted his mobile phone and pressed the memory button for the number that was so familiar to him. The phone rang three times before it was answered.

'Eddie it's Damien, how are you?'

'Fine, mate, and you?'

'Pretty good, something's come up, are you busy at the moment?'

'Not really, got a couple of drop offs for the guy round the corner I help out. Other than that I'm pretty free.'

'Fancy doing a bit of work on something then?'

'Yeah, when and what is it?'

'It's probably going to be boring. Got a call this morning from a computer company that's got a missing employee. I need someone to check out her home. I'll handle the usual computer stuff on her.'

'Okay, when do you want it done?'

'As soon as possible. This evening if you've got time.'

'Yeah, should be okay. Where is it and what does she look like?'

'Haven't got much of a description, but she lives in Sutton.' Palmer proceeded to read out the address and the few details he knew about the woman. She was fairly non-descript, being thirty-six years of age, short blond hair, about five feet four, and with what Hartley-Brown had described as a sporty appearance.

'Now, the address is a house, or so I've been told.' Palmer continued after Marston had read the details back to him. 'I don't know the road so I don't know what you'll come across. Take your camera and snap anything that goes in or out. If anyone's at home knock on the door and find out who's there. It's pretty important, but be careful you don't blow your cover.'

'Yeah, yeah. I'll get there for about six and spend a few hours there if needs be.'

'You're a good man Eddie. Ring me if anything comes up.'

'I will. Will you be at home or out.'

'Out I should think, so you'd better phone my mobile.'

'Okay. By the way, did you get anywhere on the Green case?'

'Not sure yet, his wife's looking into a few things. There may be some more work needed if you're up for it.'

'Yeah. It's a bit slack round here at the moment, I could do with the work to pay a few bills.'

'Okay, I'll remember that. Now, I must dash. You ring me if you find out anything.'

'Sure thing, talk to you later.' The phone went silent as Eddie Marston replaced the receiver on the base unit. He looked round his drab, dreary, flat, at the paint that was peeling off the wall near to the ceiling where the damp patch had reined for the past several years. He looked out of the grimy windows that needed a coat of paint onto the concrete jungle outside. Somewhere he could hear children shouting and swearing at each other. Then, as he turned towards his small, badly fitted, kitchen, he heard one of the youths crash into his door. It did not trouble him, for he was used to such things during the hour when the children from the local comprehensive took their lunches.

He looked with disinterest at the pile of mail that sat on the small table at the far end of the lounge. It had been a quiet time for him, and the local shops had had little work for him to undertake. Even Palmer had been quiet for a few weeks, which was not unusual for the summer period. Now though, Marston needed to earn some money. The bills on the table needed to be paid, and soon. He would, he considered, do virtually anything to pay those bills. He looked around him again, with the pride of a homeowner. It wasn't much by some people's standards but the dreary flat was his, all bar the mortgage, and Marston was a proud man. He'd worked damn hard in the face of adversity to get the flat in the first place and he was equally sure that a few bills would not defeat him now.

He looked at the piece of paper on which he'd written Delaney's address. He was not particularly familiar with the outskirts of Sutton and there was not much to go on. He had the afternoon to find it on the map and more importantly he had three deliveries to make for the local corner shop. He set about the task of making those deliveries.

The afternoon remained fine and passed swiftly. Palmer and Shaw walked round the park holding hands and chatting. If the missing Delaney was playing on Palmer's mind he did not show it. It was a rule of his that pleasure and work should not be combined unless absolutely necessary. So far as he was concerned the case was one of a missing person, and it was in the best of hands. Eddie Marston had an uncanny skill in making surreptitious enquiries. He could walk into a shop and ask the right questions without raising any eyebrows, and walk away with the answers. He could knock on doors and do the same thing. Palmer reflected back to one case in particular where Marston had been making some door-to-door enquiries on a block of flats where a person had gone missing. He'd ended up talking to the chap who lived next door to the missing person. He was some ex-army type and had kept Marston talking for hours. By the end of it Marston had convinced him that he was the missing person's long lost brother and the old boy had opened up and told Marston exactly what his supposed sister was like. In the end it had helped Palmer to solve the case.

Now as he walked through the park he knew that the investigation into the disappearance of Katherine Delaney was in good hands. He squeezed his girlfriend's hand, an affectionate squeeze that encouraged her to respond in a like manner. The sun-worshippers were out in the park by this time and they passed a number of people, some walking in solitude, others in pairs.

'Must do something about expanding the business,' Palmer said quite suddenly.

'How do you mean?' The woman seemed surprised by his comment, for they had been walking some distance, each with their own thoughts.

'Don't know really, but there's so many areas of investigative work I don't even look at. Take this Castle Point case. I wouldn't have a clue where to start, or what all the bits and pieces do, but that's where the big money of the future will be. The bigger and faster they build the machines the more tempting it will be for people to get involved in some form of criminal activity or other.'

'So, what are you thinking about?'

'I'm not sure.' Palmer stopped walking for a moment. 'Maybe I need to get a few people on board, people with the right skills. Then I could go out and sell those skills.'

'I see, and what kind of skills are you looking for?'

'I haven't really thought about it. Computer-based for a start, then probably someone who's into graphology.'

'Graphology, what's that when it's at home?'

'Oh, hand-writing, and stuff.'

'What, styles, signatures, that kind of thing?'

'Yeah, someone who can work out a person's character from the way they write.'

'I've got a friend who's into something like that. She's also into horoscopes and astrology. Actually she's a graphics designer by trade.'

'Could be interesting. Tell me more.'

'She works on her own as a designer. Also she's got an Internet astrology site set up – does forecasts and predictions for people. Actually I helped her get it set up. And I know she's interested in handwriting – links it in with her forecasts and stuff. I don't know how good she is, but it might be worth a chat if you're interested.'

'Could be. Have a chat with her and see if she's interested, on a freelance basis to start with. Also, if I was to expand I'd need some more folk who can do the sort of surveillance stuff you and Edie have helped out with over the past year or so.'

'Well, you could always get Eddie involved on a more permanent basis. From what you said earlier he's good at it, and he needs the money.'

'True, but he's always had other interests. I know we're good friends and known each other for years, but I kind of like our arrangement. It's informal and he can always say no if he doesn't want to do anything. Also, the thought of being his boss doesn't appeal much, I know him too well for that.'

'Fair enough, but there is an alternative you could consider.'

'What's that?'

'Bring him in as a partner, and then give him responsibility for organising the surveillance cases. That way he's still his own boss, you're getting some of the workload offloaded and he's got a vested interest in keeping busy.'

'A partner, now that's an idea. I'll think it over. Yes, that might just be what I need. I know it's been quiet the last few weeks, the summer always is. But then again, there's been enough routine stuff to keep me going, and it's only going to get busier over the next few weeks. You might have struck on something there. Come on, let's get an ice cream.' Palmer started walking with a brisk, almost playful, pace to his gait. For her part Shaw seemed content that he had at least listened to her idea.

'There is something else Damien,' she said as they licked the melting ice cream that sat on top of the cones.

'Yeah, what's that?'

'Well, I've had enough where I am. The last few months have been the final straw. I think it's more than the sod of a boss I work for, I just feel it's time to move on.'

'So, what are you going to do?'

'I think I'll start looking for a new job, see what comes up.' She sounded matter of fact about the subject.

'I see, and what does that mean?'

'It means, I might have to move away from here. There aren't many jobs around here that demand my skills. In fact apart from my place and Castle Point I don't think there are any.'

'Which means,' Palmer began.

'Which means I might have to move out of the area, which is going to be pretty hard to do now I've found you.'

'Well, let's meet that bridge if and when we come to it. First though you've got to get that other job, assuming there's one available somewhere.'

'Actually, there is, and that's what I've been trying to say for the past few days. I've got an interview a week tomorrow.'

'That's great. Where is it?'

'Edinburgh.'

'Edinburgh?' Palmer almost spat the word out in surprise. 'What the hell do you want to go up there for?'

'It's not a question of want Damien, it's a question of survival. I haven't got the job yet, and I may not. But I've been short-listed for the interview so I must be in with a chance.' Palmer looked stunned by the news and stopped licking the ice cream.

'Anything I can say or do to stop you going?' It was a weak, very un-Palmer like thing to say, but it was the best he could manage.

'Sorry, darling, but I don't think so. I have to give it a shot, and it doesn't have to be the end for us. We could still see each other and talk on the phone etcetera.'

'But Edinburgh, that's hundreds of miles away. How long do you think we'd be able to go on for?' Palmer sounded almost frightened, almost rejected, and definitely hurt. He put an arm round the woman's shoulders and pulled her to him. She did not resist, and nor did she hold back when he kissed her on the cheek, though she did not respond with her customary warmth. Palmer noted her lack of response and it poured more salt on the wound of rejection that she had opened up, a wound that had lain never far beneath the surface since Palmer's childhood.

'I don't know,' she said eventually, 'but let's not worry about it until I get the job. It may not happen.'

'It will, and if it's not Edinburgh it'll be somewhere else, and it will only be a matter of time. You're basically calling off the relationship aren't you?' His wound was now open wide, exposed for the woman he loved to see in all of its festering misery. He took his arm away from her and as if in sympathy a cool breeze crossed the path where they were standing.

'No, Damien, I am not splitting us up. I love you, you daft fool, don't you realise that? I just can't stick at what I'm doing for any longer. If there was another job locally I'd go for it like a shot, don't you understand. I want to be with you, but I have to work!' She advanced towards him but then she realised the hurt as he backed away.

'Well, just think carefully what you're doing,' was all he could say. 'Now, I reckon it's time we got back to the car. I guess you've got things to do this afternoon, and I know I have. Are you still willing to do Castle Point.'

'Yes, but only if you snap out of this silly idea that I don't care for you anymore.'

'Okay. Look, it's just the shock. I need some time to think, that's all. Do you mind if we don't spend this evening together, only I need to think things through and I won't be much company until I have.'

'Fair enough, but I need a lift back to your place to get my car.'

'Fine by me.' Palmer began the walk back across the well-maintained gardens to the car park. It took them nearly quarter of an hour and by the time they reached the gravelled area that had been cordoned off for the use of cars he was once again holding the woman's hand.

As they drove in virtual silence back to Palmer's terraced house Marston was busy with his final delivery of the afternoon. As he completed the delivery of the boxes of shopping his mind turned to the evening's surveillance that Palmer had asked him to undertake. Marston knew that he was good at surveillance he always had been, ever since he'd first expressed an interest in the work of a private investigator. It came naturally to him, the ability to watch and observe unobtrusively. Also, and perhaps it was because of his short stature and his somewhat chubby face that often bore a ruddy complexion, he had discovered that people found it easy to talk to him. Actually, on reflection, it probably had as much to do with the simple fact that he was one of the world's great listeners. Not that he was afraid to involve himself in discussions or express his views on matters of importance, because that was not the case. It was just that he knew he could learn more by listening.

It took Palmer and Shaw nearly an hour to drive back to his terraced house, and by the time they arrived it was late afternoon.

'Do you want to come in, or get back to your flat?' His question was asked just as he applied the handbrake.

'I'm not in a rush, so if you don't mind I'd like to come in. What are you going to do?'

'First of I've got to check out Delaney from the computer point of view. Care to watch what I do?' Palmer was being civil, but his voice still reflected his hurt and pain at the woman's earlier disclosure.

'Yeah, it'd be interesting. Look Damien, cheer up, I haven't got the job yet, and I probably won't get it. Also, something else might turn up, you never know.'

'Okay, I'll try, but it's not easy. I don't want to lose you, but it just seems everything's so black and white from your point of view that I don't have any way of holding onto you.' He opened the door and slammed it shut behind him.

'You do actually,' she muttered to herself before opening her own door. It was a comment that went unheard by the man she adored, as was her next, 'and that's the whole point of me telling you in advance.'

Karen Shaw opened her door and closed it so that Palmer could lock the car. Having done so he led the way up the pavement and then the short path to the blue door of his house. Once inside he turned on the computer that sat on his desk so that it would be ready for him when he needed it. By the time he'd set the coffee maker up, and the aroma from the ground beans wafted through the house he was typing in the name of the missing employee. He waited as the computer searched the database on the

CD that he was using. It located maybe a dozen possible entries. Palmer scanned them all and selected the one that he was interested in. The address matched the one that Hartley-Brown had given him a few hours earlier. Interestingly there was also an entry for a telephone number, though Hartley-Brown's details had not included that piece of information. As he looked at the laptop's screen Palmer noted down the number and a single comment on his notepad. It intrigued him that Hartley-Brown had omitted to provide the telephone number from the employee's records.

'Well, it seems like she lives where Hartley-Brown told us she does,' Palmer commented. Karen Shaw was sitting on a chair opposite Palmer and she reached round to look at the screen.

'Hey, that's pretty interesting, how did you get that?'

'Easy. I subscribe to a company that produces a database of information for the whole of the UK. I get a new one of these every year. I can find most people on this, provided they're registered on the electorate.'

'So what else can you find out about her?'

'That depends. I can do a check on the DBM database, but it's not necessarily up to date.'

'DBM?' Shaw sounded surprised.

'Yeah. Deaths, Births and Marriages. It's not widely known but some areas are electronically recording details now. Okay, she won't be on the births list – she's too old to have been put on electronically, unless someone's going back in history for it. Also, we can forget the despatches list, because it takes a couple of months to get on that, and she was last seen only a few days ago. We could look up the marriages entries and see if anything comes up.'

'So, how do you do that?'

'Basically by dialling a number, and seeing what comes up. Come on Karen, you're the computer expert, I thought you'd know about this sort of thing.'

'I do, but this is kind of specific to your area of life isn't it. I bet I could run rings round you on Internet stuff.'

'Yeah, I'll bet you could. Hold on, here comes the results.' The computer screen flickered and then suddenly the screen was filled with information. 'She's divorced according to this. Married five years ago and divorced last year. Always assuming it's the same person, which is possible but not overly probable, though the name isn't that common and our target and this woman are in the same area of the country. Shame it doesn't list her address, only the Registrar's area of responsibility.'

'What next? Anything else this box of tricks can do?'

'Hmm,' Palmer seemed unsure for a moment. 'Okay as it's you, and this is strictly off the record.' He pressed a couple of keys so quickly that the woman was unable to follow his actions. 'This next approach lets us into the flight bookings system. I shouldn't really be in here, but someone got careless with a number sometime, and as the whole thing's in script I can use a browser to get in.'

'Yeah, but only on the surface, surely?'

'No. It's used round the airport by loads of people so it's pretty open. Here, let's see if anything shows up.' Again Palmer entered the woman's name, but the screen returned no results. 'Well, it doesn't prove much really. The system only covers Gatwick, so if she were planning to leave from Heathrow, say, it wouldn't show up. Still, we know she isn't about to fly out of Gatwick. Better log off now before anyone monitors it.' Palmer pressed more buttons and then picked up the telephone.

'Eddie, it's Damien.'

'Hiya. Just getting to grips with what you want me to do this evening. Anything else you can tell me about it?'

'Nope, not even a decent description I'm afraid, other than what I told you earlier. However, the computer checks show she is registered at the address I gave you and there's a chance she might be a divorcee. Other than that nothing has come up I'm afraid.'

'Doesn't matter really. As you said earlier it will probably end up being a pretty routine case for us. I'll ring you in the morning and let you know what happened.'

'Actually Eddie, could you ring me tonight when you're there?'

'Sure, any reason though?'

'Nope, not yet, but things might change by say nine o'clock.'

'Fair enough, I'll phone you at nine, or earlier if anything comes up.'

'Cheers Eddie.' Palmer replaced the receiver and looked across the room at the rows of books on the shelves as if seeking some kind of inspiration from their wealth of knowledge.

'What's the matter?' The woman's voice broke the silence of the room.

'Nothing, I was just thinking about Delaney. It's a pretty tall order to demand two million for the return of a computer. She must have a damned good idea what the software's worth to Hartley-Brown.'

'Yeah, it does seem a lot of money. You know, I reckon there's more to this than Hartley-Brown's letting on.'

'For sure there is, the question is, what?' Palmer started drumming his fingers on the top of his desk. The action lasted for several seconds.

'Well, I can try and find out tomorrow if you want?'

'Oh I want that very much. You're the expert. From what Hartley-Brown's said, what do you reckon to this new package they've created?'

'Sounds a bit like Big Brother meets with Terminator if you ask me.'

'Sorry?' Palmer was clearly confused by her choice of phrase.

'Big Brother's always watching you. The package certainly sounds like it can home in on just about anyone's financial details. And Terminator, because at any moment the person operating it could wipe you out financially.'

'So if you have the software and the know-how why send in a ransom demand? Why not just move the money yourself?'

'There's two possibilities. One, she doesn't have the package, unlikely but possible. Secondly, she might not have the know-how needed to make it work.'

'So in either case Hartley-Brown doesn't need to pay up.' Palmer sounded momentarily pleased with his deduction.

'Maybe, and maybe not. She might not have the know-how but my guess is she could learn it in a few days, and that's what Hartley-Brown is thinking too. Which is why the demand carries the weight it does. He knows that in say three days she'll just move the money whether or not he pays up. If he pays he reckons he'll get the box back, if he doesn't pay then God only knows what havoc she'll create. So to keep this all hush, hush, he's got to pay her what she wants.'

'Which means she'll need a drop off point and that might give us a chance.'

'I doubt it. If she's clever enough to plan this then she's probably got some help from someone. My guess is they'll have worked out the drop off bit very carefully indeed.'

'You're probably right. I never did like computers, and now I'm growing to hate most of the Delaney's of this world that use them. One thing's for sure, we've got to find that box before she gets to grips with it.'

'Assuming she's got it.' Shaw's observation brought Palmer up short, momentarily lost for a response.

'But she must have. If she hasn't, then who has?'

'Don't know, but as your computer expert I have to say we're a devious lot. I'm just saying that because Delaney's gone missing and so has the laptop, it doesn't mean the events are connected.'

'You're right of course, we don't know they are, but it's a bit of a coincidence if they're not linked.'

'True, but let's keep an open mind about it for a day or so.'

'Which is about all the time we might have if Delaney is trying to figure out how to use the package. Okay, strategy time. You're going to Castle Point tomorrow. Find out what you can about Delaney and the others in the research team.'

'Okay, now can we change the subject. What do you want to do this evening?' Shaw leaned seductively over the desktop until her face was just a few inches from Palmer's. She licked her lips, suggestively, and as she did so Palmer was sure she winked at him.

'Depends on you.'

'Well, I can't stay the night for the simple reason I need some clothes for tomorrow, and with a nine start it' going to be easier to go from the flat than here. But, we do still have the evening, if you want it.'

'What about you?' Palmer sounded more hopeful than he had done for some hours

'I'm up for it. I told you I fancy you rotten. Now, do you want me to prove it?'

'Sounds fun, what do you have in mind?'

'Take-away and massage.'

'What kind of take-away?'

'Pizza perhaps, that one we had the other week was pretty tasty.' The woman was still smiling, glad that the tension between them earlier in the afternoon had faded. At times, she thought to herself, men could be particularly obtuse. Then again, she had the evening to drive the message home.

The afternoon turned into evening and Marston set off for his evening of surveillance. The traffic on the roads was as heavy as ever and the rush hour had only just started. It had been a warm day and the heat lingered into the evening. Marston made slow progress on his journey to Sutton, arriving outside the address he was planning to observe at a little after half past six. It was about the same time that Palmer placed the pizza order with the local delivery company. Marston, in his usual manner, drove carefully past the house, turned the car round and parked. It was a tree-lined road of semi-detached houses built in the nineteen thirties. Many of the houses had driveways that led from the street to the houses. There were few garages, though the off-street parking had significantly reduced the congestion on the road.

Being the end of the summer period the grassy patches that constituted the front gardens were brown and dusty. Indeed, the house Marston was watching was typical of the houses in the road. Replacement double glazing had been fitted, probably within the past few years, and Marston observed that the roof and guttering still needed attention. The driveway itself was empty though any one of the cars parked in the road could have belonged to the house's owner.

He sat and waited for nearly ten minutes before leaving his car to investigate the property. He walked up the empty drive and approached the modern, plastic-framed door. He pressed the buzzer and waited. He pressed the buzzer again and then, when a response was not forthcoming, he bent down and peered through the letterbox. The post and a local paper lay on the carpet just inside the door untouched, Marston reckoned, for a few days. He straightened up again and walked back down the drive. The house he had visited was the right of the pair of semis, and now Marston approached the front door of the adjoining property. Again he pressed the doorbell and waited. He saw the shape of the woman approaching from inside the door. She moved slowly as if her bulk inhibited movement. When she opened the door, the size and shape of her body prevented Marston from seeing much of the interior.

'Hi, I don't know if you can help me, but I'm looking for Kathy next door?' Marston had framed the question carefully, and his phoney American accent was more than passable.

'Kathy you say, and who might be after her.'

'Aw, sorry ma'am, should've introduced myself better. I'm Chuck Hardbottle, I'm Kathy's cousin.'

'Cousin, she's never mentioned a cousin. How do I know you are who you say you are?' The woman looked as if she was about to close the door.

'Well, I can't say I blame her really. Haven't seen her for maybe ten years now. Been living in the good old U.S. of A. for a while. Anyway I came over a couple of weeks ago and rang her up and she said to come over this evening, only she isn't in.'

'Well, that's not my problem. Now if you don't mind,' and the woman took a step backwards.

'Only I heard about her divorce last year and as I'm flying out at the end of the week, I was real hoping to meet up with her.' Clearly Marston's mention of the divorce struck a chord of recognition with the obese woman he was facing.

'Chuck, what was it you said?'

'Hardbottle ma'am. Do you know what time Kathy gets back usually. Only if it's going to be late, I can't really hang around. I'll have to phone her tomorrow.'

'Well, Chuck, she's usually home by now, but actually I don't think she's been around for a few days. Said she wanted to meet you here tonight, did she?'

'That's right. We made the arrangements last Tuesday, it was her first free evening.'

'Well, I don't think she's been around since before the weekend, but we don't really see much of each other, what with my angina and her being so busy. She always goes out early and comes in about this sort of time.'

'I see, well I won't take up any more of your time. Probably she's forgotten about us and she's doing something else.' Marston stepped back from the door.

'Probably, she always did seem a bit disorganised somehow. If I see her I'll tell her you called.'

'Thanks, anyway you have a nice day, ma'am.' Marston stepped back again before turning away from the house.

'And you too,' the woman called after him. As Marston walked back down the drive he heard the door slam shut behind him. Careful, in case he was being watched by the woman he had just talked to, Marston turned down the road and walked back to Delaney's house. He stood for some moments at the front door with his back turned to the adjoining semi. To any observer it would have looked exactly the way Marston intended it should look, he was writing his cousin a note. For good measure he opened the letterbox and pretended to be pushing a piece of paper through the aperture. This task completed he walked back down the road to his car.

Once he had regained the relative comfort and seclusion of the driver's seat he phoned Palmer.

'Damien, it's Eddie.'

'Eddie, how's it going? Karen, can you get the door?' The distant sound of the doorbell was just discernible in Marston's receiver. He also heard the woman respond but could not pick out the actual words.

'Not a lot happening really. It doesn't look like anyone's in at the moment. I've been to chat to the neighbour, but she hasn't seen Delaney since before the weekend.'

'So what's your opinion Eddie?'

'Well, I don't think the neighbour's the kind of person who doesn't know what's going on around her. Actually, I reckon she's a bit of a window watcher. So if she says Delaney hasn't been around since last week, then she's probably right.'

'Okay, so she isn't using her own home as a base. Not really surprising, after all it's the first place Hartley-Brown thought of looking, and I'd guessed she'd be smarter than that. Seems like she is.'

'So what do you want me to do? I could stay here for a bit, but I doubt she's coming home. There's loads of post on the doormat, more than you'd expect in a couple of days. There's also a local paper there.'

'Which are usually delivered on a Thursday, so it would be reasonable to assume she hasn't been back since Thursday morning. Okay Eddie, there's no point in staying there. Call it a night and have a drink on the firm.'

'Sure. Actually I might just do that.'

'Be my guest. Look, if you come over tomorrow we can have a chat about a few things. I've got some ideas that I'd like to put past you. Say eleven, would that be okay?'

'Yeah, any clues?'

'No, just some ideas about getting you some more of the work you're good at. Must go, dinner's arrived.'

'Okay Damien, till tomorrow.' Marston replaced the mobile phone in his jacket pocket and began the journey home.

Palmer and Shaw ate the pizza and drank the best part of a bottle of wine. The pizza was as good as Karen remembered from her previous experience, and the wine soon helped them both to relax.

'And now,' she said, 'it's time for that massage I promised you.'

'You're the boss,' Palmer replied as he placed the final few dishes in the dishwasher. Leaving it to run through its cycle he dutifully followed the woman upstairs 'So, how do you want to do this?' Palmer asked the question though he already knew the answer. The woman sitting on the end of the bed had, after all, spent some considerable part of the meal explaining exactly what she was going to do, and Palmer now needed no further encouragement. Indeed, as he stepped out of his trousers it was evident that he was very much looking forward to what was about to take place.

His shirt removed and carefully folded on the chair at the end of the bed, he lay down on his stomach as instructed, his head lying flat on the bed with his hands by his side. He was now naked apart from the pair of dark blue boxer shorts. As if to encourage the mood Karen had also partially removed her clothing. The skirt and top were discarded carelessly on the floor and now, as she sat beside Palmer she was wearing only her underclothes. She reached over his back and hung her head so that her long, sandy, hair touched his flesh. With gentle movements she swung her head so that the hair glanced tantalisingly up and down the investigator's back. After repeating this action she reached over onto the bedside table and picked up the bottle of baby oil. Having rubbed some of the oil into her fingers she proceeded to massage his shoulders. Gently at first but with growing energy as he told her how good it felt. Then, using her hands in a chopping motion she gently pummelled the area that was now covered in a fine layer of the oil. Her massage proceeded lower. Kneading, stretching, and scratching the flesh she slowly, almost tenuously, moved down his back until she reached the line of the boxers.

She stopped here and turned her attention to his legs. Taking each in turn she gently massaged first the calf muscle and then proceeded to explore the thigh until, again, she reached the boundary presented by the boxers. After some five minutes of this delectable attention she whispered two words in his ear.

'Turn over.' They were the first words that had been spoken since the start of the treatment and her voice carried a quality of seduction that Palmer instantly recognised as the voice that Karen adopted when she was aroused. He did as he was asked and with his eyes closed she repeated the performance on his chest.

This time she did not stop at the boundary of the boxers. Instead she continued over them, her fingers caressing and teasing his manhood. Although Palmer was already considerably excited by the attention that he had received Karen was sure that her touch added yet a further measure of intent into the proposal that she was preparing. Satisfied with what she achieved she straddled him, with her head facing his feet. In a moment he felt her fingers ease inside the elastic at the top of the shorts and then he felt the garment being lowered until he was fully exposed.

'Now Damien, I haven't done this before, but I want to get the message home to you that I love you, and this is the best way I know right now. If you don't like it just tell me and I'll stop.'

He felt her breath as she spoke. It played across that most sensitive part of his manhood as she leaned forward. He felt the strands of hair against his leg as she lowered her head. The sensation of heat and moisture as she attended to him was almost more than he could bear. Sitting astride him she felt his stomach muscles contract as he groaned with the pleasure he was receiving. After maybe two minutes of this most intimate of attentions she felt him rise at the same moment that she felt the first spasm, the tell-tale sign that he had reached the point of no return. Smiling to herself she thrust her head as low as was possible, ensuring that he was completely immersed in the way she was handling him. Although she could not now see what she was doing she reached over her head and between his legs. She stroked the area three times as she breathed in and waited.

His eruption seemed to last forever and though the violence of his peak was a surprise to the woman she managed to maintain position until he had subsided.

'I won't be a minute,' she said, quite clearly yet with the same seductive quality that she had used earlier. She disappeared from the room for less than two minutes. When she returned, Palmer was still lying on the bed where she had left him.

'I think you'll feel better kissing me now I taste of mint.' She reached over and placed her lips on

59

his. He responded by prising her lips apart and drawing his tongue round her teeth. He shuffled over on the bed and pulled her to him, determined that she should not now escape his attentions. After all, she was immensely attractive, clearly highly aroused, and he could not be sure how many such opportunities would arise if she went to Edinburgh.

He laid her on the bed and deftly removed her flimsy underwear. Her chest heaved slightly as he kissed her nipples in turn, offering her similar attention to that which she had just given him. Soon his free hand was exploring her ardour, ensuring that she was thoroughly aroused. He touched her intimately and caressed her until he felt the wave of pleasure seer through her body. As her arched back subsided onto the sheet he continued with his ministration though now he was more forceful. He probed her, and teased her with his mouth and fingers, until he felt her reach her second peak of pleasure. Only then did he straddle her. Then with his tongue thrust rudely into her willing mouth she felt the warmth of his body at the entrance to her body. She gasped with some surprise at his size as he entered her.

On many such occasions he took the next stage of their love-making gently for he knew his rhythmic approaches sent the woman wild, but tonight with his own emotions running high, he thrust almost wantonly into her slender body, each thrust reaching to the very hilt. With each movement she gasped as his flesh rubbed against hers. This was a new experience for her, as she could not recall him being quite so physical in his approach before, and it excited her to be treated in this way. She gasped loudly as his thrusts became stronger, sweat pouring off his body onto hers, mingling with the fluids of her own arousal. She screamed as one particular thrust forced the air out of her lungs and it felt as though every muscle in her abdomen had contracted at the same time. There was no stopping him. Gasping for breath she began to fight back, as if trying to throw him from her. But Palmer knew better, he knew that this was Karen at the absolute peak of her arousal pattern. He had taken her there before on many occasions, though not so swiftly as this particular evening. As he struggled to maintain the same rhythm of deep, penetrating, thrusts, she began to turn red. Her face, upper arms and the top of her chest became flushed with the combination of excitement and exertion. Then Palmer felt his own need. With one final movement he reached his own culmination before slowly subsiding and collapsing over the woman who had drained every last gram of what he had to offer her. Sated, and exhausted, they lay that way until their arousal had begun to subside.

'Wow,' he said finally as he raised himself so that he could lie beside her.

'Wow,' she replied, turning her head towards him. 'Did I get the message across?'

'Oh yes.'

Chapter Four

Tuesday dawned bright and sunny. After making love the previous evening Shaw had driven back to her flat in Sutton. Now she faced the short drive to Cheam village and her appointment at Castle Point Systems. She drove to the village and parked in the station car park. A gentle stroll down the road from the station brought her to the front door of office block she was due to attend. She looked briefly at her watch and decided that being ten minutes early was probably not a bad idea. She pressed the buzzer by the front door and waited. She saw Hartley-Brown's PA walk towards the door and in a moment she had been ushered into the building.

'Mr Hartley-Brown says you'll be here for a few days so I'll get you a security pass sorted out. I'm Carol by the way.' The PA showed Karen into the main office area.

'Hi, I'm Karen, thanks. So how is this all structured then?'

'Computer room's down in the basement, and there's a security door into it. I'll introduce you to some of the guys who can get you in there if you need to. The support team are on this floor, but most of them work out on site, so you won't see many of them. Next floor up are the developers, and there's a room that's been sectioned off for the research team. Again it's a locked area, but I'll introduce you to the people you might need to help you.'

'Sounds like this has all been pretty carefully organised,' Karen took up the conversation as they walked into the first office area.

'This is Ron, and he's Gary. Guys, this is Karen. The boss has called in some organisation to do an audit and he wants you to co-operate with her, okay.'

The two young men introduced themselves properly and Karen reciprocated before she was led to the stairway and the second floor. At the top of the stairs was a single desk set apart from the others. The woman sat behind the desk looked up as they reached the top step.

'Christina DeClare, meet Karen Shaw.' The PA continued speaking as the two women greeted each other. 'Karen's here to do some audit work for the boss after what happened last week. I'm showing her round, but no doubt she'll want to talk to you later.'

'By all means.' DeClare was a soft, quiet talker. Indeed she looked like an unassuming individual, though in that aspect of her character lay her strength. She was, Shaw thought, one of life's listeners and watchers.

'Say about half an hour or so?' Karen was smiling as she addressed the head of the development team.

'Fine by me. I suppose you've got to see the boss first?'

Karen looked at the PA who responded first.

'Yes. David wants a quick chat before Karen gets started.' Karen noticed the familiar use of the Managing Director's name.

'Well, see you later then,' Karen was still smiling as she was led up the second flight of stairs.

'Miss Shaw for you.' The PA had knocked on the door of the office that Karen Shaw had visited the previous day.

'Come in Miss Shaw and close the door please. Thank you Carol.'

The PA turned and left to return to her desk in the adjoining office space.

'Well, Miss Shaw, welcome to Castle Point. I take it that Mr Palmer, or at least his colleague, is making some progress.'

'I would imagine so, but I don't get involved in that side of the cases much.'

'So, where do you want to start?'

'Why not with you, and then I'd like to go and have a chat with Christina DeClare and possibly meet the research team before seeing what the support area deals with.'

'Fair enough, so how can I help you?'

'Katherine Delaney, how long has she worked here?'

'About seven years, and in all that time she has never given us any cause for concern.'

'I see, and how well do you know her?'

'Quite well, you do when you've known someone for that length of time.'

'By quite well, what do you mean, exactly?'

'She is a good colleague, trustworthy, honest, puts in a long day when she has to, that kind of thing.' Hartley-Brown sat neatly behind his desk as he talked.

'Right, and you don't believe she's walked off with the laptop?'

'Up until yesterday I'd have said no, but if she didn't then I don't understand where she has got to.'

'And if I remember correctly you said yesterday you'd visited her home, is that right?'

'Yes, on Sunday. She doesn't live that far from me anyway, so I just popped round, but there was no reply.'

'Okay, well I guess she is the main suspect at the moment, but we'd better keep our options open just in case. Now I take it you've not heard anything more about the ransom demand?'

'No.'

'And I'm right in believing that she'd be able to use the laptop to electronically transfer the funds if you didn't pay up?'

'Good God no. We do have some security you know. There are two sets of codes that are required to activate the software. The first set of codes is for testing purposes, proves the hardware links and so forth, but to unlock the power of the package a second set of codes is required. They are known only to myself and the client, which is why I had to be involved in the test run.'

'And you're sure no one else knows the codes?' Karen was relaxing now, feeling almost in her element.

'Positive. I don't even keep them here, just in case.'

'Good, so the laptop is useless unless you type in the second set of codes.'

'Correct.'

'And the first set of codes are not going to activate anything of use to whoever has taken the laptop?'

'Precisely. Now, what do you want to do round this place?'

'Talk to a few people, list the machines and configurations you've got, and see what else comes up.'

'And what do you want to do first?'

'A chat with your development manager I think.'

'Well, don't let me keep you. Any problems, just come back to me or ring me on extension 101.'

'Thanks, Mr Hartley-Brown, I'll let you know how things go.' With that Karen Shaw stood up and in a moment had descended the staircase to conduct her first interview.

As she began work talking to the Castle Point employees Palmer was opening the morning post. There was, almost inevitably, the usual pile of junk mail. For perhaps the fourth time in as many weeks they included the chain letter that was doing the rounds. It intrigued Palmer that people could be gullible enough to believe that simply by adding their name to the list of addressees and then posting on the letter to a couple of hundred other folks and sending a pound coin to the six people on the original list that one day they would receive thousands of pounds in the post. As if to show the fatal flaw in the logic of the con artist who had dreamed up the scam he was currently reading Palmer consigned it to the bin. That was, he hoped, the reaction most of the recipients would follow, leaving only the poor mindless minority with the almost impossible belief that by making a response they would soon become rich. The flaw lay not in the concept of what could happen with such a letter, but in the unpredictability of that unscientific phenomenon – human response. Palmer considered that his own response was typical of what would happen in hundreds of households that morning.

The next letter held his attention for longer. He read the solicitor's letter very carefully indeed and then examined the documents that were enclosed. John Manning, of Clarke and Manning had telephoned him at the end of the previous week and stressed the urgency of the documents. They warranted Palmer's immediate attentions, a fact backed up by the advance fee enclosed with the material. Palmer looked quickly at his watch and decided that the time to act on the solicitor's letter had arrived. He was putting on shoes when the shrill tone of the telephone distracted him.

'Damien Palmer, good morning, how can I help you?' He did his best not to sound in a hurry, and he succeeded.

'Mr Palmer, it's Dawn Green. I have the cheques you asked me to get hold of.'

'Excellent, Mrs Green, are you at home today?'

'Yes all day, bar some shopping I need to do this morning.'

'Well, I have to go out now for an hour or so. Why don't I call round this afternoon about two o'clock?'

'Are you sure you wouldn't prefer me to come to your place?'

'No need to, I'll be out and about so I might as well drop in.'

'Okay then, I'll see you about two.'

'Fine. Well I must get going. Goodbye Mrs Green.'

'Goodbye.' The phone went dead and Palmer picked up the envelope that contained the documents he needed. He took a final look at his diary and noted that Marston was due to visit him at eleven. It gave him time provided the person he was seeking was where he expected him to be.

Palmer had already undertaken some preliminary enquiries into the person Manning had asked him to locate. He'd found Paul Mathers home address quite easily. However, he'd noted that the flat was modern with an entry phone, and Palmer's experience had shown such devices were an almost guaranteed way of failing to reach the intended target for serving Process. The document was a restraining order and Palmer had been asked to serve it on Mathers at the earliest possible opportunity.

There was, of course, the opportunity to serve the document at a set of traffic lights, always assuming he could follow Mathers to work one morning, and keep sufficiently close to him so that if the lights went red he could jump out and do what was necessary. The idea did not appeal to him for long. There were simply too many possible outcomes for such a plan, though Palmer had to concede it was a scenario that he had exploited successfully on more than one occasion. Instead Palmer had decided to follow Mathers to his workplace. As a car mechanic working for one of the country's larger exhaust replacement centres Palmer had observed his quarry the previous Saturday morning as he carried out his work duties. It was, Palmer thought, the ideal place to serve the Process, and so Palmer drove round to the garage.

It was almost ten o'clock when he parked in the customer car park and went round to the reception room.

'Hi,' he began as the mechanic behind the desk looked up, 'could someone take a look at my exhaust? It's making a bit of a noise and I think it might have a hole in it.'

'Sure. Which one is it?'

'The maroon Escort in the car park. Will it take long?'

'Five minutes to look at it, and then we'll know more.'

'Oh, that's fine.' Palmer handed the keys over to the mechanic and sat down to read the out of date car magazine that lay on top of the coffee table. There were half a dozen black leather upholstered chairs for customers to use, though they were all vacant.

Palmer kept one eye on the mechanics that periodically walked past the window. Form the picture he had been given he soon identified Paul Mathers. He was a large man, with the build that Palmer associated with a weightlifter. He did not look like the kind of person who would take kindly to being served a court document, especially the one that Palmer had folded in his coat pocket.

Palmer watched the various activities around the garage for five minutes before the mechanic who'd taken his key returned.

'The manifold joint was loose. We've tightened it up for you. The rest of the exhaust looks okay, but you should have it checked again in about a year.'

'Oh, was that all. What do I owe you for that?'

'Nothing this time. Do you want us to add you to our reminder list?'

'Reminder list, what's that?'

'Just so we send you a reminder in twelve months. We do it on the brakes now, just because people forget.'

'Oh I see. Well the truth is I'm thinking about selling her pretty soon. I was going to put an ad in the paper last week, until she started making that noise. Then I thought I'd better get it sorted first. Tell you what though I've got a mate who knows one of your guys. Might not be from here, but I thought I'd get him to look her over properly before I do sell her. Are all your mechanics fully conversant with the whole car, or do you just specialise in brakes and exhausts?'

'Most of them are full mechanics. You don't know the chap's name do you?'

'Something like Matters I think.'

'Not Paul?'

'Yes, I think that's his first name. Why, does he work here?'

'You bet he does. First class mechanic.'

'I don't suppose I could have a quick word, could I?'

'Sure, here's your keys. The car is back where you left it.'

'Thanks.' Palmer took the keys and prepared to leave the office.

'Hang on, I'll get Paul for you, he's only out back.

'Cheers.' It rarely came to having to run away from such scenes but while the mechanic was out the back Palmer looked round, planning his escape route. The swing door swung open and behind the desk Paul Mathers stood, towering over Palmer, his great bulk looking like a potential candidate for the Britain's Strongest Man competition.

'Can I help you?' His voice was deep, but it did not boom as loudly as Palmer had expected.

'Yes, possibly. Are you Paul Mathers?'

'Who's asking?'

'Just someone we know said he worked here.'

'Oh yeah, well I'm Paul, so what can I do you for?' The man had walked so he stood just behind the counter, a fragile construction which Palmer had little doubt the giant of a man could easily destroy with one thrust of his powerful arms.

'Well, I've been sent by a John Manning to act as a bailiff of the Magistrate's Court in Wimbledon. I have been asked to present you with this document.' As Palmer reached into his pocket he continued speaking, always keeping an eye on the man behind the counter. 'This is nothing personal and I have no interest in what it contains. Just consider me to be the delivery boy. I have been asked to point out though, that from this moment you are bound by the contents of the document, which I suggest you read.'

The man behind the counter reached out and took the papers from Palmer. Palmer stood there as Mathers opened the document. As he began to read it Palmer was taken by surprise, for tears welled up in the giant's eyes and he started to sniff.

'Now she's stopping me from seeing my kids. She's the one that's abusing them, not me. But she just goes off to her solicitor and makes up a load of tosh. Them kids are everything to me, only now she's stopped me from seeing them.'

'Abuse, have you any proof?' he asked quite gently, quite taken aback.

'Oh no, she's far too clever for that. She lets me have them for the day and then she does whatever she does when they get home, and then she takes them to the hospital and makes out like she's really worried. I aint ever hurt a fly, though I could tell you was scared of me. Nah, she's the bitch from hell, and those kids are at her mercy now. '

'But surely the Social Services are involved? What do they think?'

'They came round once, while we were still together. I called them round you see, because the little one got a broken arm playing in the garden while I was at work. That's when we split up, when she told them I'd pushed the kid around.'

'So what happened after that?' Palmer was concerned at what he was hearing. It brought back to him the sad memories of his own childhood, not that he'd been abused by either of his parents. His elder sisters, Roxanne and Ophelia had been the

72

main protagonists of his misery as they had delighted in the mental anguish that their taunts inflicted on the young boy.

'I left her and got myself a flat and then asked for access to the kids. She didn't say no and it worked quite well for a few months. Then I got a letter from her solicitor questioning whether I should continue to see the kids unsupervised as the children were complaining about the way I treated them. Honest to God I never lay a finger on them.'

'I never said you did. And then you got this. When did you last see your children?'

'About a month ago, and then only for a couple of hours and my new girlfriend was with me.'

'And was she with you for the whole time?'

'Yeah. We went to the park, had a walk round and took the kids to the burger place for tea. Then we drove them home.'

'And they were okay when you left them?'

'Fine. Only a couple of days later she rang me up and said she was going to stop me seeing the kids because she couldn't sit around and watch what happened to them when they visited me.'

'Okay. I have a suggestion for you, if you're interested.'

'Of course, if it will help me get to see my kids again.'

'It might, but it will take time, and you must be patient. There are two things you can do. First off, you must go and see your solicitor and take your girlfriend with you. Get her to do an affidavit about what you did the last time you were with the kids.'

'And the second thing?' The tears had stopped now, and though the giant of a man was still shaking he looked at Palmer with a degree of hope in his eyes.

'Well, that's up to you. I'm actually an investigator, and serving this stuff is part of what I have to do. Another part of my work is to watch people. I have some colleagues that help me with it. So, if you wanted, we could watch your wife for a bit and see if that turns up anything. That way you'd have some independent witnesses to anything that happens. It might help, but I can't promise anything.'

'And what would it cost?'

'Well, we can work something out. Talk to your solicitor first and he'll put you in touch with me if you want to go ahead.'

'Fair enough, Mr, sorry I didn't catch your name.'

'Palmer. Damien Palmer, and look I'm really sorry that I had to be the bearer of such news.'

'That's okay, it's not your fault. I knew it was coming. And look, thanks for listening. I'll be in touch.'

'Fine. Well I must get going. Don't forget to talk to your solicitor, and mention my name.' Palmer turned and walked out of the garage and found his car parked where the mechanic said it would be. The journey home was short and Palmer arrived in good time for his meeting with Eddie Marston.

The grandfather clock in the hall had begun the sequence of chimes for eleven o'clock when the doorbell sounded. Palmer opened the door and greeted his colleague.

'Eddie, thanks for coming over. How's life?'

'Not bad, but I could do with having a few more jobs to do. It's that time of the year for the bills.'

'Always is, isn't it. Do you fancy a coffee, or tea?'

'Coffee please. So what's happening with you then?'

'Well, we've got the missing Delaney as you know, and I'm still working on the Green disappearance. Then there's this chap I served a restraining order on this morning. I think we might get some work out of him. Big guy, and I mean big, but he broke down when I gave him the Process. There are kids involved and he reckons his ex is abusing them. Might get messy, but the next few days will tell. Apart from that there isn't much.'

'So no real work for me then?'

'Hang on a moment while I get the coffee. Take a seat in the office.' Palmer left his friend and colleague to make his own way into the office. Marston sat in the so-called interview chair and looked round the room. He had an almost photographic memory, something which had impressed Palmer when they had first got to know each other. Now, as he scanned the shelves of books he stood up and went to the middle section of the third section, pausing to give it greater scrutiny.

'You've got the new Who's Who, then?' Marston called out to the kitchen. The disembodied voice of Palmer came back a moment later.

'Yeah. I wondered how long it'd take you to find it.'

'Well, you put it in an obvious place really.'

'I did?' The question sounded confused as Palmer entered the study carrying the two mugs of coffee. 'How do you mean?'

'Well, look at the shelves. The obvious place someone looks is bang in the middle. It's where your eye goes to first. Then you start to scan outwards. If you'd put it on the top shelf at the end I might not have noticed it.'

'You would.' Palmer put the coffee mugs on the coasters on top of his desk. 'Which is why I wanted a chat with you Eddie.'

'Go on,' Marston's attention was attracted in the same instance as he turned round to face the desk.

'Right, well I know we're a bit quiet at the moment, but that won't be for much longer. I reckon another couple of weeks and we'll be out of the holiday season and things will pick up. Truth is, based on what was happening before the break, I don't think I can cope with the load on my own anymore.'

'So?' The question was genuine.

'Well, I have an idea. Would you be interested in setting up a satellite office? You'd be responsible for the day to day stuff, and I'd suggest we aim in your direction the stuff you're good at, and by that I mean watching people.' The proposition was clumsy but it was out on the table for discussion.'

'You mean I run an office?'

'Sort of.'

'But I aint done that kind of thing before.'

'I know. We'd still run the business from here, but we'd get a phone line set up from your place and advertise it and so on. That way you'd get your own cases and we'd swap over stuff as necessary. All the billing and everything would go through the accountants, but it would give you a regular job and it would give me a regular pair of hands that I could do with right now.'

'Sounds good to me, but how do we sort out which cases I get?'

'Easy. You get the ones you take the calls for, unless they don't require your skills, in which case you pass them onto me. Likewise I'll hand you the stuff you're good at.'

'Okay, how long will it take to set up?'

'About two weeks I should think. We'll get the line installed and I'll get the accountant to sort out procedures and so forth. We're only expanding the business and not setting up a new one, and you become an employee, if that's okay with you.'

'Sure.' At this last suggestion Marston sounded less relaxed.

'I say employee, but we'd have an agreement that you run the satellite. It's just that until it's financially viable on its own it'd be daft to set up a new business.'

'Agreed. You know me Damien, I just like being my own boss, that's all.'

'And you will be effectively. All we need to do is have our regular meetings and keep other informed of what's happening.'

The two men continued talking for some minutes, discussing the potential of the proposed expansion. Marston clearly warmed to the idea of being responsible for part of the business operations, and was at the same time glad that, for now at any rate, it would continue to use the name of Damien W. Palmer Investigations. Finally Marston turned the conversation to find out what else Palmer might be planning.

'And Karen, is she joining the set up too?'

'She might do, but she might be off to Edinburgh soon, so I don't know.'

'Well, Damien, if I were you I'd decide what you want, and if it's her I'd do my best to stop her going to Edinburgh. I've seen you two together and I know how good you are for each other'

'Thanks Eddie, but I don't think we can support three of us at the moment, and anyway the salary I could offer her would be a lot lower than what she can earn in computers.'

'Fair enough, but it has to be worth thinking about, if she really means so much to you.'

'I get the point. Now, to change the subject, Karen is at Castle Point today and I'm expecting her to call back later with a progress report. I've got to go and see the Green woman this afternoon. If anything comes out of it are you available this evening?'

'Sure. I'll be at home probably, so just give me a ring.'

'Great. Now how about some lunch?'

'Your local I presume?'

'If that's okay, or have you got to get away?'

'No, I'm not in a rush.'

'And nor am I for an hour. Let's go and celebrate opening up the satellite office.'

'Okay.'

With that the two men left Palmer's house and walked the short distance to the public house. They selected a table in one of the secluded corners and Palmer ordered two pints of bitter. After a few minutes the waitress came and took their food order. Marston smiled at the young woman as she walked away from them.

'She's not the one who was here last time we came in,' he ventured when she had disappeared into the kitchens.

'No I don't think it was. They have a fair collection of girls that work here a few hours a week. Anyway here's to us, and the new satellite office. Cheers.' Palmer raised his glass and swallowed a mouthful of the beer.

'Cheers,' replied Marston as he followed suit.

'Tell me Eddie, if you had a wife you were thinking about leaving, how would you go about putting some money on one side?'

'Don't know really. Are we talking about the Green case here?'

'Yeah.'

'So why did you ask?'

'Just wanted your thoughts.' Palmer took another mouthful of the bitter.

'Well, I suppose you'd have to open up a bank account she didn't know about and then you'd start paying money into it.'

'Okay, but just suppose there wasn't much money. What then?'

'That's more difficult, but from what you've told me about the case I'm surprised they are as tight as they seem.'

'Yeah, my thoughts exactly.'

'But he could have made it look as though they were strapped for cash.'

'How do you mean?' Palmer leaned forward, interested in what Marston might have to say next.

'Well, suppose you had a head start and had been putting small amounts of cash away or a long time, that way you could increase the amounts slowly and probably your partner wouldn't get suspicious. That way you'd seem like you were hard up and having to economise and then all you'd have to do is keep on increasing the amounts.'

'Especially if your wife didn't have any real interest in the family finances, other than she read the bottom line of the statement every now and again.' Palmer was beginning to sound almost jovial. 'I reckon that's what old Green has done. Probably been salting money away for some years, and then in the last few months he's just increased the amount. I'm almost sure his little disappearing act is something to do with another woman.'

'What did you say he did for a job?'

'A psychologist I believe. Does some work with a health practice, but from what I've been able to find out he also did private stuff.'

'So, where did he practice from?' Marston raised his glass as he waited for the response.

'Home, I presume, or more likely he visited the homes of his clients. I can find out this afternoon.'

The food arrived and the two men set about the task of emptying the plates. It took them several minutes and during it Palmer ordered refills of the drinks. Finally the meal was over and Palmer looked at his watch.

'Well, Eddie, it's time I was going. I have to be at the Green's place by two.'

'Fair enough. Do you need a hand?'

'I don't think so, not for this. But I'll ring you later if I need you, and Karen has your mobile number in case anything turns up at Castle Point.'

The two men left the pub and walked the short distance back to Palmer's house. Marston continued walking to his car as Palmer let himself into the house to make his final preparations for his meeting with Dawn Green.

After five minutes he left the house holding his battered top-opening briefcase. He placed it on the back seat of his maroon Escort and began the journey to Wimbledon. The traffic was mercifully light and it took Palmer less than fifteen minutes before he was pulling into the driveway of 'Cedars'. The house was detached, with a shingle drive that swept across the front of the property. The two access points to the road were open with a new brick wall that separated them. The house itself was modest in size, comprising two reception rooms and four bedrooms. Palmer observed that the windows were the originals and the external paintwork required some considerable attention. Holding his brief case he pressed the doorbell. Inside he saw the

81

diminutive figure of Dawn Green appear and in a moment she had opened the door.

'Mr Palmer, thank you for coming round.'

'No problem Mrs Green, I was in the area anyway,' he lied.

'Do come in. this is our living room.'

'Very nice too. I presume your husband uses the other room for his consulting?'

'Oh no Mr Palmer, he never sees clients here.'

'I'm sorry, but now you mention it I seem to remember you saying that before. So your husband doesn't work from home?'

'No, no. He likes to keep his work well away from here.'

'I see. You don't know where that is do you?'

'No, I'm sorry. I mean I know he does work round some of the surgeries but which ones I don't know. We never discuss his work. I think he thinks it would upset me and there is always patient confidentiality to consider.'

'I see. Anyway, you have something for me to look at?'

'Oh the cheques, yes, they arrived this morning.' She offered Palmer the armchair, which he duly accepted. She went over to the bookshelf that sat in the corner of the room and rummaged through some papers.

'Here, the cheques you wanted to look at.'

Palmer took the half dozen sheets of paper and examined them. He took a notebook from his briefcase and jotted some numbers on the top page. After a few minutes he looked up and smiled at his client.

'Well, Mrs Green,' he began, 'it seems your husband has not been overly careful in whatever he has done. These cheques have all been paid into the same bank account. All I need to do now is find out which one.'

'And how will you do that?'

'Easy, we'll look up the sort code. That should give us a clue. I can't do that here, but I will do it this evening. Now, is there anything else you can think of that I should know?'

'No. I mean you're welcome to look through Stephen's things again, if you want to.'

'I don't think I need to. I had a pretty good look when you first came to me, and frankly there wasn't much of any use. These cheques, though, could be the break I'm looking for.'

'I see Mr Palmer, well let's hope so. Now, can I get you a cup of tea, or coffee perhaps?' The woman's face had brightened with the hope that Palmer had offered. She smiled now, and Palmer noticed it was a warm, friendly smile. She was a small woman, perhaps not much over five feet tall. Her dark brown hair was short, and almost matched the colour of her eyes. She was curvy, some would say slightly dumpy, though Palmer would not have used such a word.

'Tea would be nice.' He smiled back and noticed that beneath the pair of faded jeans her backside wobbled as she left the room. Palmer sat back in the chair and relaxed. He cast an eye around the room, noting the few ornaments that sat on the home-made shelves. The curtains at the window were old but the room looked loved and was well decorated.

'I won't be a minute,' the woman's voice came from the kitchen. Palmer absently listened to the sound of her feet climbing the staircase, and a few minutes later descending the same. His thoughts were far away at Castle Point Systems when she re-entered the room. The drab black top and faded jeans had been discarded. Now she stood in the doorway carrying the tray of tea things, wearing a somewhat see-through blouse and a short, black skirt. From the hem of the skirt Palmer followed the woman's naked legs down to her calf length black boots. The transformation was complete and it momentarily stunned the investigator.

'Sorry to startle you Mr Palmer, only I have a drama group that meets later on this afternoon, and I wanted to look my best.'

'Oh I see.' Palmer sounded relieved.

'Now, the tea is almost ready for pouring. Can you tell me what I owe you to date, just to keep the records straight?'

'I,' Palmer stuttered, 'don't really know.' The woman was not wearing a bra and as she leant forward to place the tray on the low table palmer was given full view of her ample cleavage.

'Well, you must let me know, and I must pay you, somehow.' It was the word 'somehow' that unnerved Palmer. In all the two months he had known the woman before him she had come across as a confused, nervous, an even frightened person. Now, dressed in the attire of a seductress, her demeanour had completely changed, and Palmer had to admit that she was an attractive woman.

'I will. Anyway, what are your drama group doing at the moment.'

'Rehearsing for a play. We do two a year.'

'Anything I might know'

'I doubt it, it's called The Chance for Change.'

'No, that's not one I'm familiar with.'

'Oh it's quite good fun. I'm playing the dowdy woman who meets up with a clever scientist who turns her into a nymphomaniac and that's when the trouble really starts. It's a sort of love hate thing if you know what I mean. Oh there I go, giving the plot away.'

'It doesn't matter, I won't tell anyone.'

'And do you think I am attractive, dressed like this Mr Palmer?'

'Yes, I have to admit you are, and it's quite a change from the way I've seen you before.'

'I know.' She knelt down and poured the tea before offering Palmer a cup. He tasted the tea and thought it was slightly bitter. The woman was still knelt at the low table. She took her own cup and sipped it before standing up. She walked over to the settee and smiled at Palmer. 'So, how are you getting on with the case of my disappearing hubby?' Her voice had changed from her usual nervous whine to one of a much deeper, more seductive, quality.

'Actually, there hasn't been too much progress, but with these cheques I hope we'll find him soon.' Palmer sipped some more of the tea. It still tasted slightly bitter but he was too polite to complain.

'Let's hope so. Stephen has a lot of questions to answer, not least of which is who the other woman in his life is.' The comment surprised Palmer who reacted to it.

'Another woman?' His expression was one of surprise. 'You know that there's another woman involved?'

'No Mr Palmer, I don't, but you think there is, don't you? I can tell.'

'It is a possibility yes, but there's nothing to suggest that is the case. Tell me Mrs Green, what else do you suspect?'

'Lots Mr Palmer, lots. Is your tea to your liking?'

'Yes it's fine.' Palmer took another sip, slightly larger than the previous one. It still tasted bitter. 'Go on, elucidate for me.'

'Well, some years ago Stephen had a fling with another woman. Doesn't matter who she was, but he did. Spent a lot of money on her, which is why we don't really have much saved up, or at least he tells me that's the case.' Dawn Green continued talking as she noticed Palmer's eyes starting to close. 'Anyway he ended that relationship, but I think he's been seeing someone else for several months now. No proof or anything just an idea.'

Palmer had put the cup back on the low table and closed his eyes as he concentrated. He heard the voice getting closer, the soft, seductive tones of the woman's voice making it difficult for him to think straight. Then he felt her standing in front of him, and sensed that her chest was just a few inches from his face. He felt her take his hand and raise it towards her.

'Are you all right Mr Palmer,' her voice was now filled with concern.

Palmer, by way of reply, opened his eyes and pulled his hand away. 'Yes, I'm fine. Sorry, it's just that when I get thinking about things I tend to close my eyes. It's an old habit. Anyway, thanks for your concern. Really I'm fine.' Her ample bosom was still a matter of inches from his face and Palmer could now see the shape of the nipple beneath the flimsy material of the blouse. He made to stand up, an action which caused the woman to back away from him.

'Are you sure you're okay?'

'Yes really. Now, if you're right about your husband having another woman then it would help me enormously if you could remember where your husband has offices, or under what name he trades.'

'Well, he'd use his own name I would think. As for where his offices are, I've always assumed he works from the surgeries he's attached to.'

'I see. Well, I ought to be getting to my next appointment, but if anything does come to mind, please let me know.' Palmer was already standing up. 'Oh, and good look for your rehearsal later on.'

'Rehearsal?' The questioning voice of the woman was lost as she recovered her mistake. 'Oh that rehearsal. Well thank you Mr Palmer and I'm sure it will be just fine.'

'And so am I,' Palmer had detected her mistake. 'Well, I must be off.'

It was half past two when Palmer started the engine of his maroon Escort. He had still not quite recovered from the transformation in Dawn Green's demeanour when the mobile phone that lay on the passenger seat started to ring. He picked it up and recognised the caller.

'Karen, how's it going?'

'Fine Damien, there's loads to tell you. I'm on my mobile out the back having a five minute break right now. Listen, I'll talk to you later on in detail but I need a favour. There's a guy called Hammond who works here – he's one of the researchers. He's got shortish mid-brown hair, he's about five foot ten and slim build. He's got brown suede shoes on today and a brown leather jacket. I'll tell you more later but I'd like him followed when he leaves here tonight. I don't know what it is but I've just got a feeling. I haven't got time to talk Eddie through it but could you ask him to be here for five and watch the guy who leaves in the yellow Esprit? It's the only one here so Eddie can't miss it. I may be wrong but I get the feeling that Hammond is not quite who he seems to be. It'd be good to know a bit more about him I think.'

Palmer had listened carefully, scribbling down the gist of what the woman was asking.

'Okay, Karen, leave it with me.'

'Cheers Damien, now do you fancy coming over this evening for dinner?'

'That'd be great. Why don't I pick up a Chinese on the way? It'd save some time.'

'That sounds good to me. Make it about eight and I'll tell you everything I've found out.'

'Okay. Better go or Eddie won't have time to get round to you. Talk to you later babe.' With that Palmer broke the connection, to replace it a few moments later with a call to Marston. He told Marston what was going on and made the arrangements as Karen had asked him to. Only when he mentioned the Esprit did Marston whistle and express the hope that Hammond was not going to drive down any open roads. Palmer reassured him that if he lost Hammond then it was not going to be a problem. The arrangements made, Palmer started the short journey from the Green's house in Wimbledon Village back to his own less salubrious abode.

Chapter Five

After Palmer's call, Marston made his way to Cheam and found a suitable place to park. As he did so, Palmer arrived home. On entering his study to place his brief case in its usual corner of the room he noticed that the red light of the answerphone was flashing. He pressed the play button and was greeted by the calm, clear voice of a female.

'Mr Palmer, my name is Ellen Morrison. I have found you through my local directory and was wondering if you could help me. My fiancé, who lives in Scotland is coming down to stay for a few days on a business trip, and rather than staying with me, he has booked himself into a hotel in Sutton. Basically I want to know if he's playing the field if you can find out that sort of thing. If you can help me please phone me on,' and she continued to leave the number. Palmer noted the details before making himself a mug of coffee.

Then, suitably reclined in his leather chair he dialled the number she had left.

'Miss Morrison, it's Damien Palmer. You phoned me earlier. Is it convenient to talk?'

'Mr Palmer, thanks for calling back. Yes, I'm on my own.'

'Well then Miss Morrison,' Palmer began though he was interrupted.

'Please, call me Ellen.'

'Well, Ellen, what can I do for you?'

'I don't really know. I've just moved down here into a flat in South Wimbledon. My fiancé is still living up in Scotland but has come down to London on a business trip. He says he's on his own, but I'm not so sure. Anyway, rather than stay with me he's booked into this hotel in Sutton,' and she proceeded to give the name to Palmer. 'Do you know it?'

'Yes, do continue.'

'Well, that in itself is so unlike Robert. Normally he can't wait to be with me. Anyway he said it was for convenience, something to do with the trains to London. We're due to get married in just under three months. The thing is I'm the one with the money, thanks to Daddy and well, I don't really like to say this, but I want to be sure he isn't playing the field. You see, I really want to trust him,' she paused for a moment

'But you want to be sure.' Palmer completed the sentenced for her. 'And how long is he at this hotel for?'

'Another two nights after tonight. The thing is, well, it's almost like he doesn't want to see me, and he won't say why, other than that he's going to be busy working until all hours of the night.' The woman was beginning to sound somewhat upset at the thought of what her fiancé might be up to.

'And what exactly does he do?'

'He's a salesman for a computer software company.'

'I see. Well, if I were to help you I would need to act very quickly. I'd need a picture and description of him and anything else you can tell me.'

'Yes, yes, I know. I've got it all to hand. I've even typed up the details. The only problem is the post won't get them to you in time.' The woman sounded perplexed.

'Well in that case I'd better come and get them from you. Are you around this evening at about seven o'clock.'

'Yes, are you sure you don't mind.'

'No, not at all. I'm out your way on business anyway so I'll just pop in.'

'Oh, one more thing, Mr Palmer, what do you think this will all cost?'

'Well, if we get lucky tomorrow night, say a hundred pounds or so. It's difficult to be precise because it all depends on what happens.'

'I see. Well provided it doesn't go above two hundred it will be all right.'

'I promise you it won't get even close to that. Now if you'd care to give me your address I'll see you later on.'

The woman read the address out to Palmer, who noted it on his pad of paper.

'Well, I'll see you in just under two hours Mr Palmer, and thank you.'

'The pleasure is all mine.' Palmer replaced the receiver and adopted the look of a man who has already formulated a plan in his mind.

Having time to kill before his evening visits Palmer removed from his brief case the copies of the cheques Dawn Green had given him. He waited for his computer to warm up and then selected the program he needed. A few moments later he typed in the sort code of the bank into which the half dozen cheques had been paid and then whistled softly when the address was returned as a High St. bank in Epsom.

Marston had arrived at the offices of Castle Point systems by half past four, giving him plenty of time to reconnoitre the area and select a suitable place to position his car. Palmer had given him no clue as to where Hammond might live so his strategy was based purely on chance. The road from the front of Castle Point systems led in two directions. The first led directly to the heart of Sutton though, as Marston had discovered in his journey to the offices, the road was strewn with those menacing bumps designed to cut traffic speed to a minimum. The second direction led back onto a main road that dissected Cheam Village and a route back to the main road leading to the motorway. Marston placed himself in the situation of being an Esprit driver and decided the speed bumps, or sleeping policemen as they are correctly termed, would be out of favour. Consequently he positioned the car so that it pointed back towards the village. Having done that he sat and waited. For fifteen minutes he waited until the staff of Castle Point systems began to leave for home. At a few minutes after five he spotted Karen Shaw leave as she made the short walk to her car that was parked somewhere in the railway station car park. Two cars emerged from behind the office buildings, though neither bore any resemblance to the vehicle he was waiting for.

A further fifteen minutes passed and Marston was becoming frustrated by the delay. There had been no indication that Hammond would be leaving late that evening, nothing that Karen had said to Palmer showed that Hammond was a workaholic.

Up on the first floor of Castle Point systems, in the secure room that had been sectioned off for the small research team Mark Hammond sat alone at his console. The screen flickered with information as Hammond typed at an impressive speed. He stood up and strolled overt to the window. As he did so he casually looked up and then back down the road. The car was still there, and the occupant was still sitting at the wheel. Hammond looked casually at his Rolex watch and mentally noted that the car had been there for nearly an hour. It was curious, but it did not bother Hammond in the slightest. He had no reason to be bothered. He returned to his console and continued his work. It had been an interesting day, and the presence of Karen Shaw, though unexpected, had not phased the genius. Her chat with him had been perfunctory and he'd been pleasant enough to her. Actually, after their discussion, he had admitted to himself that she was knowledgeable and someone who could go far in the industry. She was, he thought, wasted as a system's auditor, but it was a necessary intrusion into his working day life, especially after the disappearance of his manager Delaney and the laptop they'd set up for the demo.

Hawton and Stavers were creatures of habit, regular nine to fivers, and so they had long since left the room in which Hammond was seated. He swung his chair round to look at Delaney's empty desk. Normally she was a late worker and the last to leave the room at the end of the day, but her disappearance had left Hammond alone for the past few evenings. He heard the sound of shoes on the staircase beside the room and recognised the high heels of Hartley-Brown's PA. He heard the heels come down the steps and then ascend them again before he heard the door to Hartley-Brown's office close.

Hammond sat and waited. Six o'clock arrived and passed and still Hammond waited. Apart from himself, only Hartley-Brown and his assistant remained in the building. He looked at the screen and pressed a few buttons. A window opened for him and suddenly he had a birds-eye view of Hartley-Brown's office. The picture was in colour though it was obvious the lighting in the office was subdued. Using his mouse he panned round the office, past the filing cabinets and the table towards Hartley-Brown's desk. He scanned past the blouse that had been discarded on the floor near to the door and the bra that lay almost on top of it. He scanned across the room to Hartley-Brown's desk. As he did so the PA came into view and it was evident that she was not taking dictation. She lay with her back in contact with the bare wood of the desk, naked from the waist up, with her black skirt bunched roughly around her waist. Her legs dangled over the narrow side of the desk, and between them stood Hartley-Brown.

Hammond watched their act of lust for some minutes. He watched the way in which Hartley-Brown handled the woman, how he fondled her breasts, an act that made her arch her back. In the research room there was no sound because

95

Hammond had muted it. He watched in eerie silence as Hartley-Brown thrust into his willing PA, he watched as Hartley-Brown relaxed when he had released his energies into the woman, and he watched as she replaced her clothing after their act was complete. As he watched he occasionally pressed some buttons on the keyboard, and from time to time he zoomed in and out of the scene that was taking place a few feet above his head.

Long before the woman descended the stairs for the second time that evening Hammond had taken the CD out of its drive and returned the console to its usual mode of operation. As he heard her descend the stairs he chose to open the solid door to his office.

'Oh, hi Carol,' he said casually. Her face, still slightly flushed from her sexual experience, turned a slightly darker shade from her surprise at his presence. He continued speaking as though he had not noticed. 'Working late again?'

'Yeah. Some typing that needed doing. Off home now though. See you in the morning.'

'Sure. Is the boss still in?'

'I think so, unless I missed him leaving when I went to the girls room. Do you want to see him?'

'No. Just wanted to know if I needed to set the alarms, that's all.'

'Are you leaving now?'

'Yeah.'

'Well, hang on and I'll check if he's here.' She turned and ran back up the stairs while Hammond picked up his metallic attaché case and returned to stand at the bottom of the stairway. She came down the stairs and continued the conversation. 'He's still there, so I've asked him to set the alarms when he goes.'

'Great. Say, do you know what's on TV tonight?'

'Not much, never is,' they began walking down the final flight of stairs to the exit at the back of the building. 'What are you into?'

'Crime fiction mainly. You know, Morse, Poirot, that kind of thing. I find it helps me relax.'

'Really. I prefer the soaps or a nice game show.'

'Yeah, well they're okay, just so long as it's not one of those damn vet programmes cutting open animals just as you sit down to eat. I hate them.'

'Me too, I have to turn over if one of them comes on while I'm eating. Anyway, see you tomorrow.'

'Yeah, see you in the morning.' Hammond walked over to his Esprit and smiled to himself. It took him a minute to start the motor, the deep roar of the engine penetrating the air as it fired first time. A minute later he emerged from the car park and turned left towards Cheam Village. As he did so he looked in the rear view mirror and smiled to himself when the blue Renault pulled out to follow him. He pressed the start button on the CD player and the car was filled with the sounds of heavy metal music. Hammond smiled to himself, relaxing as he drove to his apartment. Every now and then he checked the rear view mirror and smiled at the sight of the blue Renault behind him.

Hammond drove through Cheam Village and headed towards Epsom. His apartment was on the very edge of the town, situated just off the main road. Underneath the block of apartments the designers had thoughtfully included residential parking, a secure environment that was accessed by a swipe card system. As Marston followed Hammond to the apartments he saw the Esprit disappear into that underground haven. Marston pulled over and found a place to park a short distance down the road. It was now nearly seven o'clock.

At about the same time as Marston arrived at Hammond's apartment block Palmer was making his way through the still heavy traffic around South Wimbledon. He'd located Ellen Morrison's house on the street map and was now battling his way through the side roads that led to it. Finally he located the block of flats and parked up. With his ever-present top-opening brown brief case by his side he pressed the buzzer for the flat number she had given him.

'Hell?' The questioning voice was somewhat distorted by the intercom, but equally recognisable to Palmer as eth female voice at the end of the phone two hours previously.

'Miss Morrison, it's Damien Palmer.'

'Come on up.' That was all she said before Palmer heard the buzz of the magnetic catch on the front door as it was released for him to gain entry to the building.

Palmer ascended the two flights of stairs quickly and found the door to the flat open. Behind it, and holding the door open politely for him, was Ellen Morrison. Palmer could not imagine why any man attached to such a rare beauty would want to play the field. Her long auburn hair, flowed gracefully around her smiling, pretty, face, accentuating the depth and beauty of her dark green eyes. She was casually dressed in a short skirt and loose fitting blouse, with naked legs descending into the brown, calf length boots. She was, thought Palmer, a candidate for a men only magazine, a rare beauty that had descended from Scotland. When she spoke she smiled, her perfect set of white teeth glistening in front of Palmer. Then he realised that she was tall, very tall, nearly six feet in stature. She straightened as he entered the flat, and he noticed that the movement of her breasts indicated she was wearing nothing under the blouse. She shut the door behind Palmer.

'The lounge is at the end of the corridor. Do go through.' Her voice contained only a hint of Scots, and it was clearly not her native country, either that or the public school she must have attended had all but eradicated the accent. Palmer did as he was requested and selected the settee to repose on.

'Thank you for coming round Mr Palmer.' She handed him a manila A4 sized envelope as she continued speaking. 'Here are the details you asked for. There's a picture of the rat, and some other details. I phoned him earlier and he said he was dining with a client tonight and that tomorrow night he would probably have to catch up on some paperwork. Doesn't look like he'll be coming to see me, even though he's just travelled nearly five hundred miles.'

'Hmm. Did he drive down?'

'No, flew to Gatwick and then got a taxi to the hotel. It's only five minutes to the station from the hotel, and he can get up to London from there.'

'So Miss Morrison,' Palmer was interrupted.

'Ellen please, I hate the Miss thing.' Palmer noticed the three rocks of the engagement ring that sat correctly on the third finger of her left hand.

'Well, Ellen, are you sure you want me to do what we discussed?'

'Yes, I've got to know. He's been acting really strangely for the past couple of months and because I'm the one that's loaded, so to speak, I don't want to take any chances. I have to be sure he isn't just after my money.

'But your ring doesn't look like he's hard up,' Palmer protested.

'Oh that.' She took a moment to look at it. 'Daddy loaned him the money for that. Didn't want me wearing anything that he could afford, it had to be better than that.' There was a growing degree of bitterness in her voice.

'I see. Well, we only have a couple of evenings, so I can't guarantee anything. But if you're sure that's what you want, we can try something that might work.'

'I understand. Well give it your best shot, I can't ask for anything else. Now, would you like a cup of something?'

'No thanks. Tell me, where did you meet Robert?'

'University, three years ago. He was doing a computer sciences degree and I was doing sport. We met at some conference or other and sort of fell for each other. He's actually very clever but he's got very little money – leastwise he didn't until quite recently when he got into software sales. I don't understand it all, but recently he changed jobs and he's been flying off all round the world selling whatever it is he sells. Must be doing quite well out of it I should think but he doesn't like talking to me about it.'

'I see. So you've known each other for a while now. Well, I'm sure there's nothing much to worry about – he's probably just preoccupied with his job at the moment. People in new jobs usually are to start with.'

'That's what I've been trying to tell myself, but Robert has changed. He's not the man I fell in love with, but I think he could be if I could just get close enough to him to find out what's going on.'

'Well, let's see what we turn up over the next couple of days. Now, unless you've got anything else to tell me I really must get going. This picture is up to date, isn't it?'

'Oh yes, I took it just before I moved down here, and that was a couple of months ago.'

'Okay. By the way, why did you move down here?'

'That's simple. I specialise in sport technology and the jobs are down here at the moment. It's reasonable money and we both always wanted to move down here eventually. His parents live in Ascot and mine live in Reading. I think we both went to Scotland to get a bit of freedom, you know. It just so happens Robert got snapped up by this firm in Edinburgh and I did a doctorate at the university. Then I got this job and he left the Edinburgh firm and got involved in this software sales thing, only he won't; talk to me about it.'

'Oh, right, I think I see.' Palmer didn't see, but his first rule was never to admit a weakness. 'Anyway, I must be going. I'll be in touch just as soon as there is any news.'

'Very well, Mr Palmer, now do you need any money up front as a retainer.'#

'I don't think so. I know where you are so there's no need. I'll call you in a couple of days.' Palmer had walked back to the front door of the flat. As he turned round to shake his client's hand he again admired the beauty of the woman. She deserved better than Robert Smith.

Marston sat outside the flat of Mark Hammond as the evening passed slowly by. The minutes turned into half an hour and the half hour into an hour. The hour was rapidly becoming two when a woman walked down the road. She walked with a small gait, her high heeled shoes compensating for her otherwise lack of stature. She wore a light, brown, coat for the evening air was becoming cooler as the days progressed towards autumn. Her hair was light in colour and either short or tied up. Marston watched as she approached the apartment block in which Hammond lived. For the sake of precaution Hammond reeled off three photographs of the woman as she waited to gain entry to the building. The darkness of night was beginning to fall as she disappeared from view and Marston returned to the magazine he was reading, though he kept one eye fixed on the building that was across the road and in front of him.

It was nearly eight o'clock when the woman arrived and Marston made a brief note to that effect. Perhaps, thought Marston briefly, she was a resident. As quickly as the idea had formed in his mind he dismissed it for the simple reason that she would have been able to let herself in. He mused over the magazine that he was reading and turned its well-thumbed pages at regular intervals.

At the same time as the mysterious woman had arrived at the apartment block in Epsom so too Palmer had arrived at the somewhat less opulent block of flats where Karen Shaw lived in Sutton. He pressed the buzzer to her flat and was allowed inside. In his hand, the brown paper bag indicated that he had stopped off at their favourite Chinese take-away on his journey over from South Wimbledon.

'Hiya, babe,' he said as he walked through the open door of her flat. 'How did it go today?'

'Great. Any news from Eddie? Hmm, that smells good.' Karen Shaw appeared from the bathroom, dressed only in one bath sheet, and rubbing her long sandy coloured hair with another. 'Won't be a moment, if you want to go in and serve. There's a bottle open in the fridge.'

'Okay, but really, you don't have to make any efforts on my behalf. If you want to eat like that then it's fine by me.' Palmer laughed and stepped back before the damp hair towel could connect with him.

Ten minutes later they were sat at the dining table helping themselves to the food in the foil containers.

'So,' he commented eventually, 'what is there to tell?'

'Well, lots of rumours I'd say. Not many of the people I talked to know what the research team do for a start, which kind of makes them jealous, well some of them anyway. What's more interesting are the personal rumours flying round the place. I had a long chat with Christina DeClare. Say these pork balls are good.'

'Go on. She's the development manager isn't she?'

'Yeah,' the word was muffled by the tail end of the pork ball. 'apparently our Hartley-Brown, HB if you like, is a bit of a man about town. First Christina knows about his goings on go back a few years now. Apparently he had a PA called Julie something or other, Watson I think. No it was Watkins. Well, the two of them got caught on his desk after one Christmas party and I mean, like, he was right inside her at the time. Silly man, should have locked the door.' Karen licked her lips but Palmer could not be sure she was removing the taste of the sweet and sour sauce. 'After that she left. Anyway, and there's at least two others who'll back this up, HB started up an affair with Delaney after that. It was all very hush, hush, but in a way so that everyone knew about it on the quiet. That lasted about three years or so and Christina reckons he'd had a couple of the younger girls as well during that time. Anyway, about three months they split up. Apparently Delaney took it badly and that was it really. There is a rumour going round that HB has a hard-on over his new PA but she's so prim and proper it seems unlikely.'

'And to the computer side of things?' Palmer was listening with interest, and confirmed in his own mind the first impression he gained of the Managing Director's PA.

'Not much to say really. Delaney and the laptop have gone missing. That story is all round the building, but most people reckon it's over the broken affair and that she's just taken it to spite him. Only the guys in the research team know the real score.'

'So what about them?'

'Hawton and Stavers both come across as conscientious nine to fivers. They don't seem to have too many axes to grind and they're both friendly. They're family men, above average intelligence but neither of them come across as the brains of the outfit. Without having had the benefit of chatting to Delaney that leaves us with Hammond, unless of course HB is doing his own company.' The plate of food was beginning to dwindle.

'And do you think he is?'

'Good God no, he may be the MD but he's not about to walk away from it all. Seems like he's got a wife in a hospital somewhere. Has been for about five years since she got mowed down in a hit and run. She's been in a coma ever since, and HB has no real life outside of the company. He's not someone I'd put too high up the suspect list on this one.'

'So who would you put on it?'

'Delaney. She has to be tops. But there's something about the contractor Hammond that bugs me. He's cocky, really knows his stuff, and makes sure you know he does as well, if you understand.'

'Yeah, but that doesn't make him suspicious.'

'No, but he was reluctant to talk much, didn't like it when I ran some stuff on his computer, that sort of thing. Also, he reckons Delaney wasn't really interested in the team – fancied herself in a higher job. That's not the impression I got from anyone else.'

'So why call Eddie out tonight? You said you'd explain.'

'Yeah. Well first off, Hammond has no home address listed on the company records, only a business address. Secondly he drives an Esprit. Even if he's good, very good, he won't be earning enough money to afford one of them. So, logically, the lifestyle doesn't fit, which in my book makes it worth having a closer look at him.'

'Fair enough. At least we'll get his home address. Biggest question now is, where is Delaney? Form what you said she has to be number one candidate. She was working late. It gives her opportunity. Motive, could be the split from Hartley-Brown. Means, well the laptop holds the secret to that. Okay the package we've been told about is valuable and in the wrong hands it's dangerous. But, and I've been thinking, how long do you think it would take or the banks to render it useless?'

'A couple of hours after the first breach, maybe a bit more. One thing's for sure it would cause havoc if it were used.'

'Yeah, but my guess is Delaney knows how the banks will react. No, there's something else on that computer that only she knows about.'

'Or whoever has the computer knows about. It might not be her.' Karen corrected him as she began to gather the empty cartons and plates together.

'Okay, so we've got no proof, and I guess the only way we'll ever know is when we find Delaney.'

'Fair enough, so what do you want me to do next?'

'What you went there for, a systems audit. I want to know every box, modem, screw and piece of dental floss that's used in that building. More than that, I want to know what else is on that computer, because that is what whoever has taken it is going to use it for, not this bank account thing. Moreover I doubt Hartley-Brown knows what's on it either, so you may find it difficult to find out. Now, to change the subject, how do you fancy doing some real investigative work?' Palmer stood up and helped carry the dishes through to the kitchen.

***

In the apartment above the car in which Marston was sitting Hammond sat down on the sofa and pressed the button on the remote control unit. Immediately the picture on the television changed to Hartley-Brown's office. The man was kissing the woman tenderly. As he did so he gently guided her until her back came up against the end of his desk. Slowly he popped the buttons on her blouse, all the time kissing her. Tantalisingly he caressed her breasts, first as they hid behind the blouse and bra, then with the garments discarded on the floor he continued to caress the tender white flesh, ensuring the nipple stood stiffly to attention under his ministrations. The camera was on a wide angle, covering most of the office. As the woman shuddered the gasp of her excitement could be heard on the television. He watched as Hartley-Brown gently pushed her backwards until her shoulder blades touched the cool wood of the desk. Then he raised her legs and kissed the insides of each in turn before he parted the legs further and moved in closer. The woman gasped again as Hartley-Brown, though unseen on camera, entered the woman's pale-skinned body. He took his time and as Hammond watched he felt his own ardour increasing. Then the television showed him the sequence that he had watched at first hand whilst at the office. As it did so, and as Hartley-Brown completed his act of passion Hammond smiled to himself.

'Couldn't be better,' he said.

'Absolutely perfect,' the woman sitting beside him replied. She smiled at him.

'Well, Mrs Hammond, what shall we do next?' Hammond looked into the woman's eyes.

'Jumping the gun as usual. We take our time as planned and we don't make mistakes. He'll get his desserts in due course.'

'And the snotty little investigator he's employed to follow me?' Hammond sounded slightly perturbed.

'He'll get his too. Now, I think it's time we went to bed. And don't worry about the investigator. We'll sort him out if we have to. Come on Mark, watching that disk has made you hard, and it's made me horny too. See if you can give me what he gave his PA.'

The woman, in her mid-thirties had attractive blond hair. She placed her hand around the mound that protruded beneath the man's trousers. She squeezed it firmly and licked her lips.

As she stood up it became apparent that she was quite short, maybe five foot three inches. Hammond stood with her and allowed her to escort him to the bedroom. It was not long before the couple in the bedroom were enacting their own kind of passion. Outside Marston waited patiently, determined that if nothing happened by eleven o'clock he would call it a night. It was now just after nine o'clock.

***

Palmer returned from the kitchen and sat on the sofa with Karen beside him.

'So,' she said, 'what do you mean by real investigative work?'

'Well, I got a call from a woman this afternoon. She's getting married in three months and has just moved down from Scotland, Edinburgh actually. Now, her fiancé has come down on business and instead of staying with her he's booked himself into a Sutton hotel. Not only that but he seems to be too busy to even meet up with her. She's asked me to find out if he's playing the field.'

'So where do I fit in?'

'Have you ever heard of the honey trap?'

'No, but I've got a feeling you are about to tell me.'

'Sure,' and Palmer went on to explain exactly what the honey trap involves. Five minutes later he concluded his explanation. 'So, are you up for it?'

'Yeah. Sounds like it might be fun, just so long as you won't get jealous if anything happens.'

'I won't. Anyway, it has to be tomorrow night, so you'd better make the reservation.'

'What now?'

'Yeah.'

Karen stood up and picked up the phone. She dialled the number Palmer had shown her from his diary and in less than ten minutes the reservation had been made.

'So, I'll check in after work tomorrow. What will you be doing?'

'Oh, I've got a few things to sort out as usual. You'll be all right won't you?'

'Of course, computers are my line of business and you already know that I can handle myself in bed. What are we going to do for evidence though?'

'You can write a report for me and I'll take it to the client. That should suffice for something like this. We'd need something a bit more tangible if it was a divorce case, but for a pre-marital all we need to do is state what happens.'

'Fair enough. Well I don't know about you but I fancy a nice early night. Do you want to stay?'

'Yeah why not. Say, how about a night cap? Have you got any of that whisky left?'

'Sure. I won't join you, but go ahead. I'll just go and pack a few things for tomorrow. I'll see you in the bedroom, but don't be too long.'

'Five minutes babe.' Palmer stood and went over to the small drinks cupboard. As he poured a small whisky he heard Karen opening and closing drawers in the bedroom. He sipped the whisky and walked into the kitchen area. He looked out of the window onto the road below and wondered how Eddie was getting on. There'd been no call from him so presumably everything was quiet.

It was indeed quiet. Marston had finished the magazine and was becoming bored. He continued to watch the apartment block but apart from a couple of people letting themselves into the building there had been little activity. Marston looked at his watch and noticed it was now just after ten o'clock. Impatience and tiredness finally caught up with him and he decided to call it a night. It seemed unlikely that Hammond would be leaving his apartment that evening. Marston started his car and the blue Renault began the half hour journey back to Marston's own dreary, grey fronted block of flats.

Palmer finished the whisky and rinsed out the glass before returning it to the shelf in the drinks cupboard. Then he joined Karen in the bedroom. A small suitcase sat on the floor next to her dressing table. It was closed and evidently full. Karen lay in bed, her lithe body covered by the duvet which she had pulled up to her neck. Palmer undressed and slid in beside her.

'Fancy a treat?' She whispered the offer into his ear as he turned to kiss her.

'What do you have in mind?'

'This.' She leaned over and planted her lips fully on top of his. She rolled over until she lay on top of his fit, lean, body, and as she did so he allowed her tongue to intertwine with his. He felt her take his right hand and stretch it above his head, and then she repeated the action with his left. She held the wrists with her hands, as if playing with him. He knew that if he wanted to, he could easily escape her hold simply by using his greater strength.

The bed had a fake metal headboard, with a design cut into the vertical metallic railings. Palmer felt his hands touch the railings and he grasped one in each hand, happy to play along with her game. In a moment she had achieved her aim. Deftly, and before Palmer could respond to her attentions she had the cuffs around his wrists and he found himself secured to the headboard, now her prisoner. She pulled back the duvet and slid off his body.

'Now you're my prisoner and you will have to do just what I ask if you want me to release you, big boy.' Her voice was low and seductive, and as she spoke her tongue curled round her lips.

Palmer lay on the bed, his boxer shorts failing to conceal the fact that his imprisonment had had the effect of instantly arousing him. The woman, for her part, was totally naked, her sandy mid-back length hair flowing and swirling around her body, shimmering in the moonlight that flooded through the window, the curtains of which had not been closed. Sitting beside her lover she reached down and gently placed the fingers of her right hand around the mound of his arousal. He groaned as she touched him. He felt her fingers as they played up and down the full length of his manhood, teasing him in such a way as to induce every last possible iota of stiffness into that part of his anatomy. As she touched him in this way so the covered mound grew, until it seemed that it must burst through the fragile fabric that stood between its captivity and freedom. Again Palmer groaned.

Next Karen placed her thumbs on the sides of his abdomen and slid them into the elasticated sides of the boxers. He raised his buttocks off the sheet as she expertly lowered the boxers over his engorged member and slid them down his legs until she discarded them onto the floor.

'Now, open your legs for me.' Palmer did as he was instructed and in a moment he felt the leather cuffs being secured round his ankles. Now a total prisoner he could barely move, his legs wide open exposing him fully to the wiles of the female who even now began to run the ends of her long sandy hair tantalisingly up the inside of first one leg and then the other. To Palmer it was like a small electric shock that moved up his legs pumping even more

113

energy into his already pulsating genitals. He giggled as she caressed him with her hair and she playfully scolded him for it. After she had run her hair the length of his legs maybe half a dozen times Palmer felt the warm breath on the very end of his manhood. She blew the air over the head of his organ and watched with satisfaction as it twitched from her attentions.

He felt the drops of warm liquid as they landed on his engorged member moments before she placed her hand around the end and began to stroke him. Her grip was such that on the down stroke she held him firmly, releasing the pressure before moving her hand to the top for the next stroke. This action continued for some time, each stroke being the full length of the phallus. Finally she replaced her hand with her thumb and forefinger at the same time as she increased the stroke rate, now holding him with the same grip in both directions. Palmer felt the pressure within him rising and knew that he could not hold back for long. He groaned as his pleasure overcame him and the woman felt the first twitch as he prepared to explode. Dutifully she stopped the stroking, ensuring the head of his member was fully exposed. Holding the base of his shaft tightly in her fingers she lowered her head until he could feel the warmth of her breath as her mouth immersed his arousal as far as she could manage it. She clamped her lips around him and sucked once. It was more than Palmer could take and he exploded within her.

When his eruption had subsided she continued to hold him there, teasing him now with the tip of her tongue until she felt sure the stiffness would not subside. Only then did she sit up and look at her handiwork.

'And now, for the real thing.' She smiled wickedly at the helpless man beneath her. She turned round until she faced his toes. Kneeling on the bed astride his abdomen she knelt forward giving him a perfect view of her totally exposed body. She knew she was moist from her own arousal and that this view would greatly arouse Palmer, but her motive lay elsewhere. She rummaged under the mattress until she had found what she wanted, though Palmer could see nothing except her exposed sex. Then she shifted position until the entrance to her body lay directly over the member that still glistened with her saliva. She went down on him gently until he was inserted up to the hilt. As he penetrated her she gasped from the combination of his sheer size and the angle with which the insertion was taking place. Her pleasure increased and she felt a new wetness as he slid into her.

Slowly at first she began the sequence of raising and lowering her body over him. With each stroke she was being driven wild, both by the sensations within her and by the thought of what she was about to try. With increasing speed she continued to allow him to stroke her insides until she arched her back and reached her peak. For a moment the motion slowed but his engorged member twitched gently within her and she regained the rhythm she had achieved.

'Are you enjoying this?' She asked after her second peak.

'Mmm,' he responded as he thrust his hips upwards to meet her descending body.

'Good, because I have one more surprise for you which will send you wild, I hope. Are you ready?'

'Mmm,' he replied and she took it to be affirmative. Reaching down she picked up the small device that had been lying between his legs as she had taken her pleasures. Now she picked it up, licked the end and inserted it between his legs just on the entrance below his testicles. Palmer heard the soft humming sound a moment before he felt the pressure as she inserted the device into his body. He arched violently as it entered him, more from surprise than instant pleasure.

'What the fuck's that?' He asked as the insertion was completed.

'It's called a prostate finger. Do you like it?'

Palmer did indeed like it. It was a new experience for him, and after the surprise of the rude intrusion he began to greatly enjoy the strange sensation. The woman adjusted the device so that it found the sweet spot within him and in moments he was arching his back in sheer ecstasy. As he did so she felt him swell within her until she knew he would explode. By now the explosions within her own abdomen were virtually continuous as he hammered into her. She felt the final surge as he climaxed and a moment later she felt the final spasms of her own excitement as they drained the last energies from her body. She gently removed the finger, pulled herself off his body, released the cuffs that had held him so superbly, and lay down exhausted. In less than two minutes they were both fast asleep their bodies sated from the sexual exercise of the previous hour.

It was nearly half past ten when the woman came out of the apartment in Epsom and made her way down the road to her waiting car before making her short journey home. She left unobserved, her partner equally as drained as Palmer.

Chapter Six

The rain was falling steadily as Palmer made his way to Epsom early the next morning. Being a Thursday the market stalls were already set up in the centre of the town, the early shoppers hunting for the elusive bargains. Palmer followed the one-way system to the back of the High Street and parked in the Ashley Centre car park. The car park itself provided facilities for the many shops that combined to form the Ashley Centre and also parking for the local theatre and many local businesses. Palmer parked on level four and took the glass fronted lift back down to the shopping centre. He walked briskly through the Centre's brightly lit corridors until he gained access to the High Street itself. It was nearly eight o'clock and he was in a hurry to make his appointment at the bank. Finally he stood outside the bank's front door and pressed the buzzer. A minute later the short, rather overweight, figure of the bank manager emerged from a back room and Palmer watched as he limped towards the front door to the building. Finally, and after much effort, the door was opened.

'David, thanks for agreeing to see me,' Palmer started as he went inside. With the same effort that he had made to open the door, so the short, overweight, man locked it carefully behind him.

'That's okay Damien. How are you anyway.'

'Tired, but then I'm not an early bird really.'

'Shall we go through to my office?'

'Thanks. Anyway, how are you keeping?'

118

'Oh pretty good. The wound has almost healed now, but the doctors reckon I'll be left with a limp.' The door to the office bore a simple brass nameplate that stated 'David Callan – Manager'.

'That's unfortunate, still it could be worse.'

'Yes it could have been, and thanks to you they didn't get away with anything.'

'Me and quite a few others.' Palmer reflected back to the incident several months earlier when a case he'd been working on had led him to the bank manager's desk where he now sat. The notion that an armed robbery was about to take place was, at that time, anathema to the manager who had dismissed Palmer with due alacrity. Palmer though, had followed his hunch and, together with Marston, had been outside the bank when the BMW had driven up and the three masked raiders had entered the bank. A quick call to the police was followed by some heroic action by Palmer. In less than five minutes the raiders had fled empty handed, having fired only one shot that by some quirk of fate had penetrated the upper leg of the manager. It had taken the police only a couple of hours to trace the BMW thanks to Palmer recording the index number, and within forty eight hours all three raiders had been arrested and charged. As a result Callan had good cause to be grateful.

'Yeah, but you actually stopped the bastards.'

'Well, that's history now, but I do need to ask you a favour. I know it's totally against banking ethics but I'm working on a case that's totally floored me. There's a guy who's been paying money into an account here on a regular basis and I've been asked to find him.'

'And how do you know he banks here?'

'Because my client has been paying him the money and we managed to get some of her cheques returned to her, and of course the clearing bank details were on the back.'

'So, how can I help you? You know that customer confidentiality is paramount.'

'Yeah, yeah, but my client has been ripped off by this guy and well, we're trying to keep it out of the courts by getting the matter settled, only we're beginning to talk a lot of money. What's happened is that the address she's got is only a holding address and he picks up the mail himself, so no one knows where he lives or works. I'll level with you. My client has given me until tomorrow to find this guy in the hope it all gets sorted out quietly. After that she says she'll make a public issue out of it all and that would be most unfortunate.'

'Why would that be?'

'Well, unfortunate for you that is. You see we've discovered he's using the bank to launder illegal money. I'm saying no more than that because I might have to give evidence.'

The man sitting opposite Palmer turned a significantly paler shade of white. 'So how can I help you?' The question was uttered by a voice that faltered.

'Simple really, I give you the account details. You check that regular amounts have been going into it and that those amounts have recently got bigger. You give me the guy's address and I go and encourage him to stop what he's doing. End of story and nobody need ever know where the address came from.'

'But I can't do that.' The manager was now visibly shaking.

'I appreciate your position and I can't say I blame you. Well, it was worth a try, but I don't see how I can stop the reporters and the police investigation without your help.'

'Reporters?'

'Sure, my client already knows the amounts have been paid in here so I guess the papers will want to know why you're laundering money. Anyway, as I said I appreciate your position, so I won't take up any more of your time.' Palmer stood as if he was about to leave.

'One moment Damien, you don't have the account details do you, just out of interest?'

'Sure.' Palmer sat down and handed the manager a slip of paper on which he had written the name and number of the account.

'Hang on a moment. I can't use this terminal to check it out but I'll use the one just outside if you'd care to wait.' Callan left the office leaving the door open and Palmer heard him typing at the terminal that sat on the desk immediately outside the office. Suddenly realising what was being offered Palmer stood up and idly went to stand at the open doorway. The computer screen was positioned so that he could just read what was being displayed. The screen flickered for a moment and then revealed what Palmer was interested in. he had noted the details and was sitting at the desk some moments before Callan reappeared.

'Well, it is as you say, but I can't help you anymore I'm afraid. I hope you understand the position I'm in.' Callan still sounded somewhat taken aback.

'I understand perfectly and I couldn't ask for anymore. Anyway, there are other avenues of investigation open to me so I may be able to keep my client quiet. Thanks for your time David.' This time Palmer stood up and shook the bank manager's hand. 'If you could let me out?'

'Of course, and good luck with your enquiries.'

'Yeah, let's hope so, for all our sakes.' Palmer waited until the short man had unlocked the front door before he disappeared back up the High Street to retrieve his car.

As Palmer collected his car Mark Hammond sat in front of his television eating a bowl of cereal. On the television he was replaying the sexual encounter he had recorded the previous evening. The more he watched the more he smiled to himself. There was work to do and it was going to keep him occupied for much of the day. He picked up his mobile phone and dialled the number for Castle Point systems. He reached the answerphone.

'Hi, this is Mark Hammond. Just calling to say I won't be in today as I've picked up some kind of stomach bug. Hopefully I'll be back tomorrow.' He turned off the mobile phone and turned to the table that occupied one corner of the sitting room. The laptop computer sat idle on the table and it took Hammond a few seconds to bring it to life. As he did so he extracted the CD from the box under the television and placed it in the CD drive on the right hand side of the computer. He waited for a couple of minutes as the computer completed its start-up procedures and as he did so he made himself a cup of tea. There was no rush in anything that he did and the smile remained on his face, the self-satisfied smile of a man who has complete control of his destiny.

Five minute later Hammond had opened a series of windows on the computer and was busy editing the code to a program. He pressed some buttons and watched as the scenes from Hartley-Brown's office were replayed in one of the windows. Then he clicked an icon in a second window and watched as the PA's hair turned from her dark brown colour to a paler shade. He pressed the icon again and the tone of the hair continued to grow lighter. He held the picture of a long blond haired woman up to the screen as he replayed the entire video sequence. It took nearly twenty minutes and at the end of it he seemed satisfied. He pressed some more buttons and continued to the next stage of the process. His day's work had only just begun. Through the morning he continued his work, and as each stage of the process was complete he saved what he had achieved, before editing the program that he was running so that the next stage could start. As the hands on his Rolex watch passed midday he straightened up and took the CD back to the box that sat beneath the television. He played the video again and smiled as he watched the long blond haired woman being attended to by the attentive Hartley Brown. He broke for lunch as the sequence was replayed, a lunch that he intended to fully enjoy.

After Palmer had collected his car he drove round to the address that he had written down. It was a short journey from the High Street and the semi-detached house was situated in one of the more run down roads in the area. Palmer walked up to the front door and knocked loudly three times. He waited for two minutes and then repeated the summons. It went unanswered so Palmer bend down and prising open the letterbox he peered in. Post lay on the floor just inside the door, not a significant amount, but perhaps enough for a couple of days. Palmer straightened again and walked back down the driveway to the pavement. He observed the net curtains in the lounge of the attached house move slightly as the occupant inside clearly shifted position so as to be able to continue to watch Palmer. For his part he decided to make no further enquiries and made his way back to his car, which he'd parked a short way down the road. From what he'd seen it looked as though Stephen Green was not at home.

Once in his car Palmer phoned Marston, a courtesy call to find out what had happened the previous evening.

'Eddie, how are you today?' Palmer sounded deliberately jovial for he knew that Marston was even less of an early bird than he was, and at half past nine in the morning Marston would still be feeling very sleepy. He was.

'Huh, oh hi Damien, just waking up.'

'Great. How did you get on last night?'

'Followed the guy home and he stayed there all evening. A few people went into the building during the evening but I'd say they were mostly residents as they knew the pass number on the entry system. All that is except one woman, but she could have been visiting any of the flats. I took a couple of pictures of people, but other than that there wasn't much going on and Hammond definitely stayed in all evening.'

'What time did you stay until?'

'Huh, oh about half ten or so, might have been a bit later.'

'Good work Eddie. And the woman didn't leave?'

'Nope. Guess she stayed the night with someone.'

'Or left after you did, but I'd guess she stayed too. Okay, what are you doing today?'

'Not a lot. Couple of deliveries to make after lunch then I'm free. You got anything for me to do?'

'Don't know yet. I'm in Epsom and on my way back. One thing for you though. Remember the Green case?'

'Yeah.'

'Well I'm sitting about fifty yards from the place he's put as his address at a bank his wife knows nothing about.'

'Blimey, so he's upped and left her then?' Eddie's question was accompanied by a yawn.

'Not sure yet. Got some enquiries to make when I get back. Actually, before I go I might just pop in to the land people and see what I can dig up. I'll be a couple of hours getting back and then I'll ring you.'

'Okay. I'll talk to you later.' Marston replaced the receiver before Palmer could continue the conversation. Palmer placed the mobile phone on the passenger seat and started the engine. He drove round to the council buildings and located the land registry office. He pushed open the swing doors and stood in front of the counter that had above it, on an A4 sized piece of paper, the word 'Reception' typed in bold print.

'Yes?' The clerk behind the counter was curt an almost uncivil in his manner.

'I'd like to make a preliminary enquiry into a property that I am considering purchasing.' Palmer remained polite and spoke evenly.

'Fill in this and the charge is twenty quid.' The clerk appeared to be suffering. Palmer wondered if his suffering would increase if he took issue with him. Instead he took the form that was held out for him and began to fill it in. When he'd completed the task he took out a £20 note from his wallet and handed the two items back over the counter.

'Come back in three days and you can have the information. Good day.' The clerk had now stretched Palmer's patience to the utmost.

'The form says that this is a preliminary enquiry for which I can receive the requisite information immediately. Would you be so good as to provide it for me.'

'Come back in three date and you can have the information.'

'Very well, you leave me no alternative. I would like a word with your supervisor please.' Palmer's tone of voice had become cold.

'Okay, but she'll say the same thing as I do. Pauline, customer for you.' His last sentence was called out loudly and as he spoke he relinquished the seat he had been sitting on.

Palmer waited for two minutes before a woman, who was substantially overweight for her stature appeared.

'Now sir, what is the problem?' She smiled and there was a genuine tone of warmth in her voice.

Palmer explained that he had filled in the preliminary request, handed over the required £20 and then told to come back in three days.

'I'm sorry sir but there has been a mistake.' She leaned over the counter and whispered to Palmer. 'These job scheme people don't know a thing.' Speaking louder she continued. 'I'll sort it out for you right away, and for your inconvenience we'll waive the fee.'

Palmer smiled back at the woman as she sat at the computer console and tapped in the details of the request. Somewhere beneath the counter Palmer heard the sound of the printer. In less than a minute the woman handed Palmer the printout and returned the currency note to him.

'Thank you very much,' he spoke. 'If I want further information what should I do.'

'Take this form and state what you want to know. There are several sections and an explanatory guide. The fee structure is also attached – it all depends on what you need to know. But I'd let your solicitor do it for you if you go ahead with the purchase.'

'I probably will. You've been most helpful, and thank you.' Palmer turned and left the building. There was now no doubt. The property was registered to a Mr. Stephen Green, with a first charge being secured with a Building Society. Palmer wondered if Stephen Green had any other accounts with the Building Society, not that it was of importance at this time.

Once again Palmer regained the driver's seat of his car and began the journey back to his terraced house. It was a slow journey as the mid-morning traffic was heavy. The various road works that had seemingly sprung up as if by magic overnight combined with the traffic to cause congestion that was not dissimilar to the rush hour and so it took Palmer nearly an hour and a half to return home. When he finally opened the front door to his house and picked up the pile of mail that had been delivered earlier that morning he was feeling in desperate need of caffeine.

With the mug of steaming coffee in his hand he cast a cursory eye over the mail. There were the usual items of unsolicited mail, and Palmer immediately recognised another copy of the chain letter that was doing the rounds. There were three envelopes associated with overseas lotteries and another from some entrepreneur offering him the chance to make a fortune for doing very little. These items Palmer consigned to the waste bin unopened. The final envelope caught his attention. The address was handwritten in block capital letters. Palmer placed the mug on a coaster and picked up the gold-plated letter opener and then proceeded to slit open the very top of the envelope. He extracted the single sheet of folded notepaper and opened it. As he did so he noticed that the contents had been printed using an unfamiliar style of text. The actual message ran as follows:

'If you persist in your futile attempts to find me you can be assured that I will take such action as is required to stop you.'

Palmer read the message twice and scratched his head, confused as to which case the writer was referring. He picked up the envelope and looked at the post-mark, though the mark of Sutton gave him little further information, and the time indicated it had been posted early the previous day. His hand reached out for the telephone and he dialled a number.

'Mr Hartley Brown please, it's Damien Palmer.'

'One moment.' The voice was female and unfamiliar to Palmer.

'Hartley-Brown.' The voice was impatient and formal.

'Mr Hartley-Brown it's Damien Palmer. Just checking up how things are going your end.'

'Fine I think. Your colleague has all but finished but she hasn't come up with anything yet. And how are you getting on finding Miss Delaney?'

'Some progress but mainly dead ends I'm afraid. Actually there are a few things I need to talk to you about. Could I pop over about three this afternoon.'

'Yes, I'm free all afternoon.'

'Excellent, and if you could ask Miss Shaw to attend too, I'd like to hear what she has unearthed to date.'

'Very well, I'll see you at three o'clock then. Goodbye Mr Palmer.'

'Goodbye Mr Hartley-Brown.'

Palmer replaced the telephone and turned to his computer. He started one of his numerous enquiries programs and typed in the name of Katherine Delaney. After a short pause the computer returned the results, indicating she lived at the house in Sutton that Marston had already visited. Palmer opened another window and made a different enquiry. This time he was rewarded with a blank screen, indicating Delaney held no directorships within the UK. It was what he had expected. Next he tried Mark Hammond. There were two entries for M. Hammond in the area in which Palmer was interested. The first was at the Epsom address Marston had sat outside the previous evening, while the second was in Sutton. Again Palmer selected the second screen and this time his enquiry was rewarded with the information that Mark John Hammond was a director of 'TIS Services'. It seemed unlikely that it was the same Hammond and a subsequent enquiry showed TIS was a new company that had yet to file accounts. There were two other directors, a Kathleen Westley and a Robert Smith. It seemed to be a small operation and of little interest to Palmer.

Next he entered the name of Stephen James Green. Again he was given the address where he had visited Dawn Green and there was no indication that the man was a director of any business. It was much as Palmer had expected, and as each enquiry was answered he made notes on his pad of paper. Then he reached for the phone.

'Eddie, it's Damien.'

'Hi, how are things?'

'Getting busy. Have you got a couple of hours free this afternoon to do some legwork for me?'

'Yeah, what do you want me to do?'

'Take a trip up to London and visit the central records place for me.'

'With what in mind?'

'I want you to find the birth certificate of Katherine Delaney. She's 36 now so that gives you a good idea where to start. If you don't find it then jump forward eighteen years and start looking through the marriage registers. Keep going forward until you find her. Then use her maiden name and go back to the birth registers for the right years and locate her parents. Then have a look round five years either side and see if you come up with any siblings. If you do, then have another look at the marriage registers.'

'Oh, is that all?'

'Yeah, I know it sounds complex but you'll get the hang of it. When you've finished, which will probably be late afternoon, give me a call on my mobile.'

'Okay. I'd best get going then.'

'Yeah, now you know where you're going?'

'Yeah, went there a couple of months back, remember?'

'Oh yes now you mention it. Well, good luck and don't worry if you draw a blank, I'm only working on a hunch.'

'Cheers – an afternoon on a hunch!' Marston sounded more perturbed than was actually the case. 'Right, I'll talk to you later.' Marston hung up the phone and began the journey into London.

Palmer sat back and looked once again at the note he had received in the post that morning. The words were still the same, still confusing.

After a hasty lunch Palmer made a further telephone call. There was no reply which was not particularly surprising, after all most men would be out working during the day, and he had no reason to suppose that Stephen Green would be at the address to which his bank statements were posted. Palmer sat back in his chair and swivelled round so that he could look at the shelves of leather-bound books, as if gaining inspiration. His mind drifted between the cases that he was currently involved. The disappearance of Stephen Green, he conceded, did at least now look like it might be drawing to a conclusion. All he needed to do was make some direct contact with the man, and that was something he could do that evening. Then there was the request from Ellen Morrison for some surveillance. Palmer felt sure that Karen would be more than capable of executing their plan, and it was important that he made himself available at the right time. Again he hoped the matter would be concluded in a few short hours. Then there was the mess at Castle

Point. A missing employee and a laptop were bad enough but Palmer could not help but believe he had been told only part of the story. There was something else, something so secret that not one of the employees knew about it, or at least if they did know about it then they'd chosen to stay silent. But what, apart from the information retrieval software could be worth two million quid to Hartley-Brown? It puzzled Palmer because he had long since determined that if the account stuff was Hartley-Brown's only worry he could have alerted his bankers and given them time to make security arrangements to block the Castle Point accounts. With the threat gone the blackmailer would have no choice but to give up.

As he rocked from side to side in the chair Palmer decided that there was definitely another very good reason why the laptop had to found, and why it was worth so much money to Hartley-Brown, and more importantly that the blackmailer realised it was worth so much money. The grandfather clock in the hall sounded the half hour and almost reluctantly Palmer made a move. He gathered up the paperwork he needed and placed it in his top-opening brown briefcase. Two minutes later he locked the front door behind me as he began the journey back to Castle Point Systems.

The rain was falling now as a light drizzle, though heavier falls had been forecast for later that day. Palmer drove carefully over the greasy road surfaces, and arrived in Cheam ten minutes before his appointment. Taking Karen's advice he parked in the station car park and walked the short distance to the Castle Point offices. He pressed the buzzer on the door and after a minute a young girl opened it for him.

'Damien Palmer to see Mr Hartley-Brown.'

'Come in Mr Palmer. I'll let him know you're here.' The girl led Palmer into the office and phoned Hartley-Brown's PA.

'Please, go up the stairs to the second floor. You'll be met by his secretary up there'

'Thanks,' Palmer replied and began his ascent. On the landing the familiar face of Hartley-Brown's PA greeted him.

'Mr Palmer. Please go in, they're waiting for you.' She knocked twice on Hartley-Brown's door and opened it.

'Mr Hartley-Brown, Miss Shaw, good to see you.'

'Likewise Mr Palmer.' Hartley-Brown stood up and shook Palmer's hand as he motioned for him to take a seat. 'Three coffees please Carol.'

'Yes Mr Hartley-Brown.' She closed the door behind her.

'Right Karen,' Palmer continued, 'what have you come up with?'

'Not a great deal, though you might be interested to know that Hammond has taken the day off sick. That aside there are three mainframe computers here running different systems. One of them is massive and runs the businesses for eight other organisations. That's linked by no less than thirty two modem carriers through the telephone system using permanent connections. The other two mainframes are smaller and have half a dozen temporary modem links each. Right, then there's a ring network connecting all the desk workstations through a complex set up of at least half a dozen servers. They've all got different software on them. Some are reserved for the support team, and others for the development guys.'

'Sounds quite complex to me.' Palmer was relaxed and clearly attentive.

'And now to the best bit. All the boxes are linked on the network, and I counted ten of the workstations that have modems attached to them. I make that over fifty connections to the outside world. Now, from my point of view that poses a pretty large security risk from a hacker. Moreover it gives Delaney, or whoever, plenty of opportunity to tap into these systems to transfer the funds when they have the codes.'

'But you could always unplug the modems couldn't you?' Palmer's question was aimed at Hartley-Brown but Karen replied.

'In theory yes. The desktop modems and those on the smaller mainframes are temporary connections so they could be unplugged from the telephone lines without much difficulty.'

'And,' said Hartley-Brown, 'in answer to your next question we could also remove the connections that are more permanent though it would take a few hours and we'd have to make sure no-one was active at the time.'

'Well,' said Palmer, 'until this blackmail threat has passed, that is what I suggest you do. That is, of course, assuming the blackmailer intends to use the software on the laptop to access your computers and transfer the funds.'

'That would be the logical deduction based on what they have taken and what they've asked for.' Hartley-Brown sounded flustered. 'Unless you have another theory Mr Palmer?'

'No, no,' Palmer started. 'Based on the laptop having the new software on it, and you giving the blackmailer the codes, it is a logical deduction. I take it one of your systems links directly to your bank?'

'Yes, of course we have such a link. We have a standard link that requires access codes to transfer money. We use it for accounting purposes.'

'Then we have to assume the blackmailer knows such a link exists. I take it only a few people will know that?'

'Of course. Our accountant does and the directors, but that's about it.'

'And the blackmailer.' Karen Shaw had been listening to the conversation. 'Tell me Mr Hartley-Brown. How much are your systems worth to you, roughly?'

'About ten million I should say?'

'And if the systems your clients access, such as the big mainframe, were incapacitated for say a week how much would you lose.'

'The clients would almost certainly lose confidence and leave. Let's say five million in turnover for the next year, plus an incalculable amount from loss of confidence in our security.'

'So the blackmailer must know that as well,' she said.

'But the blackmailer would also know that you could pull the plugs and stop him,' Palmer re-joined the conversation.

'True, but I dare say that she'd find a way round that. Remember that we're still waiting for the next set of instructions.' Hartley-Brown sounded quite miserable as he spoke. There was a knock at the door and the tray of coffee was placed on his desk. After the PA had left the office Karen picked up the conversation.

'Mr Hartley-Brown, if you don't mind me saying so, this is all somewhat theatrical.'

'I don't follow.' Hartley-Brown looked flustered, a fact noted by Palmer as he silently admired his colleagues intuition.

'Well, I've spent two days round your systems. The whole demand for money, the need for access codes and so on, why is it needed? Let me carry on,' she continued quickly as Hartley-Brown made to speak. 'If your blackmailer is one of your staff and they're interested in the new software why not simply steal it and walk off with it, card and all? After all it would be easy enough to sell such a unit to any number of organisations across the world, and that would be far less risky than having your system pay money into their bank account from here.'

'I don't see how?'

'Because Mr Hartley Brown,' Palmer finally intervened, 'to pay the money out of here will require the person to identify their bank account so your system can pay the money in. So, logically, I'd say my colleague is right. If it was the new software

137

that was of interest why go to all this fuss. Tell me, what else is on the computer?'

'I have no idea, and surely it isn't relevant. Whoever has the machine can't use the software until they have the second set of access codes.'

'They wouldn't be Sierra, Charlie, one, three, X-ray, hyphen, two, seven, Yankee, Charlie, Foxtrot, by any chance?' Karen was looking at a small slip of paper.

'Good God,' Hartley-Brown looked as if he were about to explode, 'where do you get them from?'

'Not relevant, but if it took me just two days, how long do you think it took your blackmailer? Rest assured Mr Hartley-Brown your blackmailer already knows the codes you think they are going to need. In theory, at least, they could transfer the money now. So, why haven't they done so?'

'I have no idea.' Hartley-brown looked pale and he was sweating profusely though the office was not unduly warm.

'I have an idea,' Palmer continued. 'The blackmailer is waiting for something, a flight perhaps, or something else. Perhaps they are waiting for the day you are due to give the demonstration to your client. Perhaps that is what they are waiting for, or perhaps there is something else. I don't think your blackmailer gives a damn about the new software. Having it on the laptop is a bonus because it makes us focus on it, when actually this person is focused on something altogether different. What if instead of trying to break into accounts, which I suspect he or she could already do, they want to do something else. What if he or she wants to destroy either you or Castle Point. What if this isn't someone who's just snatched on an opportunity to get rich? What if the money itself isn't important? What if this is a case of revenge?' Palmer's final sentence was delivered with a significant degree of force.

'Revenge,' repeated Karen, 'but what for?'

'Oh, I don't know, a disgruntled employee perhaps. Isn't it true Mr Hartley-Brown that you've been having an affair with Delaney?'

'Yes, but we called it off about three month ago.'

'Hell hath no fury like the woman scorned, or something like that. It gives her a motive. We already knows she has had opportunity, both to ensure the software you value so highly was on the laptop and then to steal it.'

'But she is such a pleasant woman. I really can't believe she'd be into revenge, apart from which point she told me a few weeks ago that she'd got herself a new partner. My PA went to a party at his place week before last.'

'Karen, can you find out who he is and where he's living. I don't suppose it occurred to you Mr Hartley-Brown that she just might be with him now?' Palmer sounded mildly irritated. As he concluded the sentence the woman left the office. She returned two minutes later and handed Palmer a piece of paper.

'Shit.'

'You know the address?' Hartley-Brown looked intrigued.

'Sort of, only the guy who lives there has gone missing as well, or so it seems. Well, we're back to the software theory. Personally I think the person already has the access codes. If my colleague can get hold of them so easily I doubt it caused our friend too much pain. That said, they still need to use your systems to get to your bank account, unless of course they've found another link that works. I'd have to say I think that's unlikely, so let's assume they are going to use your systems to get through. My suggestion would be to cut the modem connections until the threat of the blackmail is behind us. Who knows, if whoever it is can't get onto the system it might flush them out of the woodwork.'

'Very well, but we'll have to explain to our clients.'

'Why? It's Thursday today. If we take things off-line tonight and leave them off-line tomorrow then by the end of the week-end the blackmailer will be bound to try something.' Karen had regained her seat and sat looking at the carpet as she spoke. Clearly her mind was working overtime.

'And you could sort this out?' Hartley-Brown sounded concerned.

'No not tonight, I have other plans. But I could come back tomorrow morning and do it. We could make out there's a system malfunction.'

'Okay, tomorrow it is. I'll put a note out to the section heads that all the workstation modems are to be disconnected and taken to the computer room for inspection. That will cover them, and I'll leave you to talk with our engineer chap tomorrow, though I'll talk to him first.' Hartley-Brown had been cornered and he knew it.

'I'm still not convinced that there isn't something else on the laptop that's the real motive for this crime,' Palmer spoke evenly and watched Hartley-Brown very closely indeed. He saw what he was looking for, the slight twitching of the left eye that showed he had touched a nerve.

'As I said,' Hartley-Brown responded, almost too quickly, 'other than the new software I have no idea what else was on the laptop.'

'It was a company machine, wasn't it?' It was Karen who asked the question.

'Yes. Been used by a few people over the past year but mainly by Hammond, recently, for setting up the demonstration. So maybe he knows what else is on it.'

'Maybe he does, and if he comes back in tomorrow then perhaps you could ask him.'

'I could, but if he's been using it on the sly he's hardly going to tell us what he's been doing.' Hartley-Brown had begun to recover his composure.

'That is true,' Palmer conjectured, 'but I think it is more likely to be something that the blackmailer knows is on the machine, and in view of the ransom demand, it must be something that affects either Castle Point, or you directly Mr Hartley-Brown. There is no other logical explanation.'

'There is one possibility,' the Managing Director suggested. 'The blackmailer, whoever he or she is, may think there is something on the machine, but it's not there in reality.'

'True,' said Palmer, 'but you'd think that they'd check the machine before issuing the demand. Anyway we are wasting time like this. Miss Shaw has work to do, and a busy evening ahead of her, and I also must get on, though before I go I'd like a quiet word with my colleague on our own if that's okay.' Palmer's request was polite but firm.

'Sure. You can use my office for five minutes if you want.'

'Thanks.' Palmer waited until Hartley-Brown had left the office and then leaned over and spoke softly to Karen. 'There's something I know that he doesn't know I know. Have you heard of Pradonet?'

'No. Why, should I?'

'Probably not, but he's a director of that company too. I ran some enquiries earlier and they're a holding company for some Internet based venture that operates some pretty explicit offshore sites for adult entertainment, and they sell the gear too.'

'Good God that changes everything Damien.'

'Yeah I know, and my guess is he's got a load of Pradonet stuff on that laptop, and if it's worth two million we're not talking about some old slapper showing her legs off.'

'No, I suppose we're not, more like kids' stuff for that kind of money. What do you want me to do?'

'Keep focused on the accounts ruse. Pull the modems and see what happens. Leave me to work on Pradonet and see what I can come up with. Now, not a word of this to anyone. Also, you can forget

142

Hammond. He went home yesterday and stayed there on his own the whole evening according to Eddie.'

'So what are you going to do this evening?'

'Well, first I'm going to take a look at Delaney's house and then I plan to visit the invisible Stephen Green.'

'You've found him?'

'Yeah. Same address that you got off Carol a few minutes ago. Might be interesting.'

Once outside the office Hartley-Brown had gone to talk to his Personal Assistant. He entered her semi-partitioned office and stood behind her, watching the screen. The view was different to the one that Hammond had observed the previous evening and, to his frustration, Palmer's voice was too low to be picked up clearly. As he stroked the woman's shoulders he asked her the question that was on his mind.

'Do you think they know?'

'I doubt it, but we've got to get that bloody laptop back before all hell breaks loose. Left shoulder a bit harder darling please. Oh yeah, down a bit. Ahh, that's the spot.'

'And how do we get the damn machine back when we don't know who's got it, and more to the point the country's foremost PI doesn't know either. I'm not so sure it was such a good idea to bring him in on this after all.'

'But you do want to get the pictures back, don't you?'

'Oh yes, of course I bloody do. If they get out on the streets then we're finished if whoever has taken them starts dropping names.'

'Do you think it was Katherine?'

'Who else could it have been? Why, oh fucking why, did I go away on business and leave the laptop in the store? Why did she have to pick that bloody machine for?'

'Because, if it was her, she knew what was on it, and that means she knows it's worth two million for you to keep it quiet.'

'You went to her new boyfriend's place a few weeks back, what was he like?'

'Nice enough and a complete moron when it comes to computers.'

'Could he be in on it though?'

'Could be, but I doubt it. Why?'

'Well, Palmer said he'd gone missing too. Adds up to something I'd say.'

'Well, not much if they've got the machine. If they've gone missing then I don't see it helps much. We'll have to wait until they contact us again.'

'Well they're not at her place, and they're not at his place, but damn it, they must be somewhere. Right I'd best get back in there.' Hartley-Brown stopped massaging the woman's shoulder and made his way back into his office.

'Good timing,' Palmer smiled falsely. 'I have just put the final touches to our plan. Miss Shaw will isolate as many of the links to your machines this evening before she leaves. That reduces the risks I guess. Then tomorrow she will isolate the other links and that way we will simply wait and see what your blackmailer does next. Meantime I am taking direct charge of finding your Miss Delaney, though my colleague has already established that she is not at home. I do have a few other possibilities to look into, and as Miss Shaw is more than capable of handling things here, I see no reason to hang around. I'll contact you tomorrow, if there's any news.'

'Very well, Mr Palmer, and good luck with your enquiries.' The two men shook hands briefly before Palmer left the office to find Hartley-Brown's PA waiting to escort him from the building. As she had not been called to do so Palmer considered it odd that she should have been waiting just outside the door, but he chose not to raise the matter in conversation.

Chapter Seven

The car park outside the front of the hotel was nearly full when Karen pulled into it. The traffic around Sutton had been particularly busy due to a problem with the main traffic lights at one end of the one way system. Karen parked her car and made her way up the short flight of steps that led to the hotel entrance. The glass front doors slid open as she approached them and she found herself standing in the foyer. Ten minutes later she had completed the formalities of checking in and was walking to her bedroom on the third floor. The room was comfortable and boasted a king-sized bed. She looked around the room and saw the bouquet of flowers on the table, next to the ice bucket. She read the small card that was attached to the bouquet. It simply read,

'Thought you'd appreciate an upgrade. Love DP.'

Karen located the mini-bar and opened the door. Inside a bottle of champagne was already well chilled. It lay on the shelf next to the other usual mini-bar contents. She looked at her watch and noted it was seven o'clock. She unpacked her few clothes and placed the small cloth-covered suitcase on top of the wardrobe.

The bathroom was functional and she noted with appreciation the wall-mounted power shower. It took less than two minutes for her to undress and stand under the powerful jet of water as she rubbed the delicately scented shower gel into her hair and flesh. She caressed her body as she washed, pleasuring herself with the luxury of the foam and the bubbles which burst against her skin. By half past seven she had towelled herself dry, finished her hair and was wearing the almost-revealing black dress she had chosen for the purposes of the evening. She wore no bra as to do so would have disrupted the way in which the dress hung. A dark G-string and stockings completed the ensemble. Finally, satisfied that all was as it should be, she left the room for dinner.

As the lift arrived in the foyer she looked into the bar. She had already committed to memory the picture of Robert Smith that Palmer had given her the previous evening. Now she looked round and spotted him sitting on his own at one end of the bar. Without undue haste she made for the middle of the bar and ordered a dry martini and lemonade. She chatted to the barman as he prepared the drink and asked him if the bar was always as quiet as it was this particular evening. His response indicated that the room would become busier later in the evening. Finally, and with a glance to ensure her conversation was being listened to she questioned the hours of service in the dining room and stated quite deliberately that it was the one part of a journey away that she hated - eating alone. Her comment had the desired effect for after she had taken barely three sips of the drink that had been poured for her she felt the presence of a man standing behind her. He coughed gently so as to attract her attention without alarming her.

'Excuse me, but I couldn't help noticing you were on your own. Are you waiting for someone?'

'No, I'm on my own.'

'Would you mind if I joined you?' The accent was definitely Scottish, but not true Scots.

'Not at all. You here on business too?'

'Yeah. Just a few days, and you?'

'One night. I don't mind the business side of these days out, but I do so hate the evenings.'

'Couldn't agree more. Fortunately last night I entertained the client I came to see, so that wasn't so bad. Have you eaten yet?'

'No, what about you?'

'Not yet. I know it's awfully presumptuous of me, but would you care to join me in the restaurant. I'm Robert by the way.'

'Karen, and yes I'd love to. What do you do Robert? For work I mean.' Karen looked up at the man and smiled, and as she did so she licked her lips seductively.

'Oh I'm a salesman. Well, that's not strictly true. I'm actually a partner in a small company and this week I'm acting as its salesman.'

'Selling what, if you don't mind me asking?'

'Computer software. We've got a little package we're touting round the market at the moment. Been to the Middle East and the States with it and next week I've got three potential clients in different European countries to see.'

'Sounds interesting. What kind of software?'

'Difficult to explain it really, but it's to do with the Internet and it gives the user access to a brand new type of product. Tell me, why are you here?'

148

Robert Smith pulled up a barstool as he spoke and sat next to the woman.

'Well, I'm also into computers. Small world isn't it. Only I'm a designer and auditor and I'm down here to look round a company we're helping out of financial problems. All very complicated but basically I'm spending a couple of days looking for loopholes in their systems.' If she was nervous she did not show it.

'Sounds more interesting than selling. Have you got anywhere yet?'

'Not really. Only what we already knew, but I've got high hopes for tomorrow, then I jet back up to Manchester tomorrow evening. Now, if we can change the subject, only I've had enough of computers for one day. How about dinner?'

'Agreed. Shall we take our drinks through?' Smith offered a helping arm as Karen moved to slide off the barstool, an arm that she was grateful to accept. As she moved she leaned forward, enough to give the man an eyeful of her ample cleavage.

'Thanks very much. Not too many men I meet are that courteous these days. It's a refreshing change to find a real gentleman.'

'Well, thank you for the compliment. It was just the way I was brought up. After you.' He guided her gently to the door of the bar and allowed her the courtesy of leaving the room first. She smiled as she passed him, a gentle smile, a smile which Smith could not fail to notice.

Dinner was a pleasant occasion and they made small chat as they ate. Finally the coffee arrived and was served.

'Now I absolutely insist,' Smith suddenly changed the topic of conversation, 'that you allow me to pick up the tab for this. It has been a great pleasure having you for company. Not often do I get to dine on my journeys with such an attractive and intelligent woman.'

'I couldn't possibly allow you to do that.'

'But I insist.'

'Well, if you do, then I suppose I can't say no. What have you got planned for the rest of the evening?'

'Not a lot. Maybe a bit of television to while away the hours. What about you?'

'Well, I hate being on my own, especially on nights like this.' Her voice had become silky so that the words rolled off her tongue with a certain seductive quality.

'Sorry, I don't understand. Nights like what?'

'Well, charming company, a good meal, a very, very expensive bottle of wine and the thought that I'll have to go back to my room and a bottle of champagne all on my own.' She looked at the man and smiled suggestively. He took the hint and shuffled, almost unnoticed, in his chair.

'That, I have to admit, would be a shame. Are you asking me what I think you're asking me?'

'How could I know what you're thinking. If you think I like the look of you then the answer is yes, and to be blunt about it, and I'm sorry if you're offended, I haven't had a good fuck in ages and you look like you know what to do.' She whispered the last part of the sentence as she leaned towards him, again revealing her breasts. If he had failed to notice

150

before, Robert Smith could not help but now notice her bare breasts under the dress. Karen smiled to herself as she noticed he spent slightly longer than was decent looking down the top of her dress. She felt her nipples stiffen as he looked at them.

'And you can tell that just by looking at a guy?'

'Usually, yes. I'm sorry, I've ruined it haven't I? I've offended you? It's the wine talking really, makes me relax and speak my mind. I'm really sorry.' Her voice had changed to one that resonated with apology in every syllable.

'No, you haven't ruined anything. It's just not something I have the courage to ask of a lady when we first meet. Of course I find you attractive, who wouldn't! I just didn't want to offend you by suggesting anything. After all, we will probably never see each other again after tonight.'

'Which makes it even more fun thinking about it. We're less likely to get spotted being together.'

'Have you not got a partner then?'

'Oh a couple of men who I see every now and then, but it's all very ad-hoc. What about you?'

'No, no-one special. So where do we go from here?'

'Well, oh here's the waiter.'

'Waiter,' Smith called out and continued when the uniformed man arrived at the table, 'could you ensure this is all added to my bill. Room 327.'

'Certainly sir, if you'd just sign here.' The waiter proffered a slip of paper which Robert Smith duly signed.

'Thank you sir.' The waiter gratefully accepted the ten pound note that Smith handed him.

'Well,' Karen continued after the waiter had left them, 'I'm off to room 301, and if you want to join me in say ten minutes that would be very pleasant.'

'I will. Actually, if you don't mind I'll get out of this suit and put on something a bit more casual.'

'Why should I mind? I take it you don't change according to the clothes you wear?' She laughed. 'Right, see you in a few minutes.' The woman stood up and planted a surprise kiss on the man's cheek, not a long passionate kiss, more of a peck. 'And thanks again for dinner.'

Karen left the restaurant and took the lift to her floor. Once inside her room she quickly hid the card accompanying the bouquet of flowers. Then she took the bottle of champagne out of the mini-bar and selected the two champagne flutes that sat on the tray that was next to the tea tray. She placed her handbag in the wardrobe and locked the door before hiding the key under one corner of the mattress of the bed.

By the time she heard the knock on the door she was sitting on one of the comfortable chairs, ready for her guest.

'Come in, it's not locked,' she called out. The handle of the door turned and Robert Smith stood in the doorway, a large smile on his face.

'Just before I settle down, I must check that you haven't changed your mind.'

'No, you're just exactly what's been on my mind ever since I met you in the bar. Incidentally I like your casual gear.' He was dressed smartly. The light brown slacks and a casual open-neck brown shirt made Smith feel relaxed. The woman had not changed and as Smith walked towards her she asked,

'Champagne?'

'Yes please, would you like me to open it?'

There was a faint humming sound that was almost inaudible in the room.

'Please.'

'Say, can you hear that humming noise?'

'Yeah. I heard it when I arrived. Something to do with the air-conditioning according to reception. Apparently the duct goes down just past the wall. Still, it's not loud and now I've got used to it I'd forgotten it was there until you mentioned it.'

'Oh.' There was a bang as the cork hit the ceiling and then Smith filled the flutes. 'Cheers, and here's to this evening.'

'Cheers. Hmm, that's nice. Now, I hope you don't think I'm getting too forward but I'd love to know what you like to do in the bed department.' She smiled as she spoke.

'Well,' he paused for the thought, 'most things really I suppose. Not that I've ever had the chance to be that adventurous. Why, what do you like?'

'Everything. I hope you don't mind me asking, but you are normal aren't you?'

'How do you mean?'

'Well, it's silly really but I met this real hunk of a guy once, only when we got under the duvet his dick was only about two inches long and that was erect, so it wasn't much fun for me. That's what I meant by normal.' She could already see the signs of growth down the left leg of his trousers. He laughed politely before he replied.

153

'Well, no problems there. I'm fairly large and thick, so you should have no complaints.'

'I can't wait to find out.' She reached over to where Robert Smith was sitting and put a hand on his knee. 'Do you want to show me?'

'You don't waste time, do you? Okay.' He removed his slip-on shoes, stood up and removed his slacks, revealing a pair of boxer shorts that bulged furiously as his manhood hung partly erect along his left leg.

'Looks good from here,' she said smiling. 'Let's sit on the bed.'

'So you like to be in charge then? Not that I mind that.' He complied and sat on the bed. The wardrobe in the corner of the room pointed towards the window, the curtains of which Karen had thoughtfully closed. Smith quickly noted the doors were closed, and the case on top of it was no bigger than what he would have expected for a couple of nights away from home. Feeling safe in the hands of this woman he had met barely a couple of hours earlier, he relaxed as she sat beside him. She stroked his leg feeling the coarse hair as she did so, gently teasing her fingers higher up the inside of his thigh with each stroke. As she did so the bulge in his boxer shorts grew until the material was quite taut. With a deft hand she placed her hand on his mound and squeezed gently. As she did so he reached over and placed a hand on her breast.

'Sorry, Robert, but do you mind if I just touch you for now. It's just one of my quirks. I want to make sure you really enjoy this.'

'Fine by me. Tell me when you want attention.'

'I will. Now if you lie back I'll attend to you properly.'

Smith did as he was asked, and as he did so Karen slid the boxer shorts down his legs revealing the full extent of his arousal. Now, fully exposed, there was no doubt that he had not been bragging. He certainly had not underestimated his size, he was, thought Karen, huge. His shaft was at least ten inches long and very thick. For a moment she wondered if she would be able to cope with it, but the thought soon vanished as she considered that he was no thicker than Palmer, and only slightly longer. She noticed that his foreskin was intact and, using a little champagne for lubrication she rolled the skin back, revealing the frenum.

'Well, you weren't exaggerating about the size. This is going to be one hell of an experience for both of us. Do you like what I'm doing.'

'Yes, I've not had this kind of attention before. God it feels good.' He lay back and allowed her to continue masturbating him.

She stroked him now using her fingers and thumb, gently and slowly at first but with increasing strength and speed. As she did so he groaned as his arousal increased.

'I'll be finishing soon if you carry on like that,' he muttered between groans after a couple of minutes of the delicious torture.

'No you won't. Just relax, and let me handle you.' As she spoke she changed her grip so that her whole hand was wrapped around his shaft. She dribbled some more champagne onto the tip of his glans as she stroked him slowly. After a minute of this slow, deliberate, action, she felt him twitch, a sign that he was close to reaching his climax. As he twitched she relaxed her grip and grasped him firmly behind the head of his member. After a few seconds the steel girder that she had been stroking became more supple as her grasp took the heat out of the moment.

'As I said,' she smiled, 'you won't come until I'm ready for you to.'

'Wow, where did you learn that trick?'

'An ex-boyfriend taught it to me. Now, I want you to lie back and relax. I'm going to take my time over you because you've got exactly what I'm after and I want to make the most of it. So just lie there for a moment and I'll take some of these clothes off.' She stood up and removed her dress, throwing it casually onto one of the chairs. As she did so he lay back though keeping one very interested eye on the woman as she revealed more of her naked flesh.

'Do you like what you can see now?' She asked playfully, aware that the steel girder was once again as vertical as it possibly could be.

'Fantastic. Can I touch you yet?'

'Not quite, just be patient and enjoy what you can see for the moment. I take it you do know how to handle me when I let you?'

'Oh yes, no problems there, none at all. Oh, that is so good.' As he had been speaking she had once again taken the girder in her hand and now, with the foreskin rolled right back, and with a finger covered in cold champagne she gently stroked the frenum until she was sure he could almost take no more of the attention. All this time she had been sitting on

156

the side of the bed, and had been using both hands in the most intimate moments of her caresses. Now she leaned over him and gently blew cool air across the very tip of his manhood as she held firmly in her left hand. As she breathed out the cool air so her right hand began to caress his scrotum. He groaned loudly as she touched him there for her hand was cold to the touch after she had first cooled it against the side of the champagne bottle. As she continued to squeeze him she said the words he was longing to hear,

'Now you can hold my breasts.' It was all the encouragement he required. With one hand he reached out and cupped the nearest breast in his hand. The moment he touched her she felt the shiver of excitement course through her body - she could immediately tell that he was an experienced lover. Gently he stroked her breast, tantalising her and distracting her from her own attentions of his body, until at last he touched her by now erect nipple. As he held her nipple between thumb and finger she felt the small explosions deep in her body. She gasped as she reached her first peak. When she had subsided he ventured,

'Is that why you didn't want me to touch you too soon? You sure came quickly.'

'Yeah, but don't worry, Robert, I'm one of those women that loves multiple orgasms. And I have a feeling you'll manage to give them to me with no problem. Just carry on enjoying yourself.'

'Okay, but let's see just how wild you can get. I think it's my turn to do the honours, if that's okay with you.'

'Sure, what do want me to do?'

'Just lie back, I'll do the rest.' With that he gently pushed her backwards until she was lying on the bed. Unable to continue her attentions to his manhood, she draped her arm round his neck as his lips met hers in a long kiss. Her tongue was still deep in his mouth when she felt his hand on her leg. It was soft, yet firm and it sent a new wave of excitement through her body. As she had done earlier, he now proceeded to gently stroke her inner thigh, each stroke getting a fraction higher. As he stroked her in this way Karen obligingly opened her legs wide to facilitate his adventurous digits. Finally his stroking reached the flimsy material of her G-string. Pushing it gently to one side he continued, slowly at first but when he met no opposition his attentions became stronger. He found the button he was looking for and circled it with his finger. As he did so Karen arched her back and groaned with the pleasure he was giving her. He continued this way until she had subsided from her second peak of the evening.

By now she was damp with her excitement and he found it easy to locate the entrance to her body. His finger caressed the entrance, teasing it in a way that made Karen pant with excitement as her back arched in a further spasm of pleasure. Now, as he circled the entrance she raked her fingers down his back. She knew that she was approaching the point of spontaneous contraction, something she wanted to hold back on until he was fully inside her. She felt the finger slide into her body, the very tip of it seeking out the pleasure pad within her. Inevitably,

158

with such a skilled lover, it took him only a few moments to find the internal pad that made Karen feel like she was about to self-destruct. She gasped as he stroked the pad with a beckoning type of action. Then she felt it happening as wave after wave of contractions took over her abdomen. She arched her back and grabbed hold of the headboard as she reached that point of continuous peaking from which she could go no further. After what seemed a lifetime, though it lasted less than a minute she felt his finger slowly sliding out of her body. As it did so the contractions eased.

'You weren't kidding either. Now, how was that for starters?' His voice was soft, caring, and wickedly seductive. As Karen heard the word starters she began to wonder what the main course would entail.

'Starters?' She whispered as she continued to gasp for air.

'Oh yes, I've hardly begun yet. I love giving attention, especially when it is so gratefully received.'

'Well, okay, but before we go any further I think we should be sensible. We don't really know each other, so if you don't mind I'd prefer to take precautions.' If Robert was surprised by her suggestion he certainly didn't show it.

'That's fine by me Karen. What do you suggest?'

'I have something. If you lie back I'll put it on for you.'

He did as he was asked and she removed the small package that she had hidden under the pillow earlier that evening. She carefully ripped open the side of the metal foil and extracted the contents. As Robert lay back on the bed she turned her attentions back to his member. She caressed it between her thumb and forefinger until she was sure that it was as rigid as possible and then, using a small amount of champagne she wet the tip of the head. Gently and carefully she placed the condom on the top and began to roll it down the long, thick, shaft. As she did so she smiled at him as he lay there watching her. When the latex fully covered his member she reached down and kissed it. Then, and without further warning she took the head in her mouth and sucked it gently. As he gasped with a mixture of surprise and pleasure she slid her mouth down over his shaft until his head touched the back of her mouth. With infinite care now she continued until she felt the head of his member sliding into her throat. Slowly, so as to avoid any reflux reaction, she continued until the full length of his shaft was buried in her mouth. Then, and again with great care, she withdrew his member.

'You sure are full of surprises.' It was all he could manage as he lay there, stunned by her adventurous spirit.

'Well, I've had a bit of practice. Did you like the feel of it?'

'Wonderful, it felt so tight. I would probably have come if you hadn't used the condom. Now, I'd really like to get this chap pumping. Would you prefer to be on top or under me?'

'From behind actually. I'll kneel on the edge of the bed and you can take me like that,' she whispered.

With that she knelt on the edge of the bed and parted her legs as wide as she could. He came and stood behind her and placed the end of his member at the very entrance to her body. Gently at first he pushed into her. She gasped at his size but felt him slide in. When the head was fully inserted his thrust became stronger and he rammed the shaft into her up to the hilt. With a yelp of surprise she felt him partly withdraw before thrusting once again deep into her body. His action was strong and in a few moments he reached a steady rhythm that had Karen shuddering as one climax after another coursed through her willing body. Then as he reached the peak of his own excitement he thrust one final time into the depths of her body and she felt his release pulsating within her. Only as they climbed down from the peak of their excitement did she realise that they were both sweating profusely from their exertions.

'God,' she muttered as he withdrew from her, his emission contained within the protective device, 'that was terrific. Thanks Robert I needed that.'

'So did I,' he said. 'Won't be a tick, I just need the bathroom.'

When he returned a couple of minutes later he looked somewhat sheepishly at the woman and then spoke, almost reluctantly.

'I don't usually do this, but would you mind if I asked for your address? People like you don't happen to me every day. Now I know we may not see each other again but I'd love to stay in touch and if I ever did hit your neck of the woods I'd love to look you up.'

'Sure. I'll write it down for you. Now, I hate to be a bore, but it's been a long day and to be honest I'm shagged out. Only, if we spend the night together I don't think either of us would get much sleep and we've both got important and busy days tomorrow. Do you mind, only it's half ten and I really do need at least eight hours after all that exercise?'

'No, not at all. I kind of figured we'd part company afterwards, but I didn't like to bring up the subject as it would have been a bit of a wham, bam, thank you ma'am situation, and that's not what I want you to think it was.'

'I don't. I know exactly what it was,' she smiled as she wrote down an address on a piece of paper, 'and I've given you my mobile, but I forgot the charger so it's dead at the moment.'

'Yeah, I always forget something on these trips away. Forgot my shaver once.'

'It happens. Now, I don't mean to be rude, but I really could do with some shut eye.'

'Sure, and thanks. Maybe I'll see you at breakfast.'

'Maybe.'

As they'd been speaking Robert had re-dressed and now he stood at the door.

'Well, goodnight then Karen, and thanks for a memorable evening.' The door was open as he stepped onto the corridor beyond.

162

'Pleasure's mine, Robert, and good luck.' As he closed the door behind him she whispered to herself the words 'you'll need it'. With the door shut Karen walked over to the bed and smiled at the wardrobe.

'That should do it,' she said and smiled, the bathrobe wrapped tightly around her body. She reached under the bed and withdrew the small cassette recorder. She turned it off and walked over to the wardrobe. She took down the suitcase and opened it and then pressed the button that switched off the video recorder. The electronic eye in one of the studs at the corner of the suitcase was virtually undetectable, except perhaps under close scrutiny. Next she retrieved her handbag from inside the wardrobe and extracted her mobile phone. Turning it on she dialled a number and reached the answerphone.

'Damien, it's Karen, it's done, and your client will be impressed with the results. I'll talk to you in the morning. I can't wait for you to see what I've been up to this evening. You'd best be warned that you are in for the same treatment soon. Bye lover.'

While Karen was occupied by the attentions of Robert Smith, Palmer was busy elsewhere. After leaving the offices of Castle Point he drove into Epsom and firstly located the apartment where Mark Hammond lived. The gateway to the underground car park was, not surprisingly, locked. It did not concern Palmer as he turned his attentions to the entry phone system by the side of the front door. Picking a number at random he pressed the buzzer. There was no reply, and neither did he get a reply from his next attempt. It was several seconds after pressing the third buzzer, and he was about to press the fourth, when the somewhat crackly voice of a woman sounded from behind the grille.

'Yes?' The voice was enquiring but not hostile.

'Oh hi, I'm sorry to disturb you but I'm looking for a guy called Mark, Mark Hammond, only I know he lives here, but I can't remember the flat number.' Palmer sounded apologetic.

'Let's see now, not the chap who drives the Esprit is he?'

'That's the chap.'

'Oh he's in number eight, but I don't think he's in at the moment. I heard his damn car go out about an hour ago and I haven't heard it come back.'

'Oh well, thanks anyway.'

Palmer waited a few seconds and then pressed the buzzer to apartment number eight. There was, predictably, no reply. A few minutes later Palmer was sitting in his car. He drove the relatively short distance to the house that was registered in the name of Stephen Green. It was a typical 1930's semi-detached affair with a short front garden and drive space, but no garage. Palmer drove past the house and was indicating that he was pulling in when, just on the far end of the curve of the road ahead of him he spotted something, something he was not looking for. The bright yellow Esprit was incongruous in the road, and Palmer was instantly sure that it belonged to Hammond. After all, he reasoned to himself, not many folk in that area drove such a vehicle. Cancelling the indicator he continued to drive slowly round the curve of the road. He passed the

Esprit and noticed that it was empty. He drove a further fifty yards and then turned the car around. As he backed into the driveway to complete the manoeuvre he saw the figure of a man walking up the road. Palmer waited and watched as the man walked up to the Esprit, looked inside it with what could be presumed to be jealousy and then continued walking.

Palmer completed his manoeuvre and drove back up the road past the house he intended to visit. Parking the car he walked the short distance back up the road to the house and rapped out three short knocks on the knocker that was situated just below head height in the middle of the door. Palmer waited and then knocked again. Inside, the figure of a man appeared in the frosted glass panels on either side of the central divide. Closing the door at the far end of the hallway he approached the front door and with the chain in place opened it carefully.

'Yes?'

'Sorry to trouble you,' Palmer began, 'but I'm looking for a guy called Stephen Green.' The man who peered out from behind the door had short mid-brown hair and wore glasses. Other than that there was little Palmer could determine about his identity.

'Well, you've found him, but he doesn't know you, so would you mind identifying yourself?'

'James Natchworth. Sorry, you won't know me, but your wife does.'

'Wife?' The man stumbled for a moment as if deciding what to say next. 'But surely she's … I mean she's never mentioned you. Natchworth did you say?'

'Yes, actually your wife has asked me to find you.'

'Well, I suppose you can tell her that you've succeeded. Not that it will do her any good. I am most definitely not going back to her, and actually by the end of the week-end I'll be gone for good.'

'But this place, what will happen to it?' Palmer had detected something was not quite right with Stephen Green.

'Sold it. Now I have to go and pack, good day.' The man closed the door firmly before Palmer had a chance to raise any further matters. Palmer walked away from the door and then back to his car and sat in the driver's seat. There was, he thought, something odd about the man he had just talked to. He opened his brief case and rummaged around inside, but the file he was looking for was not there. Disheartened at not finding what he was looking for he started the engine and began his journey into Sutton. It was now some time after six o'clock and Palmer parked his car in one of the many side roads at the top of Sutton. He walked down the High Street, selected the restaurant which appealed to his mood, and then sat down and ordered his evening meal. His meal was not as sumptuous as Shaw's, but in his present state of mind he was glad of his own company. As he ate the garlic bread starter he began to reflect on the happenings of the previous few days and then congratulated himself that he had at least found Stephen Green, and it wasn't his fault if he didn't want to go back to his wife. Having completed his act of self-congratulation Palmer focused his thoughts on the missing laptop computer and Katherine Delaney. He was halfway through the pizza, and no closer to solving his second case for the day when his mind drifted back to Stephen Green. There was something about the man that bothered him, and as the pizza was slowly demolished, the feeling did not go away. Nor did Palmer's thoughts that he'd shared with Karen in Hartley-Brown's office, about the missing laptop, go away. Palmer began to wonder just what would be found on the laptop, assuming it was ever found, assuming the blackmailer didn't just take the money and disappear with the equipment as well. There were far too many possibilities and far too many loose ends for Palmer's liking and he resolved to attempt to reduce the number by the end of the evening.

The meal over Palmer paid the waitress and added some small change as a tip. He walked from the restaurant back to his car with a slow, pedantic, walk that showed his mind was elsewhere. Once inside the car he banged the steering wheel with his left hand as he exclaimed,

'Damn it, why didn't I think of that before? Delaney's missing, she's known to Stephen Green, and Hammonds Esprit was parked just down the road from Green's house.' Palmer started the engine and drove back to the road in which Green had the three bedroom semi-detached house. He drove to the location with a great deal of haste as if trying desperately to rectify an oversight. He drove down the road looking for the Esprit and was only half surprised that it was now nowhere to be seen.

Palmer parked his own car and walked back to Stephen Green's house. Now the house lay in darkness. Palmer walked up to the front door and peered in through the letterbox. There were no lights on and the whole house seemed shrouded in an eerie darkness despite the streetlight that was not more than a few yards further down the road. Again Palmer knocked on the door, a sixth sense already telling him what he thought he knew, that there would be no response. He waited patiently on the doorstep for two minutes and knocked again, yet received the same lack of response. Finally he walked away from the door. It was now nearly nine o'clock in the evening and Palmer wondered how Shaw was fairing.

Having regained the driver's seat of his car Palmer decided it was time to pay his final visit for the evening. He drove to the address in Cheam that he had lifted from his database earlier that day. It was a visit made more out of curiosity than anything else, but Palmer had developed a desire in his own mind to find out how one successful professional lived. It took less than ten minutes for Palmer to locate the house he was after. 'Chandlers' was a magnificent home. Complete with an attached double-garage and a drive that swept across the front of the property, it looked to Palmer as though the house must have boasted at least five bedrooms. He parked a few yards down the road and walked back. The driveway was made of concrete and Palmer ventured almost silently onto its surface.

The curtains in the front room were roughly drawn and a shaft of light poured out across the drive. Palmer noticed that dark green Beetle that was parked in front of the double garage. It did not intrigue him but he made a mental note of the Index number for future reference. His attention focused on the window from which the shaft of light was pouring, Palmer edged forward until he could just peer in through the chink of light. Hartley-Brown was sitting in the big armchair at the far end of the room. He was looking straight at the window and it was impossible for Palmer to know whether he had been observed. The fact that Hartley-Brown continued to sit there made it seem unlikely. Sitting in the chair under the window was a smaller person. Palmer could only see the top of this person's hair, which was dark in colour. It was clear that the two people were holding a conversation as Hartley-Brown gesticulated in the same way as he had done when Palmer had visited Castle-Point earlier that day. Palmer decided that it would be interesting to catch Hartley-brown off his guard. He pulled out his mobile phone and dialled a number. As the phone at the other end of the connection started to ring Palmer watched as Hartley-Brown left his armchair and walked out of the room' The person in the chair below the window remained sitting, almost invisible to the outside world.

'Hello.' Hartley-Brown sounded somewhat irritated by the intrusion into his privacy, even though it was not yet half past nine.

'Mr Hartley-Brown, sorry to trouble you this time of night but something has come up. Are you free to talk?'

'Well, yes, I suppose so.'

'Or perhaps you'd prefer me to come round to see you. The matter is quite delicate.'

'That depends where you are?'

'Well, I'm in Epsom at the moment. Whereabouts do you live?' Palmer relished the moment.

'Cheam.'

'So I could be with you in about ten minutes.'

'Can't it wait until tomorrow?'

'Well, it's just something that's come up concerning Katherine Delaney, that's all, and I'd prefer to get it sorted tonight so that my colleague can get on with his job.'

'And you can't tell me what it's all about on the telephone?'

'I could, but it's a bit sensitive and if your blackmailer is listening in on the phones it would be better to do it face to face.'

'And you couldn't have told me earlier at the office?'

'Didn't know it then, and anyway again we wouldn't want anyone listening in, would we?'

'Yes, quite, of course, well ten minutes then.' Hartley-Brown continued to reel off his address and to give Palmer directions.

'Thank you Mr Hartley-Brown. Ten minutes then.' Palmer hung up and resumed his watch at the window. He was in time to see Hartley-Brown return to the room and stand in front of the window. His face was flushed and his gesticulations were more energetic than they had been before Palmers call. The woman stood up now and continued to face away from Palmer. She walked out of the room

170

and Hartley-Brown followed her. The hall light was switched on again and then the landing light. Finally an upstairs light was turned on, and then a minute later was switched off. Then, the landing light was switched off at almost the same moment that the porch light was turned on. Finally Hartley-Brown regained his armchair and sat there staring directly at the window through which Palmer was observing his every move. Finally the ten minutes were up and Palmer walked casually round to the front door and pressed the doorbell.

'Sorry to trouble you,' he began when Hartley-Brown had opened the door to welcome his visitor. 'It's just that you can't be too careful on some matters.'

'Come in. The lounge is through there,' Hartley-Brown was clearly agitated. 'Would you like a drink Mr Palmer?'

'A small scotch would be very welcome. You may want something quite strong too.'

Hartley-Brown poured two scotches and offered one to Palmer as he gestured to the armchair under the window.

'So Mr Palmer, what is so important that you felt you had to visit me tonight?' Even if he already knew the answer, as Palmer was sure he did, Hartley-Brown managed to convince Palmer that he was mystified.

'Well, it's a bit of a story. My colleague has been making some enquiries into your Katherine Delaney. She is, as you rightly said from the beginning, not apparently at her home. In fact there's the best part of a week of post on the doormat and her neighbour hasn't heard her since last Thursday. Now, we also know that she is somehow involved with a guy called Stephen Green,' Palmer began though Hartley-Brown immediately interrupted him.

'He's not a shrink is he?'

'Well, if by that you mean a psychologist then yes. Anyway Miss Delaney has been linked to this Stephen Green – do you know him then?' Palmer decided to see what he could extract from the man sitting opposite him.

'Only vaguely. Katherine invited us to some do a couple of weeks back and Green was there. She introduced him as the man she'd met when she'd taken her sister over to see him for an appointment some months ago. Apparently it was love at first sight.'

'I see. Well, and forgive me, but I have been trying to locate this guy for some months now – his wife wants me to find him.'

'But Katherine always said that she was lucky to be with a single guy for once. You, ah, probably heard that we had an affair a while back. I am sure Miss Shaw has been made party to such gossip.'

'Yeah, she did say something. Was it you or Miss Delaney that called off your relationship?' Palmer feigned disinterest in as polite a manner as possible.

'Oh she did. She'd found Green and there was no stopping her, so far as she was concerned.' The answer, Palmer thought, was a little too quick.

'Which makes it unlikely that she'd be trying to blackmail you now – what reason could she have?' Palmer looked evenly at the man in front of him.

'I've no idea.'

'Okay, well there's something else that we have discovered. My colleague has made some other enquiries and it would appear that Miss Delaney has a somewhat interesting side-line. Not to put too fine a point to it,' Palmer lied, 'she's come up in some enquiries as being involved with a company that promotes pornography on the internet.' As he spoke Palmer watched Hartley-Brown intently. If anything Hartley-Brown turned a slightly pale colour for a moment but quickly recovered.

'And why should that be of such importance that you had to visit me tonight?' Hartley-Brown's ability to show lack of comprehension was worthy of some award. Palmer decided to play his ace.

'Well, what with your involvement in Pradonet I would have thought there'd be some possible conflict there.'

'You know about Pradonet?'

'Yes, but only because it happened to come up in some searches we were making on Miss Delaney.'

'But that's impossible, she has nothing to do with Pradonet.'

'Not directly, but she is a director of Zytecha Systema, and I understand they have a twenty percent interest in Pradonet. So I'm guessing she knows exactly what Pradonet offers its clients.'

'Web hosting and adult entertainment, and Zytecha Systema supplies the hardware and so forth.'

'Including overseas facilities so you don't breach UK law, or am I wrong Mr Hartley-Brown?'

'You're wrong Mr Palmer, and anyway my interest in Pradonet is purely a sleeping one. I put some capital in to get a couple of young guys with talent started and so I now have some shares and a seat on the board. But other than that my whole life revolves round Castle Point. So I still don't understand why you had to come and see me tonight?'

'Okay I'll come to the main reason. Once we found out about Pradonet I did some surfing, I think that's what you Internet lovers call it. Those two whiz kids sure like to advertise. It took me less than five minutes to find Pradonet's website and the links it offers. Okay so I admit it all seems legitimate enough but I couldn't help taking one of the free tours on one of the adult sites, and that was when I found what I had to talk to you about. I don't know for sure who's blackmailing you Mr Hartley-Brown though I have to now believe your suspicions were right.'

'I'm sorry, I don't follow.' Hartley-Brown sounded weary.

'Well, I found someone on the site that looks an awful lot like Miss Delaney. Actually, from the photograph on your client files I'd have to say it was her. Now, I'm only hazarding a guess that if I joined the site and got to the real material inside I'd see a hell of a lot more than just her front exposed

174

to the camera.' Palmer's gambit paid off as Hartley-Brown slumped in his chair.

'Okay Mr Palmer, so you're a good detective, even if you did get lucky. Miss Delaney posed for Pradonet about three years ago. We took some shots and paid her handsomely for them. That was shortly after we started seeing each other. She had such a great body and she was very extrovert when it came to the sex thing. I actually suggested the shoot as a joke and to be honest I was surprised when she agreed to do it. And, yes you're right, and I suppose there's no point in trying to protect her image anymore, there's a lot worse than boobs once you're inside the site.'

'And is that what she's blackmailing you about?'

'I presume so. The new software gave her the means I guess.'

'But two million for a handful of pictures, that's a bit steep isn't it?'

'Yeah, but I don't think I have much choice. If she uses the damn package we're sunk, and if she exposes me about the past then my career is in tatters anyway. So she has me by the proverbial balls and there isn't much I can do about it.' There was, thought Palmer, some truth in what Hartley-Brown was saying but, he felt sure, it was not the whole story.

'Is there anything else that I should know about Miss Delaney?' Palmer asked quite gently.

'No, you know it all by the sound of it. She posed nude and in various hardcore scenes and she got paid for it. Now, and for whatever reason, she's decided to capitalise on it I suppose.'

'Perhaps someone has seen her on the site?'

'Possible, but I doubt it. Most punters don't recognise any of the models, they're just interested in the action.'

'I see, well in that case she must have some other reason.'

'I guess so, but I haven't a clue what it could be, other than the fact that she's bent on getting rich quickly, and the package gives her the opportunity.'

'Have you heard any more since the original note?'

'No I haven't actually, and it's been over forty eight hours now.'

'Precisely, which means you're bound to hear soon. When you do, let me know immediately. Now, are you sure there isn't anything else on that laptop I should know about?'

'No, I don't think so. I imagine there's all kinds of company stuff on it, software and the like, but nothing that's worth the kind of money that's been demanded.'

'Well then Mr Hartley-Brown I'm sorry to have intruded on your evening, only I thought there might have been more to what we've uncovered about Miss Delaney. Still, you know her better than I do and it sounds now like it was just something silly she did. It might give her a reason to blackmail you, but I doubt it. Like you said I doubt anybody has recognised her. Oh well, I will just have to redouble my efforts.'

With that Palmer stood to leave. As he did so he thought he heard a sound from upstairs but it was a feint sound, a sort of creaking sound, and he could not be sure.

'Well Mr Hartley-Brown once again I'm sorry to have troubled you. My colleague will see you tomorrow at the office, and I imagine her work will be completed by lunchtime. Now I really must get going – it's quite a drive back to where I live.'

'Good night Mr Palmer, I'll sleep on what you've told me and see if anything comes to mind.' Hartley-Brown closed the front door behind Palmer who started to walk back down the driveway.

Inside the house as the door closed the person who had been hiding upstairs descended the stairway and joined Hartley-Brown in the lounge. As the person did so Palmer was already looking through the window at the point where the curtains failed to meet. This time, as the person came into the room he caught a clear view of her.

'Curious,' he muttered as he completed his walk back to the car, 'very curious.' He sat in the driver's seat of his car and switched his mobile phone back on. It alerted him to the fact that he had a voice message waiting for him. He pressed a couple of buttons in sequence and listened to the message.

Fifteen minutes after Karen Shaw had switched off her mobile phone the telephone in the bedroom rang. She reached over from the bed where she was lying and answered the summons.

'Yeah.'

'Miss Shaw, this is reception. We have a Mr Palmer down here.'

'Send him up would you?'

'Certainly Madam.'

Karen replaced the receiver on its cradle and gathered the equipment together. She had almost completed the task when there was a faint knock at the door.

'Hi,' she said as she opened it. 'What are you doing here?'

'I was in Epsom when you must have rung me , only I had the mobile turned off. When I turned it on your message was waiting, so I thought I'd stop off on the way back and see how it went.'

'Fine. He fell for me hook, line, and sinker, and in answer to your question, I think you've got all the stuff you'll need for your client.'

'And you were happy doing it?'

'Sure, you know I'm pretty broad-minded when it comes to sex. Just so you know, I saw him as all part of the job, and I have to admit it I enjoyed doing it. Don't get jealous, but he was almost as good as you are and you can be bloody sure you're in for the same treatment any day now. Just watch the video and wait for it to happen. Now, the kit's all here, and unless there's anything else I'm knackered.'

'Sure, and don't worry, I'm not the jealous sort. I'll call you tomorrow. Have a good night. Oh, by the way, you can tell Hartley-Brown in the morning that I expect to have the case resolved by the end of tomorrow.' He reached forward and kissed her tenderly and she responded to his touch, glad that the evening's activities had not interfered with their relationship. After a couple of minutes of holding her he picked up the small suitcase and closed her bedroom door behind him as he left. As he began the journey back to his terraced house she returned to bed and in a few minutes was fast asleep.

Chapter Eight

Palmer drove carefully back to his terraced house. The small suitcase sat on the passenger seat beside Palmer with the seat belt preventing it from moving too far. The case contained, Palmer considered, one of his more expensive pieces of equipment. It was not particularly delicate, but it's cost made Palmer treat it as fragile cargo. The journey home took over half an hour and by the time he turned the key in the front door the grandfather clock was chiming the half hour. Outside and hidden from Palmer's view two dark green eyes were watching him. Underneath the short hedge that divided Palmers front garden from his neighbours the three-legged jet black cat watched and waited. It might be a long night without food, but the animal had already made its decision to wait.

Palmer closed the door carefully behind him, and looked around the door into his study. He noticed that the red light on the answerphone was flashing but chose to ignore the message for the time being. He took the suitcase into the lounge and opened it. Carefully he extracted the videocassette from the recorder inside the case and transferred it to the machine attached to his TV. As the tape rewound Palmer went and made himself coffee. When he returned to the lounge the tape was ready for him. He sat back on the settee, and started playing the tape. The picture of the bed and the surrounds was good. Evidently Karen had gone to some lengths, using the device's built in monitor, to ensure the camera was lined up correctly on the expected scene of action. He heard the knock at the bedroom door and watched as Karen opened it. The sound was slightly muffled but he was able to listen with interest to their conversation. Then he watched as Smith undressed himself, presenting his manhood to the woman for inspection. It was, Palmer thought, a very good trap that they had sprung. He watched as they began their acts of foreplay and as he did so he remembered her promise to him as he had left her in the hotel bedroom barely an hour ago. In his mind he placed himself in the position of Robert Smith and imagined the familiar sensations of Karen Shaw as she performed the same acts on him. To Palmer the scenes on the TV were erotic and he became roused as he watched the couples' antics. Then, and almost too soon, the action was over and the tape went blank. As the screen went dark Palmer realised that it had actually been running for nearly an hour, and hour from which he had but to extract half a dozen shots that would convince his client what was going on. He'd not asked Karen to make a specific report on the evening's actions. She was busy enough, and with the evidence they now had, any report was largely superfluous. He turned off the TV, replaced the videocassette in a box and switched off the light. It was now nearly one o'clock, and he knew the next day would have to start early.

Taking a moment to remember the flashing red light on the answerphone he turned on the study light, walked over to the machine and pressed the button to replay the message.

'Good evening Mr Palmer. You do not know me but we have a mutual acquaintance in someone who knows you. Dawn Green is her name. She has told me much about you and what you are doing for her. I have something that may be of interest to you. If you are interested I'll be having tea on the third floor of the shopping centre in Sutton tomorrow at four o'clock. I will look out for you and will contact you when I am sure we are safe. Oh by the way my name is Sharon Whiteman. Good night Mr Palmer.' The machine signalled that the message had ended. Palmer replayed the cryptic message again and briefly noted the main details. Then he walked round his desk and turned out the study light.

Outside, the animal heard the activity as Palmer prepared to retire for the night. As it listened it decided the moment had arrived. Hopping forward to the front door it started to scratch at the wood. From within Palmer heard the faint scratching sound as he passed his study. Half thinking the sound had been imagined he turned off the study light. There it was again, unmistakable this time and slightly louder. The third such sound fully attracted his attention as he was drawn to the front door. He peered through the spy-hole but saw nothing. The fourth scratching sound clearly came from the bottom of the door. Palmer turned the key and, with the chain in place, opened the door. Gratefully the three-legged creature sidled into the house. Once inside it stopped and turned to look at Palmer, its two bright green eyes looking wistfully up at the sleuth. Palmer reached down and grabbed the animal by its scruff.

'Sorry pal, but you don't belong here.' The animal hissed as Palmer grabbed it, though he bent down to look at it more closely. 'Let's see where you do belong.' The cat had no collar and no name-tag.

'Well, that's not much help. Tell you what, it's too late to go banging on doors this time of night and I don't want to be responsible for you getting run over out there, so I guess you'll have to stay – but just for tonight.' Palmer reached down and stroked eth animal which started to purr softly. 'Okay, a saucer of milk and some chicken, if that's what you want.' Palmer laughed and picked the animal up. He took it into the kitchen and opened the fridge door. He pulled out the remains of the chicken and put some on a small plate. Then he poured some milk into a bowl. He placed the bowl and plate near the back door and turned out the light. As he left the kitchen he could hear the contented sounds of the animal combining purring with munching. Palmer left the animal to its own devices and went upstairs.

Palmer felt restless as he turned out the last of the lights. The house seemed empty as he tried to find the few hours of sleep his body needed, and there was almost a chill to the air that made him pull the duvet up to his chin. He lay there wondering, wondering what life would be like if Karen went to Edinburgh, wondering if there was anything he could do to stop her. He wondered like this until fatigue finally took him over and he lapsed into a fitful slumber, of the kind from which you wake and still feel tired. As he slept the animal downstairs decided to explore its new house, and finally it arrived in the bedroom of its new owner. Jumping on the bed it curled up into a ball and fell asleep, a sleep that was as contented as Palmers was restless.

In her hotel bed Karen Shaw was sleeping soundly. The faint hum from the air-conditioning unit failed to disturb her. As she slept she dreamed she was walking in the open country. It was a warm day and she was happy and carefree. She came to a brook where the water played joyfully over the stones, making a pleasant splashing sound as the water gurgled on downstream. She looked at her reflection in the water, a reflection that was broken by the ripples on the surface of the water. Suddenly she was aware of a presence. It was the same presence that she had become used to whilst at university, when she and her friends had moved away from mainstream religion and explored various alternatives. It was a heavy, dark, foreboding presence, though it did not frighten her. As she looked at her reflection in the water she saw it change as the wind whipped the ripples into a frenzy. She waited until the wind had passed, she always did, for after the wind she knew would come the message. In her dream she saw the message appear on the surface of the water. It appeared in the form of letters that were depicted by tongues of flames that seemed to burn through the very surface of the water. The message comprised three words – *DEATH AWAITS YOU.*

Almost as soon as the message of foreboding had appeared it had vanished, the contents swallowed up in the mist that now lurked where the message had momentarily been so evident. Karen tossed her head from side to side on her pillow as she slept. It was not time to awaken just yet and the presence she was familiar with ensured that her attention continued to be held captive. As the mist evaporated it seemed that night had fallen. Before her stood a figure dressed completely in black. The long flowing robe stretched from the being's head down to the surface of the water on which he stood. In one hand he held a shepherds crook and in the other a long-bladed scythe.

Without ceremony the being raised both implements above Karen's head and threw them at her. Just as they began their descent she stirred, the power of the vision too strong even for her. Suddenly she sat bolt upright in her bed, perspiration streaming from her face, and opened her eyes. Instantly the vision disappeared, to be replaced only by the darkness of her bedroom. She sat there motionless for several minutes, as if afraid to move. As she sat there she recalled her similar experiences at university and decided that the vision this night was on a par with some of her worst nightmares in her younger days. She reached for the switch that controlled the light above the bed and in a moment the light broke through the darkness. Still feeling insecure she stepped out from under the duvet and her naked body seemed to glow slightly in the soft light as she paced up and down the bedroom looking for a solace that would not come. It was four o'clock.

Two hours later the first rays of sunlight rose above the horizon and Karen sat there in her room with the curtains open watching gratefully as the day dawned. Sleep had eluded her since the vision and for the past two hours she had sat wondering what it all meant.

Some miles away as the first rays of the dawn sunlight filtered into his bedroom, Palmer stirred. The three-legged creature curled up at the end of the bed did not respond to her new owner's movements. Tired from his exertions of the past few days the animal continued to snore, grateful for the warmth and comfort of the room, and a full stomach. Palmer turned to face the window in his bedroom and considered the day before him. As with any other day he formed a mental plan of what he needed to do. There was of course always the possibility that something would happen to cause those plans to deviate, but he had long since found that having a plan was beneficial to the way he worked.

Foremost in his mind was the Green case, exacerbated now by the response he had received the previous evening. Of course he could not be sure that the man he'd met was in fact Stephen Green, but then the man had seemed to know the details of the case. Something troubled Palmer, and suddenly he realised that it was something he should have made sure of the previous evening. In a moment Palmer had leaped out of bed and was descending eth flight of stairs two at a time. The black creature continued to snore.

186

Once in his study Palmer turned on the main light. He walked round his desk and opened the drawer where he habitually filed the folders relating to his current workload. In a flash he pulled out the folder with the word Green printed on the front and just as quickly extracted the contents. Laying the reports and notes to one side he flicked through the small pile of papers until he found what he wanted. The picture was black and white, and it was a good few years out of date. That, and the rather crumpled state of the thin card on which it had been mounted made the picture look much older than it really was. Nonetheless the man in the picture was tall, handsome and clearly had fair hair, a stark contrast to the man Palmer had encountered at the front door of Stephen Green's house the previous evening. Of course, Palmer considered, it was possible for a man to change the colour of his hair, and even its style. Not only that but in the period of time since the photograph being taken it was possible that Stephen Green had found the need to wear spectacles, but the main contrast was one of height.

Palmer had spent some time carefully observing Dawn Green over the past few months. He knew with a degree of certainty that she could not be more than five fee and three inches tall. Looking at the photograph as she stood next to the man he judged that the man in the picture was at least six feet tall. Palmer recollected that the man at the door the previous evening was shorter than himself, probably no more than five feet nine inches tall. It was a discrepancy that made Palmer curse his own lack of attention to detail the previous evening.

Carefully he replaced the picture and papers in the folder before returning it to the drawer in his desk. That done he made his way to the kitchen and began to prepare breakfast. He had not been in the kitchen for long when he heard a purring sound behind him. He turned round and bent down to stroke the cat.

'And we must do something about finding your owners today as well.' The cat responded to his touch. 'Are you hungry again?' Palmer's voice sounded friendly, the voice of a genuine animal lover. 'Okay, I'll give you the rest of the chicken.' Palmer opened the fridge door and removed the plate on which the remains of the chicken sat. He picked off the rest of the meat and put it on a small plate. As he did so the cat sidled up to him.

'Tell you what, I'll put this outside and leave the door open for you while I have breakfast.' Palmer duly opened the door and placed the small plate of food on the flagstones outside. Obligingly the cat hopped through the doorway and began its meal. Leaving the door open Palmer took his own breakfast back to his study. There was something else on his mind, something that the man at the door had said, or nearly said, something about 'but surely she's', and then the man had changed the conversation. Palmer recalled the moment clearly as he sipped the freshly brewed coffee. He wondered why the man had changed the direction of the conversation so abruptly. As he cogitated the moment it troubled him. Finally he made a note on his pad of paper that he needed Marston to assist him that evening.

It was still early, far too early to call Marston unless the matter was of the utmost importance, which it wasn't, at least not now. As he ate the toast and marmalade Palmer contemplated his meeting with Hartley-Brown the previous evening. He mused to himself as to the reason for the presence of the PA at the house, and why she had disappeared from sight during Palmer's visit. Finally palmer contemplated the missing laptop and what it was known to contain. More importantly Palmer wondered what unknown material was also stored within the machine. The answers eluded him, though it seemed very possible that it had to do with Hartley-Brown's interests in adult entertainment and his links with Pradonet.

Palmer's thoughts were distracted by the sound of the telephone ringing behind him. He spun round in his chair and removed the receiver as the machine rang for the third time.

'Damien Palmer, good morning, how can I help you?'

'Damien, you sound bright and cheery.'

'Karen, good morning, did you sleep well?'

'Not bad to start with but I got disturbed part way through the night and couldn't get back off, so I thought I'd phone you.'

'At ten past seven, that's sweet of you. Actually I've been awake for some time myself.'

'Oh, did the video give you nightmares? I take it you watched it.'

'Yeah, and no it didn't, but it was a very good bit of work on your behalf. I'd say we got him hook, line and sinker.'

'Do you need me to do a report?'

'I don't think so. I'll make up what I don't know, but the pictures are going to speak far more than the words.'

'So,' she paused for a moment, 'what was keeping you awake.'

'Probably the cases, especially this thing with Castle Point. Also, I had a visitor on the bed with me most of the night.'

'No need to try and make me jealous, you know it won't work. So what was she like?'

'She was black, furry and has three legs, and she purred and snored all night long.'

'You've got a cat?' The woman sounded surprised and then laughed.

'Maybe. It was waiting on the doorstep last night when I got back. I couldn't leave it out there, could I?'

'Guess not, but you'd better give its owners a ring this morning.'

'I can't, it doesn't have a collar.'

'So are you going to keep it?' The woman still sounded amused.

'I guess so, for now.'

'In which case, if its black and only has three legs you'd better call it Lucky.' She laughed as she uttered the name.

'Yeah, okay, I'll think about it, but I'm not sure about the name.'

'Oh go on Damien, for me.'

'Oh, all right then, but I'll try to find its owner first.'

'Fair enough. Now I'm expecting to finish off at Castle Point this morning. Shall I give you a ring later and we can meet up somewhere?'

'Hmm, might be a bit tricky. I've got a lot on today, but give me a ring and we'll see how the day progresses. I will be in the Sutton area at some point, don't know when yet.'

'Fair enough., Well I'm off down for my full English breakfast now, so I'll call you later.'

'Yeah, cheers Karen.' Palmer replaced the receiver and went back to the kitchen. The three-legged animal had finished its breakfast and was now curled up on the back door mat. Palmer reached down and stroked it.

'Well, you've certainly made yourself at home, haven't you Lucky?' He chuckled to himself as the cat purred loudly.

***

At nine o'clock Palmer picked up the telephone receiver and dialled the number. The woman waited until the third ring before she replied.

'Mrs Green, good morning it's Damien Palmer.'

'Good morning Mr Palmer, how are you today.'

'Well thank you, and you?'

'Quite well, now, for what reason do I deserve this call?' The woman sounded slightly flustered as if she might be in a hurry.

'Well, one of my colleagues has unearthed some information on those cheques and I was wondering if it would be convenient to have a chat

191

about them later on, only it's the sort of thing I don't like to talk about over the phone?'

'Well I am very busy today but if you could make lunchtime we could meet up somewhere in Wimbledon.'

'That would be fine. Shall we say one o'clock at the big pub in the village?'

'The one by the riding stables?'

'That's it. Is that okay with you?'

'Fine, one o'clock it is, now I don't want to seem rude but I really must dash, such a frightful lot to do today.'

'That's fine by me Mrs Green, goodbye.' Palmer replaced the receiver only to pick it up again a moment later. He dialled a second number, the number of a mobile phone.

'Miss Morrison, good morning it's Damien Palmer.'

'Mr Palmer, nice to hear from you.'

'I hope you are well.'

'Yes, quite well, and yourself?'

'Fine. Now then, we've completed our initial observations on your fiancé and I was wondering if we could meet up sometime so I can give you the results, only I don't like doing this kind of thing on the phone?'

'Sure. Do you want me to come round to you?'

'No, no. I will be over your way this evening and I could pop in at some point if that's convenient.'

'Shall we say about seven o'clock then?'

'Yes that's fine.'

'And is Robert playing the field?'

'I think it's better to wait until I see you, apart from which I haven't seen my colleague's report yet. She phoned me a few minutes ago to say she'd drop it in this morning but we didn't talk for long.'

'Oh well, I'll have to wait. Must go I've got a client in a few minutes and he's just turned up.'

'Oh, I didn't realise you were at work. Well I'll see you later on Miss Morrison, goodbye.'

'Goodbye Mr Palmer.' The phone went dead and Palmer, after a moment dialled a third number.'

'Eddie, it's Damien. How are you this morning?'

'Fine Damien, and yourself?'

'Pretty good. Say are you busy this evening only I could do with a hand.'

'No, nothing planned for this evening. What is it?'

'To do with the Green case. I found where the bloke is supposed to be living, only when I knocked at the door someone else answered it. I just want to take a look round tonight and if no-one's in I thought your skills might come in useful.'

'You know I don't do entering stuff anymore Damien, but I don't mind coming along to keep you company.'

'Yeah I know you don't only this just might have some links to some pretty sick adults that prey on kids, if you get my drift. I won't know for sure until we've had a look round.'

'I'll think about it Damien. Where do you want to meet up?'

'Well, I've got a couple of things to do over Wimbledon way today and I don't expect to get back, so if I give you the address, can we meet up there about ten o'clock?'

'Yeah okay, hang on a tick while I get a pen.' There was a rustling sound over the phone as Eddie Marston located a biro from somewhere close to the telephone. 'Okay Damien, shoot.'

Palmer read out the address for Stephen Green's house and then repeated it, just to be sure.

'Okay Eddie?' Palmer asked after the repetition.

'Yeah. Ten it is. Anything else I can help you with today?'

'A couple of documents have come in for serving but they can wait a day or two unless you fancy them. Pretty boring stuff but you can do them if you like.'

'Bring them tonight and I'll do them tomorrow. Doesn't sound urgent enough for me to come over your way special like. Any more thoughts on the satellite?'

'Sure, it's starting to come together. I've contacted the accountants and done some other bits on it. Once we get the Green case and the Castle Point case out of the way I'll have a bit more time to devote to it. |Should take about a month I'd guess. You're not having second thoughts are you?'

'God, no, if anything I'm getting keener by the day.'

'Great, well I'll talk to you about it a bit more tonight. Right, well I must go there's things to do. See you at ten Eddie.'

'Cheers Damien.' Again the phone went dead and this time Palmer replaced the receiver. He sat back in his swivel chair and contemplated the day ahead. It was time to plan the actions needed and Palmer spent ten minutes doing just that. At the end of the ten minutes he looked at the short list of action points and selected the third in the list. He stood up and walked from the study into his lounge, taking the laptop computer with him. Having linked the computer to the video player he began to watch the antics of his girlfriend in the hotel bedroom the previous evening. As the video played the scenes of the sexual encounter Palmer, with his own interest increasing as he did so, pressed a key on eth computer at periodic intervals. The whole act lasted nearly an hour and by the end of it Palmer was wishing the woman was sat beside him now. Also, he had captured maybe twenty frames from the action, frames which, using the software on the computer, he could now turn into pictures that could be printed for his client.

The video was still rewinding as Palmer unhooked they laptop and took it back into his office. Ten minutes later the pictures, in glorious full colour were being printed in the cupboard at the side of his desk. As they printed Palmer compiled a report for his client. The report was easy for Karen had shared some of the details of how she had met with Robert Smith, the meal they had shared and the way he had come onto her. Palmer needed no information on the bedroom scenes, the video providing him with more than sufficient material. At the end of the report it seemed somehow unnecessary to include a conclusion but Palmer added one anyway. The two page report complete he typed up an invoice. Then, with the report and invoice also printed, he took all the pages and placed them in a large brown envelope on which he had already written the name of Miss Ellen Morrison. He sealed the envelope and ticked the item on his list of action points for the day before walking through to the kitchen and pouring himself a fresh cup of coffee.

Back in his study Palmer once again turned his attentions to the Green case. Much had happened in a short space of time, the revelation of the bank account, the location of Green's new home, and then the encounter on the doorstep the previous evening, even if that encounter had not felt quite right somehow. There was something he need to check with his client, something that could wait until lunchtime. Palmer set about the task of summarising the main points of the case to date. For good measure he also compiled an interim invoice and again placed the three pages of paper in a brown envelope. He was sealing the flap down when the phone rang.

'Damien palmer, good morning, how can I help you?' His voice sounded calm and friendly.

'Damien,' the woman's voice was low, not quite a whisper, 'it's Karen. I can't talk very loudly as I've taken a five minute break and am standing in the car-park, but something's happened'

'Go on,' Palmer sounded interested.

'Well, first thing this morning a police car arrived and two men not in uniform went into Hartley-Brown's office. Ten minutes later he came out with them and they drove off. He got back about five minutes ago looking grim-faced and asked Carol his PA into his office. He also called me in. It appears that the body they found up on Epsom Downs a couple of days ago carried some identification for Katherine Delaney, and as the police have been unable to track down her nearest relative, a sister, they asked Hartley-Brown as her employer if he could go and identify the body. Of course he obliged, but Damien, it wasn't her. Apparently Delaney has a butterfly tattooed on her inner left leg, and there was no tattoo, and also her hair colour was wrong. Other than that she looked just like Delaney. Hartley-Brown's in a real state, like he's realised something dreadful or something. I don't know what, but to make matters worse he's just received a package which I guess comes from the blackmailer. I guess you'll be hearing from him soon so I thought you'd better know first.'

'Thanks Karen. Any ideas at all what was in the package?'

'None, he hadn't opened it while I was in the room, but the writing on the label was similar to the one he got when we were there the other day. Look I'd best go before someone suspects something.'

'Cheers Karen. Let me know if anything else happens.'

The phone went dead as Karen broke the connection. Palmer pondered this latest news and sat back in his chair. It was an added complexity to a case that was already taxing his mental strengths and Palmer spent several minutes wondering why a body on Epsom Downs that was not Delaney should be carrying her identification. It simply didn't make sense unless, and Palmer stood up quite suddenly and began to pace up and down the well-trodden carpet in his office, unless Delaney wanted people to think she was dead in which case she must be linked somehow to the corpse. Palmer paced the length of his office three times as he contemplated this thought. The question he now raised in his mind was whose body had been found on Epsom Downs? Also, if it wasn't Delaney, then was the woman linked to the case or just some poor unfortunate who happened to look sufficiently like Delaney to cause confusion? Palmer was still pacing his office when the phone rang.

'Damien Palmer, good morning,' he started and was immediately interrupted.

'Mr Palmer it's David Hartley-Brown. There has been a development in the case. I was wondering I you could come over to my offices so I can update you?'

'Certainly Mr Hartley-Brown. Let's see, it's nearly eleven o'clock now and I have an appointment for lunch. Can we make it about two o'clock? Unless, of course, you want to tell me over the phone.'

'No, I don't think so, two o'clock will be fine.'

'Very well, and could you ask Miss Shaw to be there as well. I imagine her work is nearly completed so she might as well keep us up to date.'

'Sure, so I'll see you at two, and thank you Mr Palmer.'

'That's okay Mr Hartley-Brown. I take it you've heard from the blackmailer, we were expecting something so I've kept the afternoon free just in case.' Palmer lied but was sufficiently convincing for the falsehood to go unnoticed.

'Yes, the blackmailer, but I'll tell you about it at two. Now I must get on, so unless there's anything else I'll talk to you later.' Hartley-Brown's own voice was not convincing and Palmer was already convinced that Hartley-Brown was hiding something, something of a quite embarrassing and sinister nature.

'Goodbye Mr Hartley-Brown, see you later.' Palmer smiled to himself as he replaced the receiver. The case, he felt, was beginning to come together quite nicely. A few loose ends to tie up and he would know for sure. Before that though, he had the much more delicate meeting with Dawn Green to contemplate.

**

The public house in Wimbledon Village was buzzing with lunchtime custom when Palmer pushed open the double doors and entered. He walked quickly around the establishment and noted that his client had not yet arrived. He ordered a pint of bitter and took it over to the last remaining table where he sat down and began to sip the brown, frothy liquid. It tasted good and Palmer took a further appreciative swig before placing the glass on the table. He looked at his watch and noted that his client was five minutes late. It began to irritate him for he was a man of punctuality and the tardiness of others always had the same effect on him.

Suddenly, as Palmer was taking his fifth sip of beer a woman pushed open the door near to him and yelled out above the noise of the customers.

'Someone call an ambulance, there's been an accident outside and someone's been knocked over.' The woman ran up to the bar as she repeated her request and then Palmer heard her ask the barman where the phone was.

'Don't worry, I've called them on my mobile.' The man was sitting two tables behind Palmer. He was dressed in a pinstripe suit and Palmer noticed he was tall and lean as he stood up to follow the woman out of the bar. 'Show me where he is, I'm a doctor,' he added as he began to walk towards the door.

'It's not a he, it's a she, and thanks.' The woman turned and Palmer noticed her face was flushed. She half ran back to the door, knocking the arm of one of the customers causing his beer to spill.

'Hey, be careful,' he yelled after the woman as she continued, oblivious to what had happened. The doctor followed her and in less than a minute the commotion caused by the disturbance had subsided. To minutes later and Palmer's irritation had increased as his client had still not arrived. The sound of the emergency service's sirens could now be heard as the ambulance fought its way along the village High Street. Finally the blue flashing lights could be seen outside the public house and the wailing of the sirens stopped. By now Palmer had drunk the better part of half of the glass of beer and now, with the skill of a practiced hand, he drained the vessel of the rest of its contents. The glass, now empty, was replaced on the table as Palmer stood up and went to the door, something in his mind forcing him to go and witness what was happening.

Outside the establishment and on the far pavement the doctor and two paramedics were busy with the victim who was still lying apparently motionless on the path. Palmer spotted the woman who had ran into the public house a few minutes earlier and casually wandered over to where she was standing.

'What's going on?' His voice was one of surprise but remained casual so as not to arouse suspicion.

'Poor woman. She was just crossing the road when this small, dark car came belting round the corner and ploughed into her.'

'Which small car?'

'Oh it didn't stop, just belted off towards the town.'

'You didn't get its number did you?'

'What are you,' the woman was suddenly suspicious, 'some kind of reporter?'

'No, nothing like that. Only the police will need to talk to the witnesses that's all.'

'Oh, well I'm not hanging around for that, I've got better things to be doing.'

'But you're a witness to what could be a death. You've got to tell them what you saw.'

At that moment the man in the pinstripe suit stood up and Palmer noticed he had a grave look on his face. The sound of more sirens could be heard in the distance. The woman standing next to Palmer made as if to walk off.

'I'm not telling anyone anything.'

'It's your call, but I'd say from the look on that doctor's face and the way the paramedics aren't moving the victim that she's been killed. Now I'm not an expert and I may be wrong, but I'd guess if you walked away now you could be seen as some kind of accessory.'

'What? Are you the law then?'

'No, but I you saw something it could just help the police stop the driver from killing someone else, maybe even your own kid.'

'I haven't got any kids.'

'All right then, one of your relatives.'

'You reckon?' Suddenly her voice faltered.

'Yeah. Whoever it was must know they hit something and they didn't stop, which is an offence. If they've done it once, and say it was drinks related, what's to stop them doing it again?'

'I suppose you're right.' The first of the police cars screeched to a halt, blocking the main road. Palmer watched as the woman walked slowly over to where the police car had stopped. He waited until she started speaking to the WPC that had stepped out of the passenger side front door, and then he turned his attention to the scene of the accident. The victim lay on the ground with a red blanket covering her body. Only her head showed above the folds of the blanket. Palmer walked round the back of the small crowd that had gathered and was just in time to see the woman being lifted onto a stretcher. He caught a glimpse of her face as they lifted her and then backed away horrified. He now knew why Dawn Green had failed to make her lunchtime appointment and somewhere in the back of his mind the thought came to him that this had been no freak accident. Just as quickly he realised that he had to hear what the one apparent witness had actually seen.

With a sigh of relief he saw the plain-clothes detective who was emerging from the second police car and recognised his friend John Hartman. Hartman was a Detective Inspector and Palmer thought it unusual that such a high ranking officer would immediately be on the scene of what was still ostensibly an accident. Palmer moved through the crowd until he could almost reach his friend.

'John, can I have a word?' The detective spun round to look into the small crowd. He smiled grimly when he spotted Palmer.

'Damien, is it anything to do with this?'

'Yeah.'

'Okay, Constable let him through. It's okay.' Palmer was allowed past the crowd control officer and together with Hartman he walked a few yards away from the crowd.

'What are you doing on a shout like this?' Palmer's question was genuine.

'Oh, just happened to be in the area on our way back from another call. So Damien, what did you see.'

'Nothing, but the woman talking to that officer over there did.'

'But you said this was to do with the accident.'

'It is. The victim is one of my clients and she was due to meet me in the pub at one, only she didn't show, and then that woman came into the pub saying there'd been an accident.'

'Client hey, well I'm sorry Damien but she's a gonna. According to the doctor it was an instant fatality, but we'll have to wait until the autopsy to be sure. Now, what else can you tell me?'

'Only that her husband has gone missing, and that was what I was trying to do – find him, only it hasn't been easy. What I really need to know if this was an accident or deliberate. Can you talk to that woman and find out if she got any identification of the vehicle, only it might be helpful.'

'Why, do you think it was the husband?' Hartman sounded intrigued.

'I doubt it, but you never know.'

'Well, I'm not supposed to, but as it's you Damien. Give me five minutes and I'll come and chat to you.' With that Palmer walked back to the Constable controlling the crowd, thanked him and then stepped back behind the area that had been cordoned off. The blue and white tape now marked off the area of the High Street in which the body lay. Palmer waited patiently as he watched Hartman talking to the woman. He waited as Hartman conducted his other necessary enquiries and he watched as Hartman inspected the body. The pool of blood on the pavement indicated that the impact had been severe and Palmer hoped the woman had never felt the fatal blow.

Finally after ten interminable minutes Palmer saw Hartman walking towards him. With a deft handshake he palmed a slip of paper into the hand of the sleuth.

'Thanks for waiting Mr Palmer, but I don't think we'll need to talk to you any further. The information we need is all to hand. Thanks again and if we need any more help we'll contact you.'

'That's perfectly all right Inspector.' Palmer sounded polite and with his speech completed he turned and walked away from the onlookers his fist clenched around the piece of paper he had received. He gripped the paper until he had returned to where he had parked his car. Only then did he open it. The paper indicated a dark brown small car, possibly a Polo and the first few characters of the Index Number were 'P746'. It was a start but it was not enough to make identification of the car possible. Palmer banged his steering wheel in frustration as he looked at the scrap of paper.

Palmer started the car and began his journey to the offices of Castle Point Systems. It was already nearly two o'clock and Palmer realised he would be at least half an hour late for the scheduled appointment. As he realised this so the little hairs on the back of his neck began to rise with his growing sense of frustration. As he drove he kept asking himself the same question, over and over. Was Dawn Green's death an accident or something more sinister? It was a question to which he had no answer, but it strengthened his resolve to visit Stephen Green's house later that evening.

The traffic was mercifully light and Palmer covered the distance to Cheam in less than the expected half hour. Parking his car in the station car park he half ran back to the offices of castle Point and waited impatiently for the door to be opened for him.

'Hi, Damien Palmer for Mr Hartley-Brown, only I'm a bit late.' The woman was in her mid-thirties and quite attractive, but not someone Palmer recognised from his previous visits.

'Come in Mr Palmer, I'll just ring upstairs and let him know you've arrived.'

The woman led Palmer back into the office and after a brief conversation on the phone he was ushered upstairs. He rapped smartly on the door of Hartley-Brown's office and was summoned from within.

'Mr Hartley-Brown, sorry I'm late but there was an incident in Wimbledon village and I got held up.'

'Doesn't matter. I'll just tell your colleague you're here.' Hartley-Brown picked up his phone and dialled an extension. Three minutes later Karen Shaw knocked on the door and joined the two men. As she did so she closed the door carefully behind her.

'Right Mr Hartley-Brown, you said on the phone you had been contacted by the blackmailer. So the question is, what did she say?'

'Mr Palmer, what I am about to tell you is in the strictest of confidence. Nothing, and I mean nothing, must be repeated beyond the walls of this office, do you understand?'

'I understand Mr Hartley-Brown and other than any requirements of law you have my word on the matter. Now what does the blackmailer want you to do?'

'What I received this morning Mr Palmer was this.' Hartley-Brown opened the top drawer of his desk and pulled out a box, a box holding a video cassette.

'I take it that you've watched it before contacting me?' Palmer took the offered box.

'Of course. It contains a most explicit movie Mr Palmer, of a sexual nature. It shows me having intercourse with a young woman, and by that I mean a very young woman. Only it's a montage Mr Palmer.'

'How do you mean Mr Hartley-Brown?'

'Well, to look at the girl on the movie you'd think she was about twelve years old but it's not true. The scene is from this office as well, though God knows how.'

'And you don't recognise the girl?'

'No, of course not.'

'Are you totally sure of that Mr Hartley-Brown.'

'Yes, absolutely sure, this is not a girl I know.' Hartley-Brown sounded evasive and his face was reddening as he spoke.

'So you want me to believe that someone has concocted this scene from what, thin air?' Palmer deliberately sounded incredulous.

'No Mr Palmer, not exactly. But you have to believe me when I tell you that I have only had sex with three women in this office. The first was some years ago with my then PA. As I recall she was in her mid-twenties at the time. The second was several months ago with Katherine Delaney, who is in her mid-thirties, and the third time was a few days ago with my current PA and she, as you have seen is well into her twenties.'

'And what was the name of your former PA?' Palmer's voice remained even.

'Julia, Julia Wester, or something like that, I think.' Hartley-Brown sounded evasive, either that or his memory was failing him. Palmer sat and watched the other man for some moments before responding. As he watched him he wrote the name on his piece of paper.

'And there is no one else?' Palmer still sounded incredulous.

'Not in this office, and if you watch the video you will instantly recognise the desk. No Mr Palmer, whoever is blackmailing me is very clever, and I have no idea how they have put this together.'

'Do you have a player so we can watch it?' Karen Shaw sounded less incredulous than Palmer.

'Well, if you must, there's the one I used in the boardroom.'

'Just the beginning of it, I have an idea but I need to see a few frames first?' As she spoke Palmer looked at her with his eyebrows slightly raised.

'Okay, let's go to the boardroom then.' Hartley-Brown led the way and Palmer and Shaw watched the first section of the film as the apparently young girl was stripped naked and Hartley-Brown caressed her breasts.

'Just as I thought,' said Shaw after a minute. 'Can you freeze the picture there?' Hartley-Brown pressed the pause button and Shaw walked over to the screen. 'It's a genuine scene that's been touched. Look, your hands are no longer actually touching her breast. Whoever you originally did this to had a fuller bust. What the blackmailer has done is to take the original scene and change certain characteristics using some interpolation formula or something. It's very clever, but as the woman stays in essentially one place for several frames at a time it's possible to pick a frame, apply certain changes and then explode that onto the film sequence. A clever bit of programming and a few hours work is all that's needed.'

Palmer looked on with admiration as she spoke.

'And,' Shaw continued, 'it's very well done. So the question is why did whoever did this go to all that trouble? After all it doesn't fit in with their original request.'

'Precisely Karen,' Palmer was the first to respond. 'So, Mr Hartley-Brown, why has someone gone to all this trouble?'

'To ruin me I suppose,' Hartley-Brown responded, perhaps a little too quickly.

'Well, if this got out on the streets I guess it would certainly do that, but again I don't see the motive?' Palmer was watching the other man closely now.

'If this got out Mr Palmer I would be ruined and labelled a sex offender. I can only assume the blackmailer wants that to happen, or at least for me to pay a very large sum of money over instead.'

'And were there any payment instructions.'

'Yes Mr Palmer, at the end of the video. I have to make the drop tomorrow morning at eleven o'clock in the lower car-park at Tattenham Corner on the racecourse. I have to be alone and with a suitcase carrying the money, all unmarked notes of varying denominations.'

'No computer transfer then?' Karen sat forward as she asked the question.

'No, it seems like the blackmailer has either failed to get the software to work properly, or she's worked out we'd stop the online transfer from working.'

'You say she, but could Miss Delaney have the skills to construct such a video?'

'I don't know, but there is something else that you should know Mr Palmer. I received a visit from the local police. They found a body up on the Downs a couple of days ago and that body had the identity of Katherine Delaney on it. I went along to identify her, but when I got there it wasn't her body.'

'I see,' said Palmer trying to sound surprised at the news. 'So our Miss Delaney wants people to think she's dead when she isn't. I have to admit that does make her seem more likely to be your blackmailer. Incidentally, is Hammond back at work today?'

'No,' said Karen quite smartly. 'He phoned in again to say he's still got the bug, but he hopes to be back on Monday.'

'Hmm, very convenient. Now Mr Hartley-Brown, I suggest you get the money together, if you can, and go ahead with the drop as planned.

Personally I think we'll have resolved the case before then but you had better be prepared just in case.'

'You know who is blackmailing me?'

'Oh yes Mr Hartley-Brown.'

'Well man, who is it?'

'I'm sorry, but as your video clearly shows, walls have ears and eyes. I think it is best that I keep that to myself for a few more hours. Incidentally Karen, how are you getting on?' Palmer sounded self-satisfied, the sound of a man who had solved a case.

'Fine. All the modem connections are broken for the weekend and I've checked for other links and come up with nothing.'

'Excellent, well it's going to be a busy afternoon for Mr Hartley-Brown so I suggest we leave him to it. We'll be in touch tomorrow morning to see how the drop went.'

'And that's it is it?' Hartley-Brown sounded dumbfounded.

'Oh yes. We've done all we can here Mr Hartley-Brown, it's down to you now.' Palmer nodded sagely as he spoke and as he did so he wrote something on a piece of paper. He folded the paper and handed it to Hartley-Brown who opened it carefully. It said, 'We're being watched, just agree to do it on your own. We'll be with you.'

'Well, Mr Palmer, I suppose it is down to me.' Hartley-Brown looked sad, and the colour in his cheeks had visibly paled. 'Ring me ten minutes after the drop.'

'Will do, now I think Miss Shaw and I had better get on with some other work.'

'Fine by me,' the woman replied.

Five minutes later Palmer and Shaw left the offices of Castle point Systems and walked back to the station car-park.

'What the hell was all that about?' She began. 'Do you really know who's responsible for all this and were we being watched?'

'Steady, steady, one at a time,' Palmer laughed. 'Firstly, yes I think I do know who's doing this and it is not Delaney, well not on her own. Secondly the accident in Wimbledon was no accident. The woman killed was Dawn Green. We were meeting for lunch only someone didn't want that meeting to take place, and the only reason for that could be that they are afraid she knew something she might pass on, and whoever it was did not want that to happen. Thirdly I think that Stephen Green is also dead, for the same reason. The only problem is I don't know for sure and I haven't been able to find his body – yet. Fourthly, that video we saw is only a reminder to Hartley-Brown why he's being blackmailed. As soon as he talked about it the whole thing clicked into place. He's linked to Pradonet, but more importantly he's into kiddies, and that's the information that is so valuable.'

'What, pictures and so forth?'

'No. Nothing like that. Don't you think whoever made that movie knew you were bound to see it, and don't you think they didn't know you'd immediately know how it was done? Of course they did, and they were right. Now think hard Karen.

Who have you talked to at Castle Point who'd have the skills to do something like that?'

'Well, it could be a number of them really. It's not that hard with the right bit of programming and some time.'

'Which is why we had to be careful. If that person has bugged Hartley-Brown's office to get some footage don't you think they might have bugged other rooms too?'

'Could be, but there's only one camera in his office and that's a CCTV on the wall behind the door. It links to his PA's machine and it's black and white with no sound – I checked it yesterday evening. I scanned his office this morning and there's nothing else there, of that I am nearly one hundred percent sure.'

'Fair enough, so the camera has been removed. Who do you think the kid was modelled on?' Palmer sounded intrigued.

'Not his first PA, it was too long ago. Could be Delaney but from what I've heard she was somewhat curvaceous. I'd say, from a programming point of view, from a touch up artists perspective, that his current PA would be the easiest to doctor.'

'Exactly, which means that if Hartley-Brown is telling the truth, that session only happened a few days ago. Who has had time to do the work necessary to come up with what we've just seen?'

'Hammond.' The woman looked intently at Palmer.

'Precisely, and if he's involved then we have to ask ourselves how, and what is his link to Delaney, and is Delaney still alive. Remember she hasn't been seen for over a week now.'

'You think she's dead?'

'Not sure, but she could be.'

'But why leave her identity on that other body?' Shaw sounded confused.

'We don't know that Hartley-Brown was telling the truth. Perhaps it was Delaney only he's trying to cover something up. Time will tell.' Palmer reached his car and opened the driver's door.

'Are you coming over tonight?' Shaw asked the question.

'Sorry love, but I've got some work to do with Eddie. Plus I think we both need a good night's sleep. I want you up at the central car park on the course an hour before the drop off. I'll meet you up there, is that okay?'

'Sure, but what's the plan?'

'Don't know yet. Have a good evening and I'll see you in the morning.' He reached over the door and kissed the woman. 'Now, darling I've got to go, there's things to do. Take care.'

'And you Damien. See you at ten tomorrow.' She reached forward and kissed him once again before pushing past the door and walking towards her own car.

Chapter Nine

It was nearly four o'clock when Palmer drove into the multi-storey car-park behind the main shopping precinct in Sutton. He parked on the third floor and walked across the bridge from the car park to the centre. He came out on the level where the food concessions were arranged. As he walked towards them he noted that many of them were closed. Then he found what he was after and five minutes later he was sitting at a metal-rimmed round table sipping the large cup of steaming coffee. He looked around the area out of curiosity and noted that the eating area was almost deserted. There seemed nobody who resembled the person he was supposed to be meeting. With a degree of annoyance Palmer sat down to wait for the contact to be made.

An old man in a dark brown coat sat huddled at another some distance from Palmer. He sat there reading a newspaper with a half-eaten plate of food sitting on the table in front of him. To one side a young mother was trying to feed her young child as it sat in its buggy, the thought of food obviously being the last thing on its mind. As he watched the antics of the child, Palmer mused to himself that more of the food was ending up in the buggy than in the child's mouth. Palmer turned his attention to the structure of the centre, and as his eye casually looked around the ceiling his attention turned inevitably to the fate of Dawn Green. He could not believe that her death was an accident, it was just too much of a coincidence. So, the question he tossed around in his mind for several minutes was why did she have to die? What did she know, or more probably what did her killer *think* that she knew that he or she was afraid Dawn Green would tell Palmer? Then Palmer recalled his meeting with Dawn Green when she had revealed her interest in amateur dramatics. Perhaps, thought Palmer as the mother finally gave up her futile attempts to feed her offspring, the reason lay in the drama group and not out of any link between her miscreant husband and the missing Katherine Delaney. Perhaps, but not likely, he concluded. The mother was now struggling to clean up her child and the buggy and Palmer was distracted by her rather loud voice as she scolded the infant.

Palmer sipped some more coffee and continued to contemplate what Dawn Green might have known, what secret that she was supposed to have been party to, what morsel of intelligence that had ultimately been her downfall. He was still considering the possibilities when the mother pushed the buggy containing her child into the back of his chair, jolting him and causing him to spill coffee onto the table.

'Careful,' Palmer began.

'Sorry,' she replied, 'but I had to talk to you. You are Damien Palmer, aren't you?'

'What if I am?'

'Well, I'm Sharon Whiteman. I was waiting to check you weren't followed here before keeping our appointment.'

'Yes, our appointment.'

'Sorry, but I can't afford to be too careful, oh and I guess I should have mentioned the kid.'

'It would have helped. So, what can I do for you Mrs Whiteman?'

'Miss actually, but it don't matter. A friend of mine Dawn Green has spent the last couple of months telling me about you, and what you are trying to do for you. Only I thought I ought to contact you because I have something of interest to tell you, and frankly it's something I've got to get off my chest, so to speak. Only I didn't want to say anything until we met.'

'So we're here now. What is it that you wanted to tell me?'

'First off, you've got to understand that I go to the same drama group as Dawn Green, which is how we met. Secondly, for some weeks now Dawn has been worried about her husband and she's been telling me things that have scared me, to the point that once she told me her plans the other night I thought it best to get in touch.'

'Well, that's considerate of you. Do go on.' Palmer sounded less than enthusiastic.

'Well, the truth is Dawn has a pretty good idea what's been going on, only she needed you to find out for her, if you understand me.'

'I think so, go on, and do sit down.' Palmer took another mouthful of coffee as the woman sat down opposite him.

'Well, she knew Stephen had gone off with another woman, and she had a pretty good idea who. One of his clients she thought, only she needed you to prove it one way or another. Well at the drama group meeting before last she confided in me because, as she put it, she had no choice, what with me being involved one way or another.' The woman sounded agitated.

'Sorry, you've lost me.'

'Well, she found out that her husband was having an affair with a woman called Katherine Delaney, and she works with my sister. At first she was angry I hadn't told her anything and then surprised when I told her I didn't know about it.'

'I see, and how did she find out?'

'Oh she's had her suspicions for a while now, and then she found some old receipts in her husband's paperwork. They were payments for therapy sessions. There were two women he'd been seeing regularly and Katherine was one of them. Apparently she found her address from one of his files and went round and spotted them together, at it.'

'At it?' Palmer watched the woman closely as he framed the short question.

'Having sex, Mr Palmer, and at Delaney's house in the middle of the afternoon. After that she just had to find out where her husband was staying and hence her reason for calling you in. She wanted revenge Mr Palmer, and that is why I had to meet up with you this afternoon.'

'Why today?'

'Because at the last meeting she said you were about to find her husband and then she'd be off round there to get revenge for all the years he's been cheating on her. Now, Mr Palmer I don't know how well you know Dawn, but she is somewhat

218

schizophrenic. One moment she is as sweet as pie and butter wouldn't melt, that sort of person. Next, when she's angry she gets that look in her eye and begins to talk crazy. My fear is that if she gets in that state of mind when she finds her husband then she might kill him. Not only that but I'm really worried that she won't believe I was telling the truth when I said I didn't know about it all and she might come after me or Ronan.'

'Ronan?' Palmer queried.

'Yes, the kid,' she responded as she pointed at the grubby faced child in the buggy.

'I see, well thank you for telling me this, but I fail to see what I can do.'

'Well for a start don't tell her where Stephen's living, or at least tell him what's going on first. He's a nice bloke and he's put up with so much from her over the years – I've known them for about a decade. If he's decided to go off with somebody normal, I can't say I blame him.'

'Well, I don't think you need to worry for your own safety anymore. I will take your suggestion under advice and see what I can do, and I can assure you that Mrs Green will not be troubling you anymore.' Palmer did not have the heart to break the news of the afternoon's incident.

'You sound confident of that Mr Palmer, how can you be so sure?'

'Let's say that Mrs Green will shortly be somewhere where she can't hurt anyone. I may have been employed by her but my investigations have not been confined to the matter in hand.' Palmer continued to bluff his way out of avoiding the need to reveal the tragedy that had befallen Dawn Green. 'Something has come to light that I can assure you will mean Mrs Green will come nowhere near you or Ronan.' Palmer's smile was disarming, deliberately so.

'Well, Mr Palmer I hope you are right. Now I must be going.' With that the woman stood up and began to push the buggy.

'By the way Miss Whiteman, who is your sister? Just for the sake of curiosity.'

'Carol Whiteman, and for your information we don't have much to do with each other anymore, not since she got involved with her boss. Soon after she met him she changed, if you know what I mean. She used to be a really nice older sister but these last few months she's become bitter and hard and, if you'll pardon the expression, she's become pervy. I only met her boss once and he gave me the creeps – like he was pervy too.' With that final condemnation of her sister she turned and pushed the buggy away from Palmer. He sat and watched as she walked towards the bridge that led to the car park.

As she walked away Palmer looked at his watch and realised it was nearly five o'clock. He had two hours before his meeting with Ellen Morrison, two hours during which he planned to apply his thought processes to what he had learned from the somewhat flustered Sharon Whiteman. The revelation had been interesting but it had not totally surprised the sleuth. He had long ago suspected there was something about Dawn Green that had eluded him, and now he knew what. Now, of course, it was obvious that her inability to offer much help in the matter had been part of her act, part of her scheme to place a piece of cheese on the trap and to wait until the mouse came within striking distance. Palmer felt a cold shiver climb his spine as he thought how he would have unwittingly given the woman the information she had been seeking at the planned lunchtime meeting, information that might have resulted in another death.

Yet that meeting had never taken place because of her own demise, an incident that Palmer reflected on. Instinct told him that somewhere in the big picture her death was an important piece of the jigsaw, yet apart from her own murderous intentions, as stated by Sharon Whiteman, Palmer could not yet resolve the importance of her involvement. The vital link, the missing morsel of evidence eluded him as he sat and sipped a second coffee. He took his pad of paper out of his brown top-opening briefcase and began to make notes. He began with a list of names which he placed down the centre of the page. Then to either side he began drawing lines between names where he knew a relationship existed. On each line he carefully wrote what the link meant. It took him half an hour of thought before the name map was complete. Palmer looked at it carefully for it summarised what he had gleaned to date and he smiled. He knew that in the list of names was a killer, and possibly more than one. Also in the list was a blackmailer, and Palmer was not yet convinced it was one and the same person as the killer.

Finally Palmer looked at his watch and decided it was time to keep his appointment with Ellen Morrison. Picking up the one way system around Sutton he headed for Morden and Wimbledon. The evening traffic was light as he passed the rows of houses that were all built in the same style, their drab exteriors indicating a need for attention. In some of what passed for front gardens rubbish bags were piled high, whilst the cars that were parked just off the main road showed the owners almost all lacked respect for the vehicles they owned. It was a dreary road and Palmer had little doubt that behind the closed, badly painted doors, the residents would be huddled either over their evening meal, or more probably watching the television, either that or they had already made their way to the public house that was just out of sight from the main street. Finally, and having had to stop at various traffic lights Palmer turned right off the main roundabout in Morden and completed his journey past the industrial sites that sprawled alongside the main road to South Wimbledon.

Finally Palmer found the road he was looking for and parked his car. The block of flats were familiar to him and as he pressed the buzzer for the flat he required he noticed the cracked pane of glass in the downstairs flat.

'Hello?' The mildly Scots voice came over the intercom.

'Hi, it's Damien Palmer. Sorry I'm a few minutes early.'

'No matter, do come up.' Palmer heard the magnetic lock buzz as the door was released. A minute later he had climbed the two flights of stairs and found the door to the flat on the latch. He knocked politely.

'Come in Mr palmer and go through to the lounge, I'll be with you in a moment.

Palmer did as he was bade and entered the lounge. The first thing that he noticed was a smell, a pleasant aroma that he instantly found relaxing. He looked round for the source of the aroma and spotted the little oil burner glowing on top of the bookcase behind the door.

'That smells nice,' he smiled as the woman entered the room. She was dressed in a black jumper and mid-length tartan skirt.

'Yes, it's my favourite. Picked it up at the local craft market some time ago.'

'What is it?'

'Ylang I think. It's supposed to relax you and have erotic qualities. Now Mr Palmer can I get you a drink?'

'Well, tea would be nice.'

'Or something stronger, Scotch, Gin?'

'Well, I have to admit I wouldn't say no to a Scotch if you have it.'

'Of course I have it. How do you like it?' She smiled as she talked and Palmer smiled back. He genuinely liked this woman and dressed as she was, her ;long auburn hair and dark green eyes only accentuated her highlights.

'Oh neat is fine, thanks.'

'Won't be a tick.' The woman moved from the doorway of the lounge back out into the corridor and then Palmer heard her in the kitchen. She returned a minute later holding two tumblers into which she had poured very generous measures of the brown liquid.

'Cheers,' he said as they clinked glasses.

'Cheers.' She took a hefty swig of her own drink as Palmer sipped his. 'I have a feeling from the look on your face that I'm going to need this.'

'Possibly. Now, I have a report here for you, and some pictures. I suspect you will find them quite offensive.' He handed her the brown envelope and waited while she extracted the contents and looked them over.

'Well, Mr Palmer, your colleague was very thorough,' she said after she had scanned the clutch of pictures. 'Was he easy to trap?'

'From what I can gather there was no catching involved. It seemed that he was just waiting for something to happen, and I'm sorry to say it Miss Morrison but if it hadn't been my colleague, from what she said it would have been the next woman that came along.'

'Well I have to congratulate you on a job well handled, and you are sure he doesn't know about these pictures.'

'Absolutely not, my colleague was the soul of discretion.' Palmer reached with a hand behind his back and tried to massage away the tension that he was feeling there.

'That's very good Mr Palmer. I'm sorry if I don't sound shocked but I've suspected Robert's been up to something for a little while now. A t least you have saved me from the expense of the marriage and a divorce. Now how much do I owe you?'

Palmer was still rubbing the back of his neck.

'It's at the back of the report,' he offered.

'Is your neck hurting you?' She sat calmly as she watched Palmer's antics.

'Yes, I suffer from this stress thing and it makes the back of my neck really sore from time to time. Don't know why but this evening it's been giving me hell.'

'Well, I could always help you there – remember I'm a sport's therapist. Here, take off your jacket and I'll give it a rub.' She moved over to where Palmer was sitting on the settee and before he had time to protest she placed her hand gently on the back of his left shoulder.

'My God,' she said quite suddenly, 'you're really stiff there, no wonder it hurts. Here, take off your jacket and I'll show you how to relieve the pressure.'

'There's really no need. It'll pass in a minute.'

'No it won't, and anyway you've done me a favour so it's my turn to reciprocate. I couldn't let you leave like this.'

'Well, it's very kind of you.'

'Nonsense, now take off your jacket and relax. I'll have you feeling better in no time at all.'

Palmer did as he was told.

'Actually,' she said as she noticed he was now sitting awkwardly on the settee, 'you'd be better sitting in the armchair and then I can lean you forward and do it properly.'

'Are you sure you've got time for this?' Palmer's protestations were not sufficiently strong to deter the woman. As he protested he went and sat in the armchair. She placed a small cushion on his knees and gently pushed his head forward until she could have easy access to the back of his neck.

Palmer felt the warm fingers as they glided over the back of his neck, moving from the hairline to the shoulders in regular, gentle, circular movements. He felt her fingers as the little hairs on the back of his neck were caressed. Her touch was light and very soothing and in a moment Palmer began to relax. As he relaxed so his mind drifted away in a similar manner to the beginnings of sleep.

As he drifted so he felt the fingers begin to dig harder into his muscles. Still covered by his shirt she was now massaging the shoulders, a sensation that was instantly electrifying for Palmer and at the same time painful. He winced as she prodded him.

'Sorry if that hurt, but you are so tense. I really should do this lying down and with some oils, but that's up to you.' Palmer could not see that behind him her face had become slightly flushed with desire.

'Well,' he began, 'if you're sure it's not too much of an imposition?'

'No, not at all. You've saved me a great deal of money Mr Palmer,' she was interrupted by the sleuth.

'Please, call me Damien,' he winced again as she continued with the massage.

'As I said, you've saved me and my family a lot of money, so it's the least I can do for you. It's what I specialise in after all.'

'If you say so,' Palmer conceded meekly.

'Well, if you remove your shirt and then lie face down on the sofa I'll just go and get my bag. She returned a minute later to find Palmer lying face down on the sofa. He felt her touch both shoulders and the instant sensation was one of cold.

'What's that?' He asked out of surprise.

'It's a cold cream, but it will help in the long run. Now, I've got to try and get into the knots so this might hurt a bit.' For several minutes palmer lay there as she kneaded and prodded his shoulder blades. Then, as he relaxed, the aroma from the oil burner began to take over. He felt her hands move down his back but he was relaxed now and it didn't matter. He felt the way she caressed his back and he was drifting off into a land of pleasure. Her hands were firm and warm, her voice was friendly, it's trace of Scots adding to its rich quality, and Palmer was enjoying the sensations.

'Turn over,' he heard her say, and without thinking he did what she asked of him. He felt her as she massaged the front of his shoulders and her touch was very good. He felt her hands on his chest and then on his stomach. Again her touch was firm and soft at the same time. Palmer began to want this rare beauty from North of the border. He felt powerless to resist whilst she continued to caress him and then suddenly it was happening. His mind relaxed to the point where normal bodily reactions took over. He felt calm, calmer than he had done for

227

some time, yet one part of his body was already screaming out for release. She continued the abdominal massage, looking briefly below his belt line and smiling inwardly at what was evidently happening to the man. She knew it would, after all she had mastered her technique of seduction many years ago. The neck massage had been the excuse and now she was fully in control of this man she had fancied the moment she had set eyes on him.

Palmer lay on the settee as she continued to massage him.

'Do you want me to go further?' Her soft, whispered voice was almost too much for Palmer.

'If it's not too much trouble,' he replied, lamely.

By way of reply he felt the buckle on his trousers being released and in a moment she had pulled down the zip. It took her soft, expert fingers, only a few moments to release the truncheon from the confines of the boxer shorts. Palmer, still affected by the potent aroma of the burning oil, lay motionless as she turned her attentions to his manhood. He felt the strong, soft, fingers enclosed round his shaft, and he felt the way she stroked him, ensuring her ministrations obtained every last inch of stiffness possible. As she stroked him with her hand he felt the softness of her hair as it played across the very tip of his arousal. As her hair brushed him in this way he groaned.

'Now, just relax, and let me help you,' her voice filtered up through the seemingly endless caverns of mindless relaxation into which Palmer had descended. Then he felt her breath. As he did so, somewhere in his mind he thought that Robert Smith must have been a complete moron to risk losing this beauty. He felt the dampness behind the breath as she took him between her lips, and then he felt the highly enjoyable pressure of her mouth as she drew him into her. She held him like this for maybe thirty seconds before the pressure was released.

'See,' she said, as she released him, 'it's what you needed.' With that she returned him to her lips and repeated the oral massage. This time the pressure was too great for Palmer and he groaned loudly as the first pulse of desired release took over his body.

As it did so Palmer brought himself back from his reverie. He sighed when he realised that he was still sitting in the armchair and that the woman was still massaging his shoulder blades.

'Does that feel any better?' She asked him, her soft slightly Scots voice still affecting Palmer.

'Yes, it's great. Sorry but I almost drifted off there for a moment, you sure have a great touch.'

'Well it comes with the job. Now, I don't like to point it out and you needn't be embarrassed because it happens to a lot of my male clients, but you are somewhat aroused?' She laughed as Palmer looked down between his legs.

'Oh God, how embarrassing,' he muttered.

'Nothing to be embarrassed about so far as I'm concerned. Actually it's a bit of a compliment, because it means I really got you relaxed. Shame I'm your client actually because you're just the sport of guy I'd go for, seeing as I won't be going with Robert anymore.'

'Yeah, funny you should mention it, because something similar went through my mind while I was relaxed.'

'I thought it did. Tell me Mr Palmer, do you find me attractive? Sorry, I didn't mean to embarrass you but I can't understand what's gone wrong with Robert.'

'Nor can I Miss Morrison,' Palmer began.

'Ellen. I mean I am attractive aren't I?' the woman fluttered her eyelids at the sleuth who was still evidently aroused.

'Yes, I'd have to say your fiancé is a lucky man.'

'He was, Mr Palmer.' Suddenly the woman reached forward and planted a kiss right in the middle of Palmer's cheek. Still aroused by the combination of the burning oil and the effects of the massage Palmer responded by turning to the woman and pulling her to him. Their mouths joined in a passionate kiss. By the end of it her hand was firmly planted in Palmer's lap, her fingers exploring the outline of his manhood.

Palmer for his part reached a hand up and began to explore the woman's chest and then, finding no resistance, he lifted her jumper, exposing the bare flesh of her breasts. He caressed them tenderly as she began to unzip his fly. He waited until her actions were complete and then took her and lay her on her back on the floor.

'Are you sure about this?' his question was one that need not have been asked.

'Oh yes, do to me what your colleague did to that bastard.'

Palmer was now on fire. his memories of the way that his girlfriend had handled the woman's fiancé came flooding back into his mind and he determined that now was the time to render the quid pro quo. Equally he could tell that the woman beneath him was burning for revenge on the unfaithfulness of her husband to be. He felt her warm flesh as he raised the tartan skirt, finding her naked under the harshness of the woollen fabric. She offered no resistance as he positioned himself between her legs and he could feel the warmth and dampness of her body waiting for him. With a single thrust he penetrated her, with a force that seemed to say that this was making up for the actions of their partners. She gasped loudly as the force of his thrust caused her to exhale. She gasped as he continued to pound into her and as her own arousal grew she stopped marvelling at his strength, length, and endurance, and instead began to revel in her own climaxes as they arrived seemingly with each of the deep thrusts of the man who was taking her in the way that she had longed for since her days at the private school where her friends all boasted of their own conquests while she had remained a virgin.

Finally she felt him withdraw as he reached his own peak, his seed splashing onto her chest. She laughed as she watched him erupt.

'You could have stayed in, it's perfectly safe.'

'I didn't know. Hang on a second I'll get some tissue.' Palmer left the woman lying there and returned a moment later with some tissue.

'Thanks Damien,' she said. 'Well I reckon that was every bit as good as what Robert got, what about you? We are talking about the same desire aren't we?'

'Yes, I think so, only mine isn't out of revenge. You see, in my line of business you have to get to learn to accept things that other people might find odd, like your girlfriend shagging another bloke. But actually we have this pact – we both have other friends, and well, your great touch just turned me on and well, it was great.'

'Yeah it was, but I have a rule, well it's a new rule. I only shag a bloke unless we're in a serious relationship.'

'Which we're not, so I get the message.'

'I don't mean any offence, but I don't think I could cope with the pressures of being hitched to a detective.'

'It's okay, you don't have to explain. Now look, I'll leave the stuff and the invoice. If you could send me a cheque for it in the next few days.'

'You've got to go?'

'Yeah, I'm watching some poor sod tonight. I'd rather stay, but I'd best do it.' Palmer was already dressing and looked at the woman who was still lying on the floor. She smiled back up at him, with no hint of regret in her eyes. When he was dressed Palmer reached over and kissed her gently.

'Well, I won't say until next time, but if you need my services again you know where to contact me.'

'Sure do, and don't worry I won't say anything to anyone. This was just for revenge so far as I was concerned, and I think that was your reason too wasn't it?'

'Something like that. Now, don't catch cold. I'll see myself out Ellen.' Palmer collected his belongings and in a moment he had closed the front door to the flat. Inside the woman smiled warmly to herself. Perhaps after all, she thought, there was something she could still share with her fiancé – a life of unfaithfulness together. After all, she knew of one other couple that thrived on it.

Chapter Ten

It was nearly eight thirty when Palmer drove away from the house of Ellen Morrison. As he drove he contemplated the events of the day and the matter that was now almost to hand. He had an hour and a half before he was due to meet Marston at the home of Stephen Green and decided to use the time to drive past the semi-detached property registered to Katherine Delaney. He found the property easily enough and parked his car before walking back up the pavement and the driveway to the house which was shrouded in darkness. He knocked on the door twice and noticed that there was a newspaper stuck half out of the letterbox. It looked like a local free newspaper and Palmer concluded that no one had been at home since at least the previous day. He turned and was about to walk back down the drive when a red/brown coloured Corsa turned into the drive. Even before he had time to react the driver threw open the driver's door blocking his exit. She stood up and Palmer reckoned she was in her mid-thirties. Though quite short in stature and with short blond hair, her attire gave her a sporty appearance.

'Yes?' The one word was spoken with politeness.

'I was just looking for the owner of the house, seems like she's out.'

'I'm the owner, who's asking?' The woman was closing eth driver's door. When she'd done so she stepped back and opened the rear door.

'Oh, I'm Damien Palmer, pleased to meet you at last Miss Delaney.'

'You know my name, but I don't recognise you. Who are you and what is your business here?' The woman now began to sound nervous.

'I'm sorry. My card, you'll see I'm a private investigator. Actually you can phone your boss Mr Hartley-Brown if you don't believe me, only he was worried about you seeing as you seemed to have disappeared.'

'Well, I'm back now, so there's nothing to worry about.'

'Well, perhaps you could tell me where you've been this last week?' Palmer's query showed that this turn of events had taken him completely by surprise.

'Edinburgh actually, on holiday, not that it's any business of yours. Private Investigator hey, why would the old fool want to get you involved?'

'Well, it's a long story. Do you mind if I come in with you?' The woman had retrieved her suitcase from the back seat and was starting to walk to the front door.

'Why not, it should be interesting to hear whet the old bugger's been getting up to.' There was no love lost in the woman's tone of voice. Ten minutes late they were sitting in Delaney's front room.

'So Mr Palmer, how come you got called in to find me? You see I'm intrigued to know why my boss should want to have me investigated in such a way.'

'Well, for a start on the night you disappeared a rather valuable piece of equipment also went missing from your place of employment.'

'Valuable, what do you mean?'

'A computer Miss Delaney, a computer on which you had loaded some top secret software that you and Mr Hammond had been working on.'

'Top secret software, is that what he told you Mr Palmer?' She laughed as she stood up. 'Tea, coffee, I'm dying for a drink?'

'Tea please, what do you mean, what software?'

'There's no secret software in Castle Point Mr Palmer, it's all very routine financial package stuff. So what were you told?'

Palmer looked at the woman and followed her into the kitchen. As she filled the kettle he told her the story that he had been given by David Hartley-Brown. At the end of it she turned and looked evenly at the sleuth.

'Well, take it from me, Mr Palmer, there was no top secret project or anything like that, there's been no special card developed and no special codes or demonstration or anything. It's pure fabrication.'

'But your disappearance at the same time? How do you explain that?'

'I don't. My disappearance was nothing of the sort. I told Hartley-Brown over a month ago that I was taking a week's holiday. Actually I've been to Edinburgh and got myself a new job. Doubtless you've heard about the affair I had with David. Well, when he ended it I began to find working in that place unbearable. Then I found out he was

236

doing it with his secretary, jumped up little tart. Well that was the final straw. I saw an advert for this job and I had an interview on Monday. They ha others to see but they offered me the job there and then. Well, I had to look round for accommodation so I spent a few more days up there. I'll be resigning on Monday and putting this place on the market. Shall we go back to the lounge?' The tea was poured and the woman offered Palmer a mug. They walked back to the front room and regained their seats.

'If you don't believe me Mr Palmer I have the letter of appointment in my case.'

'Oh, I believe you, but there are a few other things that don't add up. For example, if you didn't take the computer then who did?'

'I don't know Mr Palmer, and frankly it's not my problem, though David has pissed off so many of his staff since he took on his new secretary that it really could be just about any one of them.'

'And if the software was so mundane why would someone think it's worth him paying over a million quid to get it back?' Palmer deliberately underplayed the amount involved as he looked for a reaction from the woman. It was not forthcoming.

'I'm sorry Mr Palmer I have no idea, and as I've already told you, I'm not that interested anymore.'

'I see, well Miss Delaney, a body was found on Epsom racecourse the day after you disappeared, Thursday week, and that body was carrying two credit cards in your name. How do you explain that?'

'Well, Mr Palmer, if you are such a good detective you will note that those cards were cancelled last Friday, and they were cancelled from a hotel in Edinburgh. I can't explain how I came to lose them but as soon as I got to Scotland I noticed they were missing. Nothing else, just two credit cards, so I called up the firm I have a security arrangement with and they handled it from there. I can give you their number if you want?'

'Save it for the proper authorities Miss Delaney, the police will be keen to talk to you seeing as there's a murder involved.'

'You can't think it's me, I was in Scotland at the time,' the woman sounded indignant.

'I didn't say when the death had occurred Miss Delaney, and no I don't think it was you. Actually some things are beginning to add up quite quickly now. But there is one thing that intrigues me. The police contacted your boss and took him to identify the body. From what I've heard he initially thought from the face that it could have been you, even though the hair was dyed a darker colour. But the clincher was that the body didn't have a tattoo of a butterfly or something on the inner left thigh.'

'A red admiral, Mr Palmer, and I didn't realise the old man was that observant.'

'You don't by any chance have a sister do you?' Palmer asked the question and watched the woman closely. She paused, a fraction of a second too long, as if deciding what to say.

'No Mr Palmer.' Her voice had faltered.

'I see, well it was just a stab in the dark, but it's curious that your boss was nearly caught out.'

'Well I'm sorry but I can't help you with that one. Now, Mr Palmer, I've had a long day and I'm getting tired.'

'And the police will want to talk to you shortly,' Palmer interrupted her chain of thoughts.

'Can't it wait until tomorrow?' Her voice was tired but not quite pleading.

'I don't know, but I will have to let the DI in charge of the case know that I've found you – it really is very important.'

'Yes I suppose so, go on then, phone them from here if you want.' Her consent finally convinced Palmer that she was telling him the truth about the Castle Point situation. He pulled his mobile phone out of his pocket and dialled a number.

'John,' he said a few moments later, 'it's Damien. Sorry to catch you at home but I thought you'd be interested to know that I've located Katherine Delaney. Her boss told me earlier today that you're looking for her in connection with the body on the race track a few days ago.'

There was a pause as Palmer listened to the voice on the other end of the line.

'Been to Edinburgh for the week, cancelled her cards from the hotel up there and has got herself a new job up there – she went up for the interview. All verifiable and easy to disprove. I think you can form your own judgement.' There was another pause.

'Okay, what time?' Another pause.

'Fine I'll tell her, and I'll see you tomorrow too. Night John.' Palmer replaced the mobile phone in his pocket. 'Right Miss Delaney, no need for you to go there tonight but DI Hartman would like to see you at Sutton station at eleven tomorrow morning. Just ask for him at the desk. You know where the station is?'

'Yes, and thank you Mr Palmer.'

'Don't thank me, thank the inspector when you see him.'

'I will. Now, I don't want to seem rude but I have to unpack.'

'And I must be on my way too. Well Miss Delaney, I hope this all sorts itself out quickly for all our sakes.'

'It will Mr Palmer, it will.' She showed the investigator to the front door and closed it softly behind him.

As soon as the door was closed Palmer turned and in the same instant that his line of vision met with the car, he stopped. He stopped sand bent down so that he could examine the front bumper of the vehicle. Even in the dim light there was no question that the off-side portion of the bumper was dented, quite badly dented. Palmer stood up and rubbed his chin before continuing his walk back down the driveway.

As he walked down the driveway she picked up her phone and dialled a number. There was no reply, and there never would be again. Somewhere in the back of her mind she made the numbers all add up and as the tears welled up in her eyes she banged her fist onto the top of the newel post at the bottom of the stairs.

***

Palmer drove from Delaney's house round to the home of Stephen Green. The journey took him just over ten minutes and Palmer knew that he was in good time for his rendezvous with Marston. He passed Green's house shortly after nine thirty, turned his car round and parked. The house was shrouded in darkness, and with the curtains open it was evident that no one was at home. Palmer sat and waited. As he did so, he reflected on the evening's events; the curious meeting with Sharon Whiteman and her revelations, the attractive and therapeutic Ellen Morrison, and finally the unexpected encounter with Katherine Delaney. Palmer turned on the car's radio and tuned into a local station. The news round-up for the half hour was in progress.

'And, tonight, police have issued a further appeal for witnesses who were on Epsom Downs the Monday before last. Anyone who was in the area from about ten o'clock that evening, until six o'clock the following morning are requested to contact their local police station. And there's still no confirmation of the identity of the body, so if anyone has a missing female relative, who could be described as being in their mid-thirties, about five feet four and with blond hair, the police would also like to hear from you.' Palmer switched off the radio, and the depressing news faded into the night. Palmer looked out of the window of his car onto the dark, empty street, and wondered just who might have a relative matching the description. He suspected the police would be inundated by calls from all manner of people who had lost a loved one, even if their description did not even vaguely resemble the one that had been issued.

Suddenly he became aware of a man approaching his own vehicle. The man looked slightly overweight, and even from a distance, and despite the dark coat he was wearing, Palmer could not help but recognise Eddie Marston. Marston walked slowly, and as he passed Green's house Palmer noticed that he turned to look at the property. His turn of the head was executed perfectly, as if something had attracted his attention for a moment. No one, Palmer figured, would suspect what Marston was doing. In that precious moment, Marston made a mental picture of the front of the house, a picture that told him all he needed to know.

The passenger door of Palmer's car opened and Marston joined Palmer.

'Eddie, punctual as ever. How's things?'

'Fine. What do you reckon?'

'I was about to ask you the same thing. Personally, I reckon the place is empty. I've been here about twenty minutes now and there's been no sign of any activity, and it looks like all the lights are out.'

'Well they are at the moment. Also, all the front windows are double-glazed, and they all look locked shut.'

'So we won't get in that way, then.'

'No, not without making one hell of a racket.'

'We could try round the back,' Palmer suggested.

'We could, but if that's all double-glazed then it might prove impossible.'

'Fair enough, but I want to give it a go.'

'You're the boss. How do we get round the back? Only, I didn't see a side gate.'

'Yeah. There's an alley runs down the back of the gardens. I think it comes out in the side road up there,' and Palmer pointed back up the road. From what I remember seeing the other evening, the house has a back gate leading onto the alley.'

'Good. Well, we'd better count the houses. Don't want to break into the wrong one by mistake.' Marston grinned. 'Anyway, you were going to tell me why this is so important.'

'Yeah. Green's wife, he's the guy who owns this place, died earlier today. Only Green seems to be involved with Delaney who, incidentally, is alive and just returned from a holiday in Edinburgh.'

'She's *what*?' The incredulity in Marston's voice was clear.

'Been on holiday to Edinburgh. Says she got back sometime today. So that rules her out of the Castle-Point case. Anyway, it seems like Green may be involved with someone else, and if I'm right, that someone else is also involved in something that isn't very nice.'

'Kiddies?'

'Yeah, which is why I want to find out what we can from inside that house.'

'Right. There's nine houses to the end of the alley from this end. I counted them off while I was walking up to you.'

'You sure, Eddie?'

'Positive. Now, if we're going to do this, let's get on with it. Are you ready?'

'Yeah.' The two men left the car and walked to the side road. Palmer located the alley and they walked slowly back down it, counting off the garden gates as they did so. At the ninth gate they stopped. Palmer tried the latch, only to find the gate bolted from within.

'Damn, it's locked. Have to reach over.' With that, Palmer hoisted himself up onto the gate and leaned over. 'Only a single bolt at the top.' He reached over and slid the bolt back. 'There, that should do it.'

Palmer lowered himself to the ground and tried the latch again. This time the wooden gate opened easily. 'After you,' Palmer smiled at his colleague.

The two men slipped into the garden and Palmer carefully closed and re-bolted the gate behind them. The back of the house revealed a set of sliding patio doors from one room, and a back door that evidently led into the kitchen. There was also a window in the kitchen but it was obviously locked. Palmer tried the kitchen door and found that it was also securely locked.

'Damn. Have to try the patio doors.' Marston was closest to the doors and tried the nearest one. It was locked. Carefully he took the three steps over to the farther door. He depressed the button and pulled the door. Silently it opened for him.

'Phew,' Palmer breathed. Then he sniffed the air. 'What the hell's that awful smell?'

'I don't know. Smells like a dead rat or something.' Marston replied.

'Or dead body. Now, take it very slowly and carefully. We don't want to disturb anything.' Palmer reached into this pocket and withdrew the small torch he was carrying. He flashed the light across the room and determined it was empty. He took two steps into what was evidently the living room and stopped. The smell, now he was fully inside the room, was much worse. He reached into his pocket and withdrew a handkerchief, which he then placed over his nose.

'You look round here. I'm going upstairs.' Palmer quickly walked out of the room into the hallway and began to climb the stairs. As he did so, he became aware of a sound. At first it was a bit like a loud humming sound, a sound that got louder with each step he climbed. By the time Palmer had reached the landing the hum had turned into a buzz. From the landing there were four doors. The first was open and, using the light from his torch, Palmer immediately determined it was the bathroom. The second door was closed, as was the third. The final door, at the end of the landing was open. It was clearly being used as a storeroom. Palmer flashed the torch around the small room and decided it would take all night to check it properly.

Behind the first of the closed doors he found the source of the sound. At first the light from his torch picked out the double bed. On it lay a body, a male body. There was blood everywhere, over the sheets and the chest of the corpse. The mouth of the corpse had been taped with strong, brown tape, evidently to stop the victim from crying out.

Palmer gagged as he picked out the gruesome scene before him. The eyes of the corpse were wide open with fear, and the hands were still lashed to the bedstead with the same brown tape. The body was naked, except for the covering of blood that had oozed out of the chest and abdominal wounds. But what made the scene so wretched was not the state of the now-rotting corpse, but the flies that had taken up residence in the room.

In the same instant that he spotted the body, Palmer stepped backwards out of the door, closing it as if trying to shut out the horror of what he had just witnessed. He stood on the landing for several moments gulping in air behind the handkerchief, trying hard to recover from the shock. Finally, he descended the staircase.

'Find anything,' Marston began as Palmer entered the living room. 'Christ, you look like you've seen a ghost.'

'Dead body,' Palmer gasped, 'up in the main bedroom. Been stabbed about six times, and a few days ago at least. This awful smell is from up there, and it's covered in flies. Anything down here?'

'Nothing. So, is it Green?'

'Yeah, I reckon so. The hair matches Green's. Other than that, it's hard to say. We'd better get out of here. Make damn sure you don't leave any prints.'

'I haven't. Had my gloves on all the time. You?'

'Yeah. The same. You checked the back of the sofa?'

'No.'

'Right. I'll just give it a once over, then we're out of here. God, that smell is awful.' Palmer took two steps in the direction of the sofa and lifted the first cushion. The sofa had evidently either been kept clean, or had recently been cleaned. He lifted the second cushion, again without result. The third cushion was lifted and Palmer was about to replace it when he noticed the small notebook pushed down the side by the arm. Carefully, he lifted it out, scanned the pages and replaced it.

'Seems like Green's list of clients. We'd better leave it for the police to find.'

'Any interesting names?' Marston asked casually as they opened the patio door and let themselves out.

'Delaney stands out. Other than that there's about twenty other names and addresses. It would take half the night to note them all down and we don't have that kind of time. We know where Delaney's been for the last week, so she can't have been responsible for this.'

'She could have been if she did it before she left.'

'She didn't. Some bloke answered the door here the other night don't forget. My guess is that Green was still alive then, though I have to admit the body looks like it's been decaying for longer than that. It just doesn't add up.'

'Well, if it is more than a week old, Delaney could have done it.' They were walking back up the alley to Palmer's car.

'True, but if he's been dead all that time, it doesn't make sense.' Palmer sounded as confused as he felt.

'Unless this whole thing has been planned for a very long time and Green got wind of it, and he threatened to blow the whistle.'

'Maybe. Right, we need to alert the authorities. Where's your car?'

'Round the corner, back there.' Marston pointed back in the direction of the house.

'Okay, I'll take you there. Then, just drive home. Tomorrow morning I want you outside Delaney's house bright and early. She's supposed to be going to the police station – all I want you to do is make sure that is where she goes.'

'And what will you be doing?'

'Karen and I are going to watch Hartley-Brown hand over two million quid to somebody.'

Palmer left Marston at his own car and drove back round the corner. He switched off the engine and dialled the number of the local police station.

'Oh yeah, hi,' he drawled, when the desk sergeant answered the call. 'I don't know if you can help me, but I was supposed to be meeting a mate of mine at his house tonight. Only when I got there it's all in darkness and when I pushed open the letterbox there's this horrible smell coming from inside, like something's rotting. Only I'm a bit concerned because when I saw him a couple of weeks ago he said that he didn't feel too well. Could you send somebody round to have a look.'

The desk sergeant was attentive as Palmer spoke and promised to send a car round as soon as possible. He noted Palmer's name and location and the address he was supposed to be visiting. In a moment Palmer ended the call and waited for the arrival of the police car. He had not intended to hang around but he had remembered his visit to the house a few nights previously and was concerned that his fingerprints might still be detectable round the door. It seemed logical to state openly that he had been there before.

Palmer waited calmly as the minutes ticked by. After nearly half an hour he noticed the police car as it edged its way down the road looking for the house. Palmer left the relative warmth of his own car and went to greet the officer.

'Are you Mr Palmer, sir?' the officer looked up as Palmer approached him.

'Yes.'

'And what seems to be the problem?'

'Well, I'm a private investigator. Here's my card. I had an appointment to meet Stephen Green this evening. He lives in that house over there.'

'He's one of your client's, sir?'

'No. His wife is, and I needed to talk to him?'

'And his wife lives here?'

'No, officer, they are separated. Anyway, I was due to meet him here at ten tonight, only the house is in darkness and there's a strange smell if you open the letterbox.'

The police officer looked at Palmer with a degree of suspicion before replying. 'So, what makes you suspicious, sir?'

'Well, we met a couple of weeks or so ago and Mr Green said at the time he didn't feel very well. I know he's a quiet sort of chap, and my enquiries have shown he hasn't been at work for some time now, so when I encountered the smell, it worried me.'

'I see, sir. Well, if you'd just wait here, we'll go and take a look.'

'That's very considerate of you, officer.' Palmer looked evenly at the officer and waited while he went to examine the house. His colleague remained in the car, waiting and watching Palmer closely. After two minutes the Constable returned. He leaned in through the open window and spoke briefly to his colleague.

The conversation over, he straightened up again and waited for his colleague to exit the car.

'We won't be a minute, sir, only I need to effect an entry, and we have procedures to follow. So if you don't mind waiting here for us?' The question was really rhetorical as Palmer realised he had no choice in the matter.

'Of course, officer.'

The two Constables walked back over to the house and a few moments later Palmer heard the sound of glass breaking. He waited a further four minutes before the second Constable returned. His face indicated that he had found the body, and that he had not recovered from the ghastly revelation. He stood on the pavement and radioed for assistance before walking over to Palmer.

'I'm afraid this is going to take a while longer, sir, and we're going to need a statement from you. It's a bit of a mess in there.'

'What do you mean, officer?' Palmer feigned ignorance.

'I'm sorry, sir, but I can't say. It will have to wait for CID. They're on their way.'

'In that case, officer, I guess we'll just have to wait. Tell me, do you know Chief Inspector Andrews?'

'Yes, sir, why?' The Constable sounded confused.

'Oh, good, he's still there. Must be three years since we last did a round together.'

'A round, sir?' The Constable was now more than mildly intrigued.

'Yes, we used to play golf at least twice a month. There were four of us. Ken, that's Chief Inspector Andrews, John Hartman, he's a DI at Wimbledon, and Andy Braddock, he's also a DI, based in Sutton.'

'You're well acquainted, sir.'

'Very, Constable, very.' Palmer remained reflective. He'd had many dealings with the three senior officers over the years, but their relationship went back further than that. They went back to their latter years at school, years when they had formed an unshakeable friendship. For some years after leaving the school they had all gone their separate ways, Palmer becoming a bank clerk, while the other three had begun training at Hendon. Then they had been posted to different stations and begun the natural progression of their various careers. Yet their friendship had remained, and the trust that they had developed during their time at school. Then, a few years previously, all three officers had been

251

posted back to the South of London and so the regular rounds of golf had started. They had continued for some time until pressures of work had made it progressively more difficult to arrange suitable times and venues. Now they met on an ad-hoc basis and Palmer, being the odd one out, made special efforts to keep in contact with the three officers who had been such a help to him on more occasions than he cared to remember.

The sound of sirens wailed against the night air and the two police cars suddenly appeared round the corner of the road. They screeched to a halt outside Green's house and four men clambered out. A third vehicle also arrived and a single, somewhat distinguished man alighted. He carried a black bag and was escorted by the first Constable into the house. He was not in there for long – less than ten minutes.

'It's okay Sergeant,' Palmer heard him speak as he came out of the house. 'We'll need to do a full PM, but that can wait for tomorrow. He's all yours now.' The man looked grim as he stood there in his suit and coat, the black bag hanging limply by his side.

The next person to leave the house made a bee-line towards the police car where Palmer was standing.

'I understand from my Constable that you phoned this in?' The man looked evenly at Palmer. 'It's all right Constable, you can leave us alone. I know Mr Palmer well enough to know he won't bite me. Damien, how are you?'

'Yes, sir,' the Constable walked away from the car.

'Quite well, Ken, and yourself?'

'Pretty good. So, what's happened here then?'

'You tell me. I had an appointment with a chap called Stephen Green at ten tonight. Actually I'm doing some work for his wife – they're separated, and I needed to talk to him. I saw him a couple of weeks ago, and he needed time to get some information together for me. The thing is, Ken, there's more to it than that.'

'There always is with you, Damien. Is this going to take long?'

'Nope. I was due to meet his wife at lunchtime today, except she got run over crossing the road to the pub we were going to meet in. That's not your problem though. I've left that one with John. So, what I was actually going to say tonight to Green was that his wife was dead. Actually I thought he might be involved. One other thing. I did try visiting him a few days ago, but the guy who opened the door and said he was Green clearly wasn't. I checked the photograph when I got back home. What's happened in there?'

'Well, I'm not supposed to say, but as it's you. There's a body upstairs and, as you noticed the smell, you'll probably realise it's been there for a while. We'll have to wait for the post-mortem, but I'd say it's been there at least a week, and probably longer. Now, this other bloke you saw a few days ago – how many days ago?'

'A couple of days. Said he was Green and that he was about to sell up and go abroad. Seemed a bit nervy.'

'And how would you describe him?' Andrews was clearly interested and started taking notes.

'Early to mid-forties, mid-brown, short hair, wore glasses. I didn't really get much of a look, because he kept the chain on the door. To be honest, I was expecting Green to open the door and so I didn't really take too much notice, and what he said didn't really raise any eyebrows either – it was fairly predictable for the situation. Of course, I know now that the chap I saw couldn't have been Green.'

'Why not?'

'Because you reckon he's been dead for a week or more.'

'But I didn't say it was Green in there. It could be someone else.'

'True,' Palmer sounded surprised.

'Look, Damien, I really can't say one way or the other. There's no ID on the body or in the room. But, as it's his house, there has to be a chance. Now, I'm going to need a statement out of you. Do you want to do it now, or tomorrow?'

'Tomorrow if that's okay. Shall we say about noon?'

'Okay. Just ask for me at the desk when you get there. Now, we've got a busy night ahead of us here. I'll see you tomorrow.' The two men shook hands and Palmer began the short walk back to his own car. The road was blocked with police cars and from the far end of the road a black van was arriving. Palmer turned his car around and made his way out of the estate using some back roads. He journeyed home in silence, contemplating the double deaths of the day.

***

The sound of the entry-phone interrupted Karen Shaw as she watched the television. It was just after eight thirty and she had settled down to a quiet night in. She stepped into the hallway of her flat and picked up the handset.

'Yes?' she enquired.

'Miss Shaw? Floral delivery for you.'

'Yes, I'm Shaw, who's it from?'

'Can't say. There is a card, but it's sealed in an envelope.'

'Oh, right.' You'd better come in. I'm up two flights.' She pressed the buzzer, thinking that Damien must have sent her a nice surprise. Even as the delivery boy was climbing the stairs she hoped the flowers were her favourites – red roses. They were bound to be, after all Damien knew she loved them. She heard the fire door to the landing open and was standing by the door when the man outside knocked. She looked cautiously through the spy hole. The man was turned away from the door, his baseball cap covering the back of his head. In his hand was the bunch of flowers, and yes, they were roses.

Karen unlatched the door and began to open it. As she did so, the man turned round. The grin on his face and the gun held in his other hand only added

255

to Shaw's fear as he pushed her roughly back into the hallway. In a moment the door was closed and she was reeling from being pushed backwards once again. She looked up at the man and recognised him immediately. Even as she recognised him he tossed the bunch of flowers on the floor and placed his hand hard against her mouth, preventing her from screaming.

'You see this gun?' he whispered savagely. 'One scream, one yell, and it's your last. Understand?'

Karen nodded in agreement and felt his grip on her face loosen. Her shoulder hurt where he had pushed her against the wall, and now as he pushed her into the lounge, the same shoulder made violent contact with the door frame. She winced as it did so, and tears welled up from the pain.

'Hammond,' she whispered back, 'what the hell are you doing here?'

'All in good time, Miss Shaw, all in good time. In a minute we will be leaving here, and I want you to do exactly what I tell you.' He still held her face, but the grip had loosened.

'Leaving? I don't understand.' Karen was acting with a great deal more bravery than she felt, and her shoulder was bruised and painful.

'You will. You see, people that meddle in other people's business take their life in their own hands. You chose to meddle in my business by getting involved with Hartley-Brown, and now I need something to bargain with. You have aggravated my plans and made them much more complex than they would have been. He's going to pay me a large sum of money tomorrow, and I need to be sure that none of your pathetic friends try to stop me, so I am simply taking you as a sort of insurance policy. Now, do as I say, or else.'

Karen nodded, realising that she had little choice but to comply with the demands of the man who still held her head in his right hand.

Hammond arranged the flowers on the table, in the form of a crude wreath. He took the card and removed it from the envelope, before placing it in the centre of the arrangement. With tears of pain still seeping out onto her cheek he made Shaw look at the arrangement.

'See what the card says,' he whispered in her ear. The words were familiar.

'Death Awaits You. What a charming message.' The sarcasm was heavy but at the same time she shuddered involuntarily as she remembered where she'd seen the words before.

'Yeah. We'll leave them here, just in case lover boy comes round to see you.'

'He can't.'

'Why not?'

'He doesn't have a key.'

'Oh well, we'll leave them anyway. A nice homecoming present for you after this is all over – always assuming nobody tries to stop me. Right, it's time to go. My car's round the back, and no funny business or I'll use this thing.' For good measure he pressed the barrel of the revolver into the woman's abdomen. She nodded.

Five minutes later she was seated in the passenger seat of his Esprit. Actually she was slumped there, because at the very moment he opened the door and with due courtesy showed her into the passenger seat, he brought his hand round over her face and held the pad against her mouth and nose until he felt her body go limp. The chloroform took effect quite quickly and Hammond was careful not to continue its application to the point where suffocation would have occurred. So with his hostage unconscious in the passenger seat, Hammond began the short journey to his matrimonial home.

Chapter Eleven

Fifteen minutes after Palmer left Delaney's house, she was sat in the bath, soaking up the rich bubbles from the expensively scented foam bath that she had added to the water. There were still tears in her eyes, and her face was one that expressed a mixture of grief and anger. It was a grief that related to something she instinctively knew had happened. She did not know that at the very same moment the pain of the grief was flowing through her that a police car was parking outside the driveway to her house.

The sound of the doorbell startled her and without thinking, she stood, wrapped a towel around her curvy body and half-tripped down the flight of stairs. Almost in a trance she opened the door. Outside stood two people, one male, the other female, and each bearing the uniform of the police force.

'Yeah?' Delaney was having difficulty comprehending the situation. As she spoke she struggled to keep the towel wrapped round her body.

'Katherine Delaney?' The question was asked by the WPC.

'Yes. What do you want?'

'I'm WPC Newman and my colleague is PC Standish. May we come in for a moment?'

'Why?'

'It really would be better if we could come in. Do you mind?'

'I suppose so. Come in.' Delaney stood back from the door and ushered the constables into her living room.

'You'd better sit down ma'am,' the male constable spoke softly.

'Sorry, I don't understand? I thought I was coming to the station tomorrow to tell you where I've been?' Delaney sat down and as she did so she fought to keep her body covered by the towel.

'Sorry ma'am, I don't understand. That's not what we're here for.' The female constable spoke with clerical efficiency, though Delaney could tell that she was apprehensive about something. Delaney also began to realise that for whatever reason these officers had come to her house at this hour of the evening, it had nothing to do with her stay in Edinburgh, or other events during the day. She sat in her armchair, and displayed growing anxiety at what she might be told.

'So, in that case, why are you here?' Delaney looked from one to the other officers as she asked the question.

'You are Katherine Delaney, nee Westley, aren't you?' The woman was obviously in charge.

'Yes,' Delaney faltered as she began to realise what was coming.

'Miss Delaney, I'm afraid we have some bad news for you.'

'Go on.'

'We found a body on Epsom Downs a few days ago, and we have reason to believe that it might be your sister, Julia.'

'Oh.' Delaney slumped at the news, but managed to continue. 'And why do you think that?'

'Well, at first we thought it was you, Miss Delaney, but your boss confirmed that it was not. We've made some enquiries that lead us to think that it may be your sister.'

'But surely her husband could tell you if she's alive or not?' Delaney was crying now.

'Her husband? Yes, well, we haven't found him yet, and he's not at the matrimonial home.'

'No, he wouldn't be. They split up about a year ago.' Delaney bit her lip as if deciding what else to say.

'Actually ma'am we were hoping you would be willing to come with us and identify the body. Only it's important we get the identity established as soon as possible.'

'Yes, yes, of course I will. Look, sorry, this is all a shock. Can I have five minutes to get dressed?'

'Of course, ma'am. Now is there anybody you'd like us to contact to come with you?'

Again Delaney paused to think. 'No, I don't think so, thank you. Now, if you'll give me five minutes.'

Five minutes later Delaney descended the stairs. Dressed in a dark blue tracksuit and jogging shoes she picked up her handbag and the house keys and followed the two police officers to their car, which was parked at the end of Delaney's drive. Delaney stayed silent in the back of the car as she was driven to the mortuary.

Delaney shivered with anticipation as the front door of the mortuary was opened, and she entered

261

the cold, grey building. Preparations had obviously been made in advance of her arrival, for she was not ushered down the long, concrete corridor to the main part of the mortuary itself, but instead she was shown into a small room. In the room was a window that opened onto a further room. In this room was a bed and on the bed, covered by a sheet lay the body. At the head of the bed was a small table and on the table was a vase of what looked like fresh flowers. The room, thought Delaney, looked just like a hospital room but without all the gadgetry and wires.

The police officers stood calmly behind her as she waited, her face a few inches from the cold glass. In the other room stood the same technician who had shown Delaney to the room in which she now stood. She looked up at the window and nodded gently before proceeding to pull back the cover over the body's head.

'Oh God.' Delaney put her hand to her mouth and turned away from the window, tears already pouring down her face.

'Is that your sister?' the WPC spoke softly, almost with reverence. 'I'm sorry Miss Delaney, but we do need you to confirm it verbally.'

'Yes, that's Julia. How did it happen?'

'I'm sorry, we don't know that yet.'

'Where did you say she was found?'

'On the Downs, by the gallops. Did she go there often?'

'We went up there sometimes, and I think she used to go up there with her husband, before they split up.'

'Ah yes, her husband. That's a Mark Hammond, isn't it?'

'Yes, but as I said, they split up about a year ago.'

'And do you know his whereabouts now?'

'If you mean do I know where he lives, then the answer is no. I do know where he works, because I got the bastard the job. He works as a contractor for Castle Point Systems.'

'I see, and you don't know where he lives.'

'No. Since they split up he's kept himself to himself. Made life very difficult, me being his boss, but thank God he's only got another month left on his contract. We won't be renewing it. Anyway, I'm resigning on Monday – I got a new job in Edinburgh while I was up there.'

'I see.' The WPC was beginning to irritate Delaney. 'And Mr Hammond, do you know if he was still in touch with your sister.

'I doubt it, but you'll have to ask him that. I don't suppose you know where he is, do you?'

'We're making some enquiries, but it may take some time. Now we know where he works we'll be able to talk to the owner first thing on Monday.'

'How did she die, officer? I want to know. I need to know.' Delaney sounded angry, confused and shocked.

The WPC looked at her colleague before continuing.

'We do know that she was hit over the head with a blunt instrument and that the cause of death was asphyxia.'

'You mean she was knocked unconscious and then strangled?'

'Yes, I'm afraid that it looks like that. But, if it's any consolation, the pathologist believes she was unconscious before she died, so she probably didn't feel anything.'

'And, was she, oh God, was she attacked in any other way?'

'If you mean, was she sexually assaulted, then the answer is no. There are other bruises but they are minor and consistent with some kind of struggle taking place. Now, do you want to go in and sit with her on your own for a while?'

'Can I?'

'Yes, just take as long as you need. We'll wait outside for you.'

Delaney left the room and was met outside by the technician. The technician expressed her sympathy and Delaney was shown into the room and left alone with her sister. She sat on the chair that had been considerately placed at the top end of the bed for her. Her sister's face was still exposed, a pallid face that expressed a deathly serenity. Delaney reached over and kissed the corpse's forehead and then placed her hand gently on her sister's hair. Delaney waited until the door clicked shut behind the technician before she spoke.

'Julia, I'm going to get the bastard that did this to you. This was never meant to happen, you know, even if things didn't work out as you planned. Well, they haven't worked out how I planned either, not now. I just wish it could have been different. Don't worry baby, we always said we'd get revenge on whoever hurt the other one. Well, I guess it comes down to me getting revenge, and I will. Now,' she sobbed, 'you get the rest you deserve. No more pain, no more suffering, no more fear or deceit. Just rest.' She brushed her sister's hair with her fingers and sat in the chair allowing her tears to fall.

After what she considered to be a decent period of time, she stood up and walked to the door. Outside, the two police officers were holding plastic cups and chatting. Delaney looked one more time at her sister, made the sign of the cross, and bowed her head in solemn respect before she opened the door.

'Are you ready?' the PC reacted first.

'Ready. Will you take me back, or do I get a cab?'

'We'll take you back, just so long as you're sure you're ready.'

'Quite sure.' Delaney looked round for the technician, thanked her for looking after her sister, brushed away the fresh tears and started to walk to the door. Fifteen minutes later the police car sat at the end of Delaney's drive and she was assuring the officers that she did not need any company and that she would be all right. Five minutes after that she was inside, the front curtains closed, and pacing up and down the living room floor.

At about the same time as Katherine Delaney was identifying her sister's body, Hammond arrived at the house where he had lived with his wife until a year previously. The house was shrouded in darkness as he drove the Esprit up the driveway. The garage at the side of the semi-detached house was larger than usual, and had an up and over door that opened automatically as the car approached it. Moments later the door was closing behind the car. Once in the garage Hammond walked round to the passenger door and opened it. He dragged the semi-conscious Shaw out of the car and round past the bonnet. The garage had a connecting door to the house and Hammond opened it and propelled the groggy woman into the hallway beyond. He pushed her through the dining room door that on the other side of the hallway, and sat her in one of the carver chairs. When she was slumped in the chair he pulled the small bag off his shoulders and untied the top. With consummate skill and a practiced hand he taped her wrists to the side of the chair and the woman's legs to the front legs of the chair. Then he waited for her to regain consciousness.

While he waited he quickly checked the house. It was cold, as if death itself had passed through the building some time earlier. It was also empty. Julia Hammond had not been at home for several days, and during that time nothing had been touched. Hammond looked round the house and searched the drawers and cupboards. It was a cursory examination, as if he just wanted to check that everything was where it should be. He'd been in the house for over two hours, and it was approaching midnight, when he heard Karen Shaw beginning to wake up.

'Where am I? What's going on?' she muttered as the effects of the chloroform began to wear off. Hammond entered the dining room and stood in front of her. 'What are you doing here Mr Hammond?'

'Shut up, or I'll gag you. No one knows you're here, and the neighbours are old and deaf, so we won't get disturbed. Now, if you do exactly what I tell you, you won't get hurt and everyone will get what they're interested in.'

'Sorry, I don't follow.'

'You will. Tomorrow Hartley-Brown is going to pay me two million quid and then I'm off out of the country for good. Now, if you and your friends hadn't got involved everything would have gone smoothly, but your meddling ways have just made it all more complex. So now I need a hostage – you. Are you going to co-operate willingly, or have I got to make you?'

'How do you mean?'

'Will you do what I tell you, or have I got to force you?' He had the revolver out now and he lightly rubbed the barrel of the gun over the woman's chest. Shaw sensed that he was enjoying the power he had over the incapacitated woman and it unnerved her. She looked down at her wrists and realised she was in a hopeless position, and totally vulnerable. 'What do you want me to do?'

'First off, we're going to phone your partner, the one who's been following me. We're going to change our plans for tomorrow. I want him to bring the money, not that pervert Hartley-Brown. Then he can have you in return, once I know the coast is clear. Got it?'

'I think so. Do you want me to dial the number?'

'No. I'll dial, you just give me the number.' As he spoke, Karen realised that Hammond did not know it wasn't Palmer who had been watching him, but rather it had been Marston. She called out Palmer's telephone number as Hammond pressed the numbers on the keypad of his mobile phone. When he'd done that he pushed the phone up against the woman's face and for good measure placed the barrel of the revolver none-too-gently between her breasts. As the phone started to ring, he smiled knowingly.

'Damien,' she said after a minute, 'it's Karen. Something's happened.'

Palmer had been home for a few minutes and was about to retire. 'Go on babe, what.'

'Damien,' the voice was male, 'that is your name, isn't it.' The voice was also quite hostile.

'Yes, who are you?'

'That doesn't matter. What does matter is that I have your friend sitting here with me. She has something to tell you, so listen very carefully to her. Do you understand?'

'Yes.' There was a pause.

'Damien, it's Karen. Hammond has kidnapped …' and the line went dead.

Palmer stood up from the swivel chair behind his desk and rubbed the back of his neck. As he did so, the phone rang again.

'Sorry,' the male voice greeted him, 'but she didn't say what she was supposed to say. So instead, I'll tell you. Tomorrow morning I am due to receive a certain package from a guy called Hartley-Brown. Seeing as you chose to get involved in this, I want you to deliver that package, on your own, and with no pissing me around. No cops, no sightseers and no private dicks, or the lady will have an appointment with death. Do I make myself clear?' the voice was calm and Palmer could hear a woman sobbing in the background.

'Yes, you are perfectly clear. Before I hand the money over I want to see that Karen hasn't been harmed in any way.'

'Sorry, that's not part of the deal. The money first, then I release her and Hartley-Brown gets his precious laptop back. Now, eleven o'clock, and don't be late.' The line went dead and Palmer replaced the receiver. He rubbed his neck again and phoned Hartley-Brown.

'Mr Hartley-Brown, I'm sorry to phone you so late. It's Damien Palmer and there has been a development.'

'Can't it wait for the morning. Don't you know what time it is?'

'Perfectly. It's just after midnight. Now, Mr Hartley-Brown, one of my colleagues has just been taken hostage by your blackmailer and he is threatening to kill her if we do not comply with his wishes. Now, I need you to agree to do what I am going to ask you, otherwise you will leave me with no choice but to hand the whole thing over to the police. Do you understand me, Mr Hartley-Brown?'

'Yes. What is it you want me to do?'

'I want you to meet me at Castle Point at ten o'clock tomorrow morning. Have the money with you in a suitcase.'

'Yes, and then what?'

'And then you wait there while I take the money to the rendezvous. Then he says he'll hand over the computer and his hostage. We don't; really have much choice. If we don't do it his way then he'll probably kill his hostage and you won't get the computer back.'

'And I must get the computer back. Who's he got as a hostage?'

'Miss Shaw.' Palmer felt angry at the developments of the night. How dare this man, Hartley-Brown, be allowed to escape from the scene of danger, and Palmer and his friend be put there instead.

'Oh God. So do you know who the blackmailer is?'

'Yes, it's Hammond. Now be frank with me Mr Hartley-Brown, why would Hammond do this?'

'Because he developed the software an knows what it's worth?' The suggestion was lame and Palmer felt the little hairs on the back of his neck rise with his ire.

'I don't think so, Mr Hartley-Brown. I think Hammond has another reason for this. But if you're not going to tell me what it is, then I can't force you. I'll meet you tomorrow at ten. Goodnight.' Palmer slammed the receiver back onto its cradle and spun his chair round to look at the shelves of books that lined his study. He turned the laptop on and waited for the machine to complete its start-up procedure. Then he selected the icon that would link him to the Internet. It was as if an unseen hand was guiding him as he logged on using the process that was familiar to him.

After a few minutes he typed in the web site address for Pradonet and waited for the screen to refresh. Absently he clicked on various links, links that took him into the very heart of the Pradonet site. Suddenly he was confronted with a list of links to other sites, sites that offered pictures, videos and other material of a highly adult nature. Palmer started to scroll through the list, and noticed that as he scrolled the nature of the sites changed from adult to teens. He looked at the sites now listed and held the mouse over one of the links. He looked with interest at the address and clicked the mouse twice. The screen changed and he found himself looking at a site that he was sure should be banned. With the reaction of one that knew such things existed, but wished they didn't, he returned to the first page of the Pradonet site. Somehow it looked different to Palmer. The images on the screen all looked the same, but in the bottom right corner there was now the symbol of a small, golden key. Palmer was intrigued and placed the cursor over the key. He clicked the mouse twice and waited as the screen went black.

After a few seconds, Palmer realised he was being offered access to a very secretive site, the kind of site that few even realised existed. The screen was prompting him for a user identity code and a password. Palmer, of course, knew neither, but he was still angry at Hartley-Brown. Then, again as if an unseen spirit were guiding him, he remembered something that Karen Shaw had once told him.

It had been one particular case he'd been working on some months earlier when he'd been faced with a similar situation. Then she'd told him something that he would never forget.

'If you don't know the user id, or a password, try the obvious,' she'd said. 'You'd be amazed how many people use their own names and think nothing of it.'

So, he typed in Hartley-Brown as the user and then typed in a password of 'David'. He waited in anticipation that his entry would be rejected. The screen went black and Palmer waited to see what would happen next. Suddenly the words 'Hello, David,' appeared at the top of the screen. A moment later a second line of text appeared: 'Searching for database...'

Palmer waited. He could scarcely believe what was happening before his eyes. Then a third line of text appeared. 'Logon to Pedosys is not possible. Remote logon authority not found.'

In the instant that the line appeared, Palmer realised what he had unearthed, and at the same time why the blackmailer knew he had such a valuable laptop. It was now half-past midnight and Palmer sat at his desk making notes on his pad of paper. After half an hour he sat back and smiled to himself. He knew now for certain that he had found the key, quite literally, to this case. It had begun with a sophisticated form of security that would only be known by the privileged few and Palmer doubted he could repeat it without the notes in front of him. Doubtless the Pradonet software stored up certain information as a user paged through the various web pages in a certain way. If they then returned to the front, or Home, page the software would recognise the pattern of the previous access and display the key – very clever, very clever indeed. Then, just to make sure of their security, each authorised user had something on their own computer – some sort of authority code. So, when signing on it was only possible to get into the site if the person actually had the user identity code, the passwords, and an authority code on their machine. Palmer congratulated himself on his deductions, and then decided whatever lay beyond the screen he had become stuck on, that it must be sinister, very sinister indeed. Finally, sure that he had noted the web site addresses correctly he turned off the laptop.

Then Palmer sat in the office, his forefingers placed under his chin as he contemplated his next move. There were still a number of loose ends to tie up in this case and the next morning would be his last chance to conclude matters. Palmer sat at his desk and made several, almost unreadable, notes.

The notes provided a gruesome catalogue of deaths, names and dates. At the centre of the list was David Hartley-Brown, a man who had started out as the victim, and now looked to Palmer as if he was about to get his just desserts. There was also the unfortunate Stephen Green and his wife Dawn. They were both dead of course. Then there was Katherine Delaney. She'd been part of the investigation for some days, yet her story about being in Edinburgh for a job interview had been easy to verify. There was, of course, the case of Ellen Morrison and her fiancé, Robert Smith, to consider, but that was totally separate, and its timing had been a coincidence.

Then there were Hartley-Brown's personal assistants. The first one, Julia Westley, had disappeared some time ago, and then there was Carol Whiteman. Palmer had seen at first hand that she was involved with Hartley-Brown, but where, if at all, did she fit in with the case he was investigating?

Palmer looked in his desk drawer and pulled out the envelope that Marston had given him earlier that evening. It was the result of Marston's visit to the record office the previous day. He opened the sealed envelope and withdrew the page of notes. He whistled softly at its contents and cursed himself for having not read the document sooner. It changed nothing, but finding out that Delaney had been born Westley made a big difference. Palmer noticed that it was now nearly two o'clock. There would be no rest for him that night. With Karen a prisoner somewhere, he knew he would not sleep. It was better that he concentrated on the case and tried to influence its outcome, and that is precisely what Palmer spent the next few hours doing – contemplating.

***

At the point when Karen had phoned Palmer she had decided that she had to let him know who her kidnapper was. She doubted that Hammond would kill her, after all he needed a hostage. So she blurted out his name. She had barely spoken it when

274

she felt the sting from the back of his hand as it crossed her face. In the same instant the phone was taken away from her and he terminated the call. She felt the bruise on her cheek rising as the hand came back across her face for a second time. This time she was waiting for it and moved with the direction of the movement, reducing the effect of the slap. It still stung her cheek.

'Now that was a stupid thing to do,' Hammond said, 'and you see where it gets you.' He made the second call and issued his instructions while Karen Shaw sat helplessly in the chair, the pain of the two vicious slaps bringing tears into her eyes – tears that flowed down her stinging cheeks.

The call was soon over and Hammond turned to his hostage once again.

'Right, it's going to be a long night, and I don't think you'll be very comfortable there, so I suggest we try some other arrangement. I need a few minutes to think.'

'What's this all about?' Karen spoke softly having regained some composure.

'That is none of your business.' He sounded mildly irritated.

'Well, indulge me.' Her voice took on a definite note of pleading. 'We've worked out that this accounts and codes thing is a scam, and that this has all got a lot more to do with Hartley-Brown as a person. So, I'm just curious to know what the guy has done that's worth two million quid, that's all.'

'Actually, for him it's probably worth more than that, but we, I mean I, did some checking and two million is about all he can lay his hands on.'

'But what's worth two million to him?'

'His freedom for a start. The alternative will be to lose everything he currently owns and he'd be looking at a minimum twenty years behind bars.'

'But you only get that kind of sentence for something like murder.'

'Exactly.'

'Okay,' she sounded surprised. 'So what has he done that's worth two million to him?'

'You might as well know,' Hammond sounded tired and resigned to divulging his reasons, 'not that what I'm going to tell you will do you any good. Doubtless you have discovered that my wife was once his personal assistant.'

Karen looked blankly at the man so he continued. 'Yeah, she was his PA when we first met. And everything was fine. We'd been going out with each other for about a year when we had an accident and she got pregnant. That was in the September. Then at the Christmas party Hartley-Brown took his opportunity. He hadn't met me by this time and I was away on business so I couldn't be at the party. He took Julia into his office and raped her. He pretended he was drunk afterwards, but his actions deeply affected Julia. A month later she miscarried and well, things weren't the same after that. We drifted apart and she needed psychiatric help. Then this contractor's job came up and I applied for it. I already had it in mind to get my own back on the guy, and as Julia had left before we got married I figured that Hartley-Brown wouldn't know who I was.' He paused and walked round the room for a moment.

'But there was someone who instantly recognised me – Kath Delaney. Actually she was Julia's half-sister – same Father. Now Kath had been married and was divorced, though she'd kept her married name, and she had the same kind of ideas as I did – revenge for her half-sister. So we set up this scam. I had a few contacts and they agreed to help, and it was all going smoothly until a few months ago. Kath had been making a play for Hartley-Brown, but then he employed that new secretary of his and he didn't want Kath anymore - and that really pissed her off, because she lost control of the bloke we were about to get even with. It made things tricky.' He walked behind the chair.

'Now I should say that I split up with Julia about a year ago and Kath and I have been an item for a while now. So we set up this scam and well, the old fool leaves his precious laptop lying around. Normally he keeps it by his side, like a co-joined twin. Anyway, I feed his PA some bullshit and we pretend to load some software on the laptop. Actually I'm hacking in to see what's so special about it. And that's when we found out just how valuable it all is.'

'What did you find?'

'Internet sites, contact names, passwords, the lot. That bastard has been running a paedophile ring for years and it's all linked through the Internet. That information is priceless and if it gets out it will finish him off, let alone get him a hefty sentence. Anyway, I got some pictures of Kath and we hacked into one of the Pradonet sites and added them in. It had nothing to do with Hartley-Brown – he was only interested in the kid's sites. But we figured he'd be too scared to say otherwise, if it came up in conversation, and it gave us another plausible reason to go after him.'

'So Katherine Delaney is in on this as well?' Karen stared intently at the floor.

'Of course she is.' His voice began to carry a mocking lilt to it. 'We thought about it and then decided we wanted to clear off and start up a new life. That's Kath and me. So we decided to raise some capital, and hence our demand.'

'But won't Julia complain about you running off with her half-sister?'

'No, I can honestly say she is no longer part of the equation.'

'What do you mean?' Karen sounded shocked and fearful.

'I mean, she is no longer part of the equation. She won't cause a fuss, and neither will anyone else who gets to know about out little plan.'

'Such as who?' Karen had her eyes fixed on Hammond.

'Well, her psychiatrist for a start. Not really his fault, but Kath took Julia round there a while back and it seems they got talking as sisters do. Actually I think Kath let her in on it because she was getting scared. Bad move that, to get scared and start talking. You see, it all came out under the hypnosis session she had half an hour later. So Kath pretended to be interested in the guy – she had to find out what he knew. Also, if she was involved with him it made it less likely he'd spill the beans. Actually she did very well. But then his bloody wife started looking for him and Julia, the silly woman, said to Kath, that she was going to write to Green's home address and tell his wife what was going on between her and Green. Julia was about to spoil everything, so she had to be seen to.'

'You mean, the body on Epsom Downs? The one everyone thought was Delaney for a while.'

'That's the one. She'd been a real pain to live with for years, and she wanted everything out of our divorce. Seeing as I was leaving the country in a few days anyway, it seemed the logical thing to do. Now I can sell this place through an agent and get the funds transferred to wherever I am. That left two problems, Green and his wife.'

'And what happened to them.'

'Green was easy. Kath set him up brilliantly. About two weeks ago she arranged to go and see him and they started this love scene in his bedroom. She pretended she was into bondage games and tied him to the bed. When he was helpless she simply killed him and walked away. The only trouble was, she left some things unfinished, and she left her dabs all over the place. So a few nights back I went over to clean the place up. God it stank by then but the place is clean now. By a stroke of bad luck, your colleague turned up while I was there. I fed him a line that he seemed to swallow.' Hammond was becoming more confident that his plans were fool proof.

'Anyway, after that killing, Kath disappeared to Scotland. She wanted to start a new life up there, with her original name. She was there when her half-sister died so she couldn't be implicated in that.

Green's place was spotless and so she could act the distraught relative and just disappear. That left Green's wife. While Kath was in Scotland she left her car at my place. It was easy to borrow it and tail the woman, and it's a lot less conspicuous than a yellow Esprit. Actually I saw your colleague arrive at the pub in Wimbledon while she was looking for a parking space. I guessed she was going to talk to him, as I knew by then that he was looking for her husband. So I had to take my chance and the only thing that came to mind was a hit and run. Again, it gave Kath an alibi, because she was coming down on the Edinburgh train at the time and had a ticket to prove it.'

'Seems like you've thought of everything?' Karen sounded frightened and condescending.

'I think so.'

'So why tell me this now?'

'Why not, it doesn't make any difference. Your colleague has worked most of it out now, but he can't do anything while I've got you. Tomorrow he comes and hands over the money and I hand him the laptop. Then I simply do to him and you what I've done to the others. Finally, no one knows the story anymore and I get out of the country before anyone can start to piece it all together.'

'And Delaney?'

'Well, she's become a liability. It's a shame, but when she wanted to go to Scotland it didn't fit in with my plans. She knows about tomorrow's meeting – after all, half the money is supposed to be hers. Of course she doesn't know that I killed Julia.

So, with a bit of luck I can catch her off guard and, proverbially, kill three birds with one stone.'

'You're sick!'

'If you say so, but I'm not the one tied to a chair, and I'm about to walk away with two million quid.'

'And the laptop/'

'Oh, that will be found next to your dead colleague. With his dabs on it and Hartley-Brown's business stuff, and all the paedophile stuff, the cops will think they were in it together. They might even think that Hartley-Brown killed you all because you knew what was on the laptop. I don't really care.' He was now standing in front of the woman and he looked at the bruises on her face. He touched them with the tip of the barrel of the revolver and she winced.

'So,' she said, as she felt the barrel of the gun trail down her neck to her chest, 'what happens tonight?'

'Well, I could leave you here, or I could take you upstairs and make you more comfortable. It depends on you, really.'

'Personally I could talk all night. For example, what is going to happen to your Esprit? It's a valuable car, isn't it?'

'It'll go to the airport and in a few weeks it will be classed as abandoned. Then it will probably be destroyed. I don't really care. Now, I think we need our beauty sleep, so it's time to get upstairs. I won't be a moment.' With that Hammond walked out of the room. Karen heard him climb the stairs and a moment later descend them again. Then he re-entered the room.

'Okay, I'll do your hands first.' He slit the tape binding her wrists to the arms of the chair and then pulled them behind her. She felt the cold metal as he clamped the handcuffs around the wrists, securing her hands behind her back. Then he released one leg and again felt the cold metal as the cuff replaced the tape. The action was repeated on her other leg and then she was told to stand. As she stood, Karen realised that the cuffs around her ankles were separated by a short chain. The cuffs allowed her some movement, enough to walk with small steps, but nowhere near enough to even contemplate escape. She allowed Hammond to guide her towards the staircase and then she was pushed up the first few steps.

'I need a pee,' she said when they reached the landing.

'Okay, but don't do anything stupid. It's in there.' He released one handcuff around her wrists and as she turned to look at him she saw the revolver pointing at her chest.

Five minutes later she was propped up on a single bed, her left hand cuffed to the headboard.

'Right, that should keep you out of trouble for a few hours. Now don't do anything you might regret.' Hammond turned out the light and left the woman trying to get comfortable. He retired to the other bedroom, the one he had shared with his wife before they had separated, before he had killed her. He lay on the bed and opened a small paper package. He inhaled the contents and lay back as the hallucinogenic effects began to take over his body.

Chapter Twelve

The first rays of sunlight filtered through the early morning sky and came to rest on Palmer's desk. As they did so he stirred, the motion of a man who had spent a restless night and who had finally fallen asleep at his desk. His body craved the sleep it needed and finally, in the small hours of the morning, Palmer relented and closed his eyes. Now, with the first rays of warm sunshine, he was brought back to consciousness. There were a few hours to go and there were things to do. He roused himself, showered and shaved and then made breakfast. He always drank his coffee on the strong side, but this morning it remained black.

Palmer noted that it was only seven o'clock as he closed the front door to his terraced house. He drove through the almost empty streets of Wimbledon and passed on into Sutton. He parked behind Karen Shaw's block of flats and walked round to the outer door. The entry-phone awaited his attentions and Palmer punched in the number she had given him some moths previously. The door buzzed as the magnetic catch was released, and Palmer slipped inside. Quickly he ascended the staircase that was so familiar to him. Facing the door to Shaw's flat he stopped and pushed the door gently. He smiled to himself as he realised she had not double locked it. Taking a thin piece of plastic from his pocket he eased it between the door and the frame. Then, pushing gently on the door he eased the plastic up the door until it reached the catch. With a deft movement he felt the door give and in a moment he was standing in the hallway.

He looked quickly round the flat and spotted the roses laid out as a wreath on the table in the lounge. He looked at the card that formed the centre piece and read the terse message, '*Death Awaits You*', which stared at Palmer from the table. He felt a dryness begin to form in his mouth, the dryness he associated with the mixture of growing anticipation and fear. He checked the other rooms and decided that his girlfriend had left the flat in a hurry. He found a handbag in the bedroom and located the keys to the flat. He pocketed the bunch of keys and left, carefully locking the door behind him.

Five minutes later, Palmer was sat in his car, his laptop seated on the passenger seat. Palmer pressed some keys urgently and was rewarded with over a hundred directory entries for the name, Hammond. He repeated the exercise and the display showed a handful of results for the name Westley with initials of 'J' or 'M'. Still too many to check out in the short time available. Hammond, he felt sure, would not have taken Karen back to his apartment. It was too obvious, and Hammond was too clever to make such a simple mistake as that. After only a moment's deliberation Palmer decided Hammond would also not have taken Karen to Delaney's house. Again the location was far too obvious. He repeated his directory search for the name, Hammond. This time he restricted the search to an area around Sutton. This time he was rewarded with only four responses for those having an initial of 'J', or 'M'. Of course, Palmer considered ruefully, the address he was looking for might not be included in the directory. He looked at the list of four addresses and located the nearest one on the map.

Palmer started the car and drove the shot distance to the house he had located on the computer. It took him less than ten minutes before he drove slowly past the semi-detached house. He noted the curtains were still drawn, perhaps not surprising for eight o'clock on a Saturday morning. He also noted the larger than average garage adjoining the side of the building, and the empty driveway. As he drove past he contemplated stopping and waiting to see what, if anything, happened. Instead, he drove down the road and stopped before turning to the map again and locating the next address.

This time the drive took nearly quarter of an hour. The second house was large, detached and had a sweep past drive with two gateways. Palmer noted the silver BMW in the driveway and the stickers in the upstairs bedroom that clearly indicated the room was occupied by a teenager. Palmer decided the house was not the one he was looking for.

At quarter to nine he drove past the third house on his list. It was another semi-detached property, and the dirty, battered, white Fiat in the drive was clearly not in keeping with Hamond's style. The first three addresses had all been in the area of Sutton. Now Palmer was faced with the longer journey out to Epsom Downs itself. He'd left this address until last, if only because it was in the same area as the rendezvous later that morning. He located the road and began the journey. As he did so he picked up his mobile phone and dialled the number for Marston.

'Eddie, it's Damien,' he spoke after a moment. 'There's been a change of plan. Hammond has kidnapped Karen and is demanding I make the drop this morning. I don't think Delaney need worry us anymore, so could you be up at the course this morning by ten thirty?'

'Sure. Is Karen all right?'

'She was last night when he phoned me.'

'And have you called the cops?'

'Nope. I don't want her getting hurt and he warned me off them. So, it's down to us. Once she's free we can get them to catch him.'

'Okay, if you say so. What do you want me to do?'

'There's a car park just down the road from the drop area. Wait in there until you see him arrive and then try to follow him.'

'But he's got an Esprit,' Marston protested. 'What chance have I got against that?'

'None. But he's hardly likely to stay in the country if he's done what I think he's done, so all we need to know is which airport he's heading to, and with the traffic he's not going to get far away from you until he hits the motorway at Reigate. We'll know which airport he's headed for by then.'

'But doesn't your computer tell you that anyway?' Marston still sounded unconvinced.

'Sorry, but there's three M. Hammond's book in for flights this afternoon that I could find, two at one airport and one at the other.

'Okay. I'll be there, and Damien, take care.' Marston sounded less than enthusiastic about the morning's events.

'Cheers Eddie, and you look after yourself too. Don't act the hero. If he gets away from you, just let him go.'

'No worries there, mate. My old crate is well past being heroic. See you later.' Marston broke the connection and began his preparations for the morning's events.

Palmer reached the house in Epsom Downs at half past nine and immediately realised his journey was wasted. The large detached house oozed an opulence that was well beyond what even Hammond could have dreamed of. The Ferrari sports car stood gracefully in the driveway, as its owner lovingly cleaned it. Palmer judged the woman to be in her early forties. She looked up as Palmer drove past slowly, but his mind was already focusing on his next destination, the offices of Castle Point Systems.

Palmer drove carefully back to Cheam. Although he had literally passed less than thirty metres away from Karen Shaw earlier that morning, there had not been the slightest indication that this had been the case. To Palmer the attempt to locate the house had failed, and now he would have to go through with the drop.

He arrived at Castle Point Systems and parked in the deserted car park behind the offices. He was alone and had time to think before he heard the sound of Hartley-Brown's car as it joined his own.

'Mr Palmer, good morning, how are you today?'

'Fine, and yourself Mr Hartley-Brown?' The question was civil, though Palmer was feeling decidedly agitated by the situation that had arisen. It had made his neck and shoulders stiff from the tension he was feeling.

'As well as can be expected. Any further news from Hammond?'

'No, and I don't expect there will be.'

'Do you want me to come with you?'

'No. He was quite explicit that I was to turn up alone. I suggest you stay here and I'll phone you after the swap has been made.'

'And if it goes wrong?'

'Let's hope it doesn't. All I want is my colleague back and hopefully to recover your laptop.'

'You must recover it. There must be no handover if the laptop isn't handed over to you.'

'I understand your position, Mr Hartley-Brown, but you must understand that my prime concern is the release of Miss Shaw, and the eventual arrest of Hammond for the crimes he has committed.'

'And those crimes, what are they?'

'Well, from my estimation, he is either responsible for, or a partner in, at least two murders and possibly more. I do not intend that this morning's activities should increase the tally.'

'But I simply must get the laptop back.'

'I heard what you said the other day, and I too would hope to recover it. If we fail then doubtless the police will succeed later on. Now do you have the money?'

'Yes, in the suitcase in the boot of my car.'

'Right, well it can stay there for a few more minutes. I figure it will take me about ten minutes to drive to the drop point, maybe fifteen if the traffic is bad. That gives me half an hour. Now, Mr Hartley-Brown, if you don't mind I'd like to take a look at Mr Hammond's computer in the office.'

'Why?'

'Because that video he sent you was filmed in your office and he must have had some means of doing that. I'm not a computer expert but I doubt he has had the time or opportunity to cover his tracks completely.'

'Oh, well okay then.' Hartley-Brown sounded apprehensive. 'Let's go indoors, then.' Palmer followed the Managing Director of Castle Point Systems into the office and into the secure office of the research team.

'Is Miss Delaney involved in all of this?' Hartley-Brown asked him when the security door was open.

'No, I don't think so. Actually I'm pretty certain she was booked off on holiday.'

'You know, I think she did say something about that, now you mention it. Well, thank God for that. So it was Hammond all the time?'

'Looks like it. Now, which is his desk.'

'This one.' Hartley-Brown pointed at the desk Hammond had occupied for the past several months. Palmer moved over to the desk and turned the machine on. He waited impatiently as it powered up then he selected a sequence of menu options, scanning the further options that were presented to him. Finally he found what he was looking for and clicked the option. In a moment a window opened up on the screen and the window was filled with a wide-angle shot of Hartley-Brown's office.

'Well, Mr Hartley-Brown, that seals it and explains how he made the video. I still don't understand why he did it, or how he made your PA look so much younger.'

'It's as Miss Shaw stated the other day – a bit of clever programming. As for why he did it, I can only guess he was trying to scare me.'

'And did he?' Palmer looked evenly at Hartley-Brown.

'Yes he did, as a matter of fact.' If Hartley-Brown was hiding anything he was not going to reveal it now.

'One final thing, Mr Hartley-Brown, does the missing laptop have a card in it that allows you to connect to the Internet using a mobile phone?'

'Yes, it does actually. Most useful if you're out and about.' Hartley-Brown looked momentarily startled at Palmer's question, a reaction that did not go unnoticed by the sleuth.

'Yes, I suppose it would be. So what kind of connection does it require?'

'A multi-pin plug linking the two devices.'

'Ah, I see, and was that taken too?'

'Yes, it would have been in the carry case, why?'

'It's just nice to know whether Hammond can use the laptop in the car park to send out information if he wants to. It pays to know all the facts, Mr Hartley Brown, that's all.' Palmer smiled at the man, the meaning of the smile lost to the managing director. 'Right, I think we've cleared up the mystery of the video, though I still don't fully understand why he did it. I think it's time I was on my way. Just check I've got your direct line number.' Palmer took a card out of his coat pocket and examined it. He read out the number and waited for Hartley-Brown to confirm that it was correct. 'Okay then, let's get the money.'

Palmer led the way back out of the research room and waited for Hartley-Brown to check the door was fully closed behind them Then they walked back to the car park and Palmer transferred the suitcase from Hartley-brown's car to his own.

'I'll ring you when the drop has taken place. Then we'll come back here, so just wait for us, and don't worry. Everything will be fine.' Palmer sounded a good deal more confident than he felt. Two minutes later he left the office car park and picked up the main road from Cheam to Epsom. The traffic was moderate for a Saturday morning and ten minutes after Palmer had left Castle Point he turned off the main road into Epsom and headed for the Downs and the racecourse. He was in good time and drove at a steady pace past the large houses that led up the road to the Downs. At the end of the road he could clearly see the great, glass-fronted grandstand, and took the road the led down the side of the racetrack itself. At the other end of the home straight was his destination and as he neared the entrance he noticed that there were a few other empty cars already parked there. On his left he passed the car park where Eddie Marston was already waiting. Palmer felt sympathy with the man who would end up with the task of following Hammond's Esprit in his own, much less powerful, car.

Palmer parked his own car at the far end of the car park, the front of the car facing the entrance. It was a few minutes to eleven and Palmer sat back in the driver's seat to wait for Hammond's arrival. He did not have to wait long. The roar of the powerful engine, as Hammond gunned the car down the approach road, and the bright yellow distinctive colour, brought Palmer's attention to the matter in hand fully to the fore. He opened the door of his own car and waited while Hammond parked thirty metres from his own. In the passenger seat of the Esprit sat the hostage. Palmer thought Karen Shaw looked tired and scared. He was right.

'You got the money?' Hammond's question was spoken with clarity and confidence as he walked towards Palmer.

'Yes.'

'Okay, let's have it then.'

'Not so fast! First I want to see the laptop and to ensure Miss Shaw is all right.'

'Fair enough, I suppose.' Palmer thought Hammond was just a bit too confident. As he watched Hammond return to the Esprit he was unaware of the dark coloured Corsa that had just pulled into the car park. After a moment Hammond returned carrying a soft carry case.

'The laptop, as promised.'

'Show me.'

Hammond stood about five metres from Palmer and unzipped the case. Inside, Palmer could see the device.

'Okay,' continued Palmer, 'and Miss Shaw?'

'She's in the car. When I have the money, and you have the laptop, I'll be leaving here. She comes with me as security until I get to where I'm going, then I'll let her out. Any, and I mean any, attempt to stop me will result in her instant demise. Now, the money, if you please.'

'Palmer walked round to the back of his own car, followed by Hammond. He had just opened the boot of the car when he felt the sickening blow on the back of his head as the butt of the revolver ground into his skull. He slumped and fell to the ground.

'Nice doing business with you, sucker,' Hammond laughed. He picked the suitcase out of the car and started the walk back to his own car. Reacting to the situation, Karen had opened the passenger door of the Esprit and was starting to climb out of the car.

'Get back in there, or I'll shoot you,' Hammond yelled at her. Then he became aware of the engine of the Corsa as the throttle was pushed to the floor. The car lurched forward and he became aware that it was headed directly for him. He started to run, trying to reach the safety of his own vehicle. The suitcase was bulky and heavy and it slowed him significantly.

In that same instant Karen looked behind her and saw the car racing towards her. She desperately tried to close the door as the car neared her. She had just made it back into the passenger seat when the car tore past her, its momentum tearing the passenger door clean away from the Esprit. The headlong flight of the car continued as the passenger focused her attention on the man ahead of her. She felt the thud of flesh on metal as his body met with the bonnet of the Corsa. She saw him being lifted off the ground as his broken, twisted body was catapulted into the air.

Karen sat, numbed and shocked, in the remains of the Esprit as she saw the Corsa heading for Palmer's car. She knew that Palmer, though out of sight, must be behind the vehicle. At the same time as the body of Mark Hammond flew into the air the suitcase and laptop were flung to one side. With the impact of the body on her car, the Corsa's owner reacted by slamming on the brakes of her car. At the last moment she spun the steering wheel and swerved to the right of Palmer's car, hitting the barrier at the end of the car park.

As she did so, he began to recover from his own ordeal. He clambered, groggily to his feet and surveyed the carnage that lay between him and the Esprit. Karen was already running towards him and the Corsa had come to a stop, the sound of its horn adding to the pain already searing through Palmer's brain. Palmer reacted slowly, his head a mass of tortured, painful flesh. As Karen reached him he called out to her.

'Call an ambulance, and the police, Karen. Here, use my mobile. Fuck, why did this have to happen?' He left her to make the call while he staggered off to the Corsa. He pulled the driver's door open and lifted Katherine Delaney off the steering wheel. The sound of the horn melted away and the throbbing in his head began to subside.

'Miss Delaney, can you hear me?' he asked. He felt the woman's pulse in her neck. It was weak, and blood was seeping from her right ear.

'Mmm. Revenge is so sweet. Julia, I said I'd do it, and I did.' Katherine Delaney opened her eyes, looked at Palmer, took a gasp of air, closed her eyes again and died.

Palmer felt the pulse stop and watched for a moment as the trickle of blood continued to ooze out of her ear. Realising there was nothing more he could do he went and looked at Hammond. Hammond's own body lay on the car park, a twisted, broken body that was equally past helping. The sound of sirens filled the air and Palmer sat down on the ground to wait. Karen Shaw came and sat beside him and put her arm round him.

'You okay?' she asked.

'Yeah, I think so. God, what a mess this is. Look, it's not the right time or place, but I've been thinking. That's my trouble, I always think too much, but I never thought this would happen.'

'What are you trying to say, babe?' The woman continued to hold him.

'Well, I've had a lot of time to think over the past few hours and I've been thinking what life would be like without you, so I have a suggestion to make.'

'Which is?'

'Why don't we get married?' Palmer looked nervously at the woman, the dry taste of fear at her inevitable rejection already present in his mouth.

'Is that a proposal?' She looked stunned by what she had heard.

'Yes, I guess it was. It's the best I can do right now, but I'll do it properly later on when we've got this mess sorted out.'

'Okay.'

'Okay, you want me to do it properly, or okay, you'll marry me?'

'Both. Now, just wait for the ambulance to arrive.' She held him close to her and he responded by putting a hand on her arm.

Chapter Thirteen

The restaurant was busy that evening. Damien Palmer, now fully recovered from the blow on the back of his head sat at the table. Beside him, his fiancée, Karen Shaw beamed at him. Across the table a somewhat bemused Eddie Marston looked at the couple opposite him. The starters had been eaten and now the main courses were sat in front of the three diners.

It had been a long day. Palmer had given an explanation of events to his good friend, Detective Inspector Ken Andrews, who had been part of the team called to the scene. The laptop had been recovered and Palmer had handed over the web addresses he'd carefully copied down the previous evening. It had taken the police less than an hour to check out Palmer's story and ten minutes later a squad car had visited the offices of Castle Point Systems. David Hartley-Brown was under arrest and facing a long spell in prison if found guilty. Carol Whiteman had also been arrested and was facing conspiracy charges. Hammond, of course, was dead, as was Katherine Delaney.

'Now,' Eddie spoke quite softly, 'before we get stuck into this, I would like to propose a toast. To my two friends, may God forgive your folly at getting engaged. Seriously though, to you both, and all my best wishes.' The three glasses clinked and they tasted the champagne.

'Thanks Eddie,' said Palmer as they lowered the glasses to the table, 'and don't forget a groom needs his best man. Can I count you in?'

'Sure. It'd be an honour.' Marston smiled. 'Anyway, Damien, you said you'd tell us all about it tonight.'

'I did?' Palmer smiled. 'Okay then. Well, it all began with a man who panicked. David Hartley-Brown knew all the time what was on the laptop.'

'Which was?' Marston interrupted the sleuth.

'Names, addresses and a lot of information on a paedophile ring he'd been running for several years. So, he needed to get that laptop back, at almost any cost. His life and liberty depended on it. I should explain here that Katherine Delaney was sister-in-law to Mark Hammond. Hammond's wife, Julia, was half-sister to Delaney. Delaney was a divorcee and she'd just kept her married name. Hartley-Brown had never met Hammond before he went there as a contractor.'

'Hang on a minute, you've already lost me.' Karen was still smiling at her new fiancé as Marston asked interrupted Palmer. 'Where does Julia fit into all this?'

'She was Hartley-Brown's secretary when she was going out with Hammond. From what Karen said earlier, she got raped by Hartley-Brown and then lost the baby she was carrying. Anyway, Delaney, and Hammond both swore to get revenge. What they didn't realise at the time was Hartley-Brown's activities.' Palmer stopped for a moment and chewed a mouthful of food.

'Say, this is good. Okay, so they set out defraud Hartley-Brown. They set up a scam for a contract and made it all look very authentic. I think they planned to take him for a few hundred thousand. Then, and I think it was Delaney who spotted it first, they noticed how Hartley-Brown always kept the laptop very close to him. It was suspicious. Anyway, they couldn't believe their luck when he left it lying round the office one day. Hammond told his secretary, Carol, that he'd left it there so they could install the software for this top-secret project they were working on. She fell for it and handed the machine over. It was only after Hammond examined the machine that he discovered what else it contained. At this point the game plan changed, and the stakes went up considerably.' Again Palmer ate a mouthful of food.

'Now, after her miscarriage, Julia Hammond went off the rails and as a result she started seeing a shrink called Stephen Green. His own marriage was far from secure and he was setting himself up in practice in the Epsom area. I think he used hypnosis on Julia and Hammond, or Delaney, got scared that she might have told him about their plan for revenge. It was a risk they couldn't take. Delaney made it her business to meet with Stephen Green and to start an affair with him. She'd done the same thing before with Hartley-Brown, and it was all part of the plan to reduce suspicion and find out what she could about the man. With Green she wanted to find out what Julia had told him, though I doubt she was successful. It was too big a risk for Hammond and Delaney to take, so they arranged for Delaney to get him into bed one evening. She just had to tie him up as if she was playing some bondage game. Then she went downstairs and let Hammond in to finish the deed.' Palmer stopped and sipped the champagne.

'Okay, so that accounted for Green. Then, and it was my mistake, I accidentally told Hammond that I was working for Dawn Green. It was the night I knocked on Green's door, and Hammond opened it. I didn't know who he was, and I guess he was there cleaning up after the murder a few days previously. Anyway it scared him to think that Green had a wife and he must have panicked himself into believing she might know something. Worse, she might even tell me! So she had to be killed. He used Delaney's car – I spotted the damage to the bumper last night, knowing she had the perfect alibi, as she was in Edinburgh at the time. I think Hammond had found Green's home address from his diary, and that he simply watched Dawn Green, waiting for his opportunity. It wasn't ideal, but I'm fairly sure he saw me enter the pub while she was parking her car. He couldn't take the chance of us meeting and he didn't know we'd talked only a few days beforehand. So he panicked and decided to run her over.'

'But why today's events?' Marston had almost finished his meal.

'Well, Hammond didn't know that in the short time that Katherine Delaney had been home that she'd been visited by me, and by the police. They informed her that her half-sister was dead and got her to formally identify the body. It was a shock because Hammond had always assured Delaney that he was divorcing Julia. However, as with Green, he couldn't risk Julia talking about the revenge plan, so he decided to kill her, and Delaney realised it was what he had done. She also knew about the two million and decided it was time to exact some revenge of her own. She'd already got a new life planned in Edinburgh, and she was reverting to her maiden name of Westley. Also, she couldn't easily be implicated in any of Hammond's misdoings, and with him planning to leave the country he was hardly likely to come back and tell all. So Delaney decided to kill Hammond and take the money for herself. She wasn't interested in the laptop. That could be left, and she knew it would implicate Hartley-Brown in a number of serious matters, so she could get revenge on him too. In her shocked, bereaved state of mind, it all made sense.' Palmer ate some more food and smiled at his fiancée.

'Anyway,' he continued, 'she panicked in the car park. Actually I think she flipped completely. Her sole interest was in killing Hammond, which she achieved, but she never gave herself a chance. Her speed and the effect of the impact were her own downfall. I'm just glad she swerved to miss my own car.'

'So am I.' Karen squeezed his upper leg affectionately with her hand.

THE END